The Last Woman

The Last Woman

JOHN WILLINGHAM

Fort Worth, Texas

Library of Congress Control Number: 2025017852

TCU Box 298300
Fort Worth, Texas 76129
www.tcupress.com

For Wendy,
and to Emily, Thomas, and Anne
for the lives they have made

CONTENTS

CHAPTER 1

Tascosa, Texas, 1939

Never had she considered abandoning the town until the new people blew in, offering up a dose of modern-day America that she could not abide. For twenty years she was Tascosa's sole resident, an old woman of mystery, alone in what was once the wildest cowtown in Texas before it became the last. She kept her alias—Frenchy—derived from her knowledge of Cajun French, although her trail to Tascosa back in 1879 had turned to dust along with those who had followed it. No one else could track her down now even if they could remember what she had done. Safe in this deserted town, empty of all except herself, she had found that herself was enough. She damn sure didn't need the newcomers and their world. But could she live with them at all?

Her only close neighbors had been the wild creatures of the Panhandle Prairie, most of them coming and going by night, occasionally killing one of her chickens that had flown the coop or rooting around in what little was left of her garden. She used to see some farmers and ranchers when they rode into Tascosa for mail, but these days most of them drove in their pickup trucks down to Vega and then on to Adrian so they could have dinner at the Midpoint Café. People said the place was exactly halfway between Chicago and Los Angeles on a road called Route 66. Like everything else since the turn of the century, the big road avoided Tascosa. What used to be the heart of the old West wasn't even on the road to the new West anymore.

At first she had welcomed the home for troubled or neglected boys, housed in the old courthouse with room enough for about ten youngsters and a small crew to teach and take care of them. But at the moment, she was at odds with the place after she was told to leave their so-called library, set up in the old Jenkins and Dunn Saloon. The saloon was a special place for her, a point of destination when she and Mick set their sights on Tascosa. That the people had turned it into a library didn't upset her at all—saloons she'd worked in, and books she still loved. When she showed up with one of the older boys who had invited her as a guest, she noticed a few books here and there, but projected onto a whitewashed wall behind the walnut bar was one of those picture shows. She'd only heard of picture shows and newsreels and such; this one was right in her face.

Spat out of a borrowed machine in a series of flickering frames, would-be cowboys rode shooting and hollering after a bunch of white men done up like cigar store Indians. How could anyone take such a thing seriously? And there was a silly woman, somebody's sweetheart, in one scene feigning bravery and in the next wilting like a begonia on boot hill. Disdain was a reaction Frenchy sometimes indulged, and it was what she showed at the old saloon that day. It was also what she received in return. Now she was angry, yes, but disappointed in herself besides. *Damn it, those people, they got to me. And those smart-aleck boys. Why? Oh, to hell with it. But she knew her mind would circle back to it later on.*

So here she was with people once again living nearby but she felt more truly alone, housebound beneath a sky so big and on a prairie so broad that it was hard to imagine their end. For so long, she had been the last person in Tascosa, though seldom feeling alone. Now she was the last woman, and alone was what she was.

Since Mick's passing, it had been her habit, weather permitting, to take a stroll down to the creek before cooking supper. The evening twilight had a kindness about it, nudging the brush and fractured rocks into the shadows, along with the harshness of the desolate plains. During the long days, she would sit on the porch if the weather allowed, sipping sweet tea or coffee and often reading a book. But now all she did was sit out there gazing at what was left of the town, and remembering.

Sometimes she thought she could hear Mick's voice, especially when she was out in the hard-packed yard next to the well he had dug, or when she swept off the front porch where they had sat talking, arguing, planning and for a few years, dreaming. She had kept no locks of his hair and none of his clothes, and they had never posed for photographs. Doc Shelton did take two bullets out of him, one well aimed and the other not. Frenchy had put them in a black velvet drawstring purse, never once untied.

This morning the porch did not beckon. She poured a cup of coffee and sat quietly at the kitchen table, her palms down, side by side, the coffee untouched, and her mind on the previous day. Suddenly, she straightened up in the chair and shouted, *"No!"* slapping the table and wishing it was the face of the man from the boys' home who had pointedly asked her to leave the Jenkins and Dunn Saloon. *Her* saloon during the town's heyday. She drank some coffee and glanced around the kitchen, for the first time noticing a crack in the adobe wall, near the ceiling. She squinted to see if any light was coming through. There was, but not much, so no need to fix it now. Or ever. The rest of the wall looked solid, as durable as the ground from which it was made.

Her eyes quickly shifted to a shelf next to the stove. Beside a stack of towels and some knitted potholders was a leather-bound notebook, one Mick had used for keeping the accounts of his livery stable when the business began to grow. The time may have come, Frenchy thought, to reconcile some accounts of my own. Not matters of dollars and cents but of loving and losing and killing and surviving. She knew all of that was gone, but there were debts to be paid.

She retrieved the notebook, dusted it off, and opened it to the first page. She was conscious of a smile as she read on, remembering Mick's way of spelling certain words—"honour $10 payment in oats and paint for centre stalls"—as he was taught to do back in Ireland. Here and there he had made some notes: "Bought two new waggons this date, good for freight," and "The new mare might serve for Frenchy, if I can get her to ride it." She smiled again. She never did ride that mare.

When she opened the notebook, an old ruler had dropped out, landing on the red cedar countertop. Frenchy left it there. Left it there, but aware of its presence. She adjusted her spectacles—they never seemed to sit exactly right. The hard wire bridge was tight on her nose and the long stems circled around the top of her ears. One thing was for sure, the damn spectacles wouldn't fall off. She sat down at the kitchen table, used a paring knife to sharpen her stubby pencil, and began to write. *In the year 1859, I was born in Baton Rouge with the Christian name of Catherine and baptized in the Catholic Church.*

She wrote nothing else for several minutes as she came to terms with the implications of that sentence, knowing what would have to follow: why she left Baton Rouge; why she used an alias; why she came to question the religion of her birth. She thought of Father Miguel, the only priest north of Amarillo, on whose shambling form the hand of God seemed heavy. They had a bet on who would die first. She told him he'd better take care of himself or she would show up at his funeral and make a little speech. The thought made her lips move toward another smile. So many years had passed since three genuine smiles had appeared on her face in the course of a single day. Remembering is what brought them on—but as quickly it could take them away.

Frenchy put the pencil down and refreshed her cup from the pot on the stove. Now that she'd decided to pay those debts, she didn't want to waste any time, as much as she liked to revisit the entries Mick had made. At her age, she could not only see the sheer cliff at the end of the trail, but could kick some pebbles off the edge. And watch them fall.

She hurried back to the table and sat staring at the pencil, but it was like a wand directed at her, commanding her to begin. She picked it up, sighed deeply, and put it to paper.

Baton Rouge, Spring 1877

The priest in St. Mary's parish fancied himself an artist and the sisters all seemed to adore his paintings. Especially those of the Virgin Mary. His name was Father Jean and he was transferred from a much larger parish in New Orleans. He came over to St. Mary's Academy for Girls and said Mass in the small chapel from time to time. He would ask Sister Francine to send the girls with what he called "the sweetest faces" over to his rectory near the church so he could use them as models for his paintings. One of those girls was my friend Louise Pennette.

CHAPTER 1

One day after a Mass honoring the Visitation of the Blessed Virgin, Sister Francine tapped me on the shoulder outside the chapel. I thought it was Sister Brigid or one of the schoolgirls because the touch was almost gentle. Not what any of us expected from Sister Francine. Next thing I knew she was whispering in my ear—"Catherine McCain, Father Jean has chosen you for a painting."

Sister Francine thought it was odd. She said she was un petit peu surprised. I was more than a little surprised, and said so, that the priest or anybody else could believe I looked sweet or talked sweet. Louise yes, but me—no. Sister Francine told me that maybe I wasn't all that bad looking but my behavior did not reflect much inner beauty. At the time I didn't know there was such a thing.

Frenchy put down her pencil. "Inner beauty," she muttered, dismissing the notion that Sister Francine could have seen such a quality in anyone. Frenchy did not recognize it in herself, but she had come to see its fragile presence within her pretty childhood friend Louise. As for her friend and former accomplice from Arkansas, Mamie Jackson, it was stubbornly intact, unaffected by Mamie's outward appearance. And then came a sharp and sudden image of Mamie, that first shocking smile, revealing the warmest of souls if one could only see.

CHAPTER 2

Frenchy's mail was still delivered to the old courthouse less than half a mile from her place, but no longer by men on horseback or in freight wagons. Now that the courthouse was taken over by the home, the place was busy with the boys getting their lessons done, the cook frying up a meal, or the boss man gravely intoning a message from above. Frenchy had put off interrupting them to get her mail, especially after the row over the picture show. The nearby farmers and ranchers generally picked up their mail once every two or three weeks. Frenchy knew most of them; a few still brought her plums or molasses or the occasional smoked quarter of beef. They were all from the old days, too, back when the mailmen would ride out from Vega, get a free meal at one of the restaurants still open in town, and spend the night. Not with Frenchy, understand. She wasn't the last woman then, not by a long shot. Young she was in those days, but with more knowledge than women twice her age about the many perils of what people call love.

In Baton Rouge, the sisters at St. Mary's tried to tell her and the other girls about men. During her three-year journey from Baton Rouge to Tascosa, Frenchy had learned her own kind of truth. One thing she could say for sure was that most of the sisters didn't know shit about men. What they knew were rules, rigid and stuck in time, and how to teach girls to read, write, shut up, and pray. Frenchy took to reading and writing, and one sister—Sister Brigid—encouraged her to read more widely. It was their secret, although it should not have been.

Looking out the kitchen window, Frenchy saw the boys from the home trudging past on a work detail, heading west with their backs to the morning sun. *I hope they work till their grubby hands bleed.* She was not feeling at all charitable toward them only two days after the picture show. They were probably on their way to cut wheat or prairie hay or dig postholes for barbed wire fences. They were following a flat-bed wagon that carried hoes and shovels and pitchforks, while the boys carried scythes for wheat. The tines on the cradle scythes were shaped like giant claws or the curved rib bones of ancient mammoths that people said used to roam this country. The boys swung those scythes back and forth all day, taking turns at tying off the wheat into shocks. Or they cut prairie hay when the weather would be dry enough to let it cure. That was hard, hot work most of the time. When Frenchy was a girl, she pulled cotton near Baton Rouge and could affirm that farmwork, among other things, can turn a person toward a different way of life.

She sat down at the kitchen table and opened the notebook to the page begun the day before, feeling some regret at leaving Mick's figures and notes behind. Tucked inside the notebook again was her old wooden ruler, used by Mick to draw lines for his ledgers and to mark his place for the next entry. Now it was only marking her place.

One time, Sister Francine had grabbed that very same ruler from Frenchy's hand and rapped her knuckles with it, sharp side down. Nobody ever took it away from Frenchy again. She had kept it for more than sixty years to remind her that what's hers is hers and damned be to anybody who thinks otherwise.

She studied the ruler, its fractional markers down to one-eighth of an inch, the bronze, beveled edge almost untarnished. "H. Chapin and Sons. Connecticut," she murmured. There were scratches, but the wood—maple, beech, she did not know—was solid, with more heft than she remembered. Slowly, she reached for the ruler and picked it up. She turned it over, aware of the initials she would see carved on the back.

* * * * *

As she and Sister Francine left the small chapel that spring day in 1877, Catherine McCain was thinking about her friend Louise, who had seemed so proud after seeing her likeness in Father Jean's most recent painting. Father Jean didn't bother to explain his art or provide any justification for it. He left that to Sister Francine. "Now that you have seen yourself in our Blessed Virgin Mary, you can more readily emulate her," Sister Francine had told Louise. Catherine knew this because the next day Louise took her aside. "Cather*ine*, what is the word 'im-you-late'?" Louise knew more Cajun French than she did English; sometimes she and Catherine would converse in that dialect, but not when the sisters were listening and quick to correct their French or demand that they speak in English. Catherine picked up the Cajun dialect from her mother, born Marie Fleurot.

Although Catherine was confident that she knew what the word meant, she promised to look it up and provide the exact definition. Louise wasn't a frequent visitor to the library, but Catherine was. The library at St. Mary's had half a dozen dictionaries, four in English and two in French. Catherine discovered that the word "emulate" was French in origin. The old meaning was "to rival; to compete." The newer definition made more sense: "to imitate, be the same as."

The next day she waited for Louise beneath the sprawling magnolia that dominated the small chapel courtyard. Louise was often the first to arrive at the chapel and the last to leave, usually taking several minutes to kneel quietly after Mass and reflect on the readings of the day or imagine the spiritual workings of the host within her. Catherine, meanwhile, was breathing in the lemony springtime scent of the tree in full bloom and running her fingers across the dark green leaves, letting the tension she often felt during Mass fall away. The tension began when she was a young girl, hearing Mass at the church with her mother. She knew that her mother had no love for anyone or anything, including the church. Marie Fleurot McCain's half-hearted participation in Mass, her breath often smelling of alcohol, hardly inspired Catherine to believe. Her mother no longer attended Mass, having received enough money from Catherine's uncles to pay for the schooling at St. Mary's. Marie McCain was easily satisfied that the religious instruction Catherine received from the sisters would suffice, along with an occasional chapel Mass. So the church and school became Catherine's foster parents; she owed them, and did not come to them freely. Because she had been given no choice but to believe, she found it difficult to do so.

At last Louise came outside. Her face was still in a reflective mode. Catherine gave her a little bump to get her attention. "Louise! I looked up 'emulate.' It just means you're supposed to be like the Virgin Mary."

"Ah! Well, that is easy. Every boy I know smells bad or acts like a pig." Then, more soberly, "Yes, to be like the Holy Mother, yes."

"Sister Francine would say you should be good in every way. You should be selfless and very devoted." Catherine fought hard to keep a straight face. She didn't care for preaching or being preached to.

"Ah, I see that. *Oui.* Selfless." They began walking away together, but Louise stopped. "But if I'm selfless, my filthy brothers will eat all the cakes!" She muttered on in Cajun French, gesturing wildly with her left hand, the one not holding the missal. The sweetness so present in Louise was rarely evident to her brothers.

"Your brothers really are a bunch of pigs. You tell Marcel I will slap the freckles off his damn face if he tries to kiss me again."

"Oooooh! I will tell Sister you use bad words, Cather*ine*!"

"I'm almost eighteen years old and about to get out of this place so I'll use any damn words I please."

They walked facing the hot and ponderous afternoon sun, but their way was shaded by giant live oak trees, the dark, leaf-heavy branches almost making an arch over Main Street as the girls headed west. There was an orphanage next to St. Mary's academy, and the girls walked past it. Catherine headed to her small house on Laurel, three blocks north of the penitentiary grounds. On their way, they passed the smaller boys' academy.

"*Mon Dieu*, let us pray that my brother Marcel has to stay after school again today," said Louise, giggling. "Oh, but here is little Gabe. Look at his big smile, he sees you, his *chérie*!"

Catherine watched as Gabe came over to them. "Hello there, Catherine McCain, and how are you today, you lovely Irish lass?" Gabe was the only male in St. Mary's Parish who could get away with such talk. For a boy of seventeen, his voice was already deep, smooth—almost musical, Catherine thought. She let him go on because she liked the sound, and knew very well that he did too. Gabe tried to ignore Louise, standing next to Catherine, whose sole attention he wanted. "I know a quiet and shady place, not far from here, where the oak leaves join with the breeze and speak to young people of love."

"That's enough, Gabe! And I'm only half Irish. Don't forget my crazy Cajun mother."

"If only I could."

* * * * *

Catherine's mother wouldn't care if her daughter walked home with smelly, tobacco-chewing Marcel Pennette, but Gabriel Celiot was as black as his Haitian father's tall top hat, a freedman's son and one of five such students in the boys' academy. With him Catherine could not be seen by her mother. Yet it did happen once, one week past. Catherine and Gabe had taken the long way to her house that day, talking nonstop.

"This place, this town of the red stick, I do not like it," Gabe had said. "The French named it Baton Rouge because in those years the Indians placed a long red pole painted with blood, high on a bluff above the river, as a warning to others. In Haiti, we have the green mountains, the palm trees along the beach, the clear water of the Caribbean Sea. Here we have none of those things."

Catherine had heard all of this before. She wanted out of this place even more than Gabe did, and she was absolutely determined to leave. "So why are you here? Why the hell are you here, Gabriel?" She knew better than to remind him of the violent history of his native country.

Gabe tried to stand as tall as Catherine. "You talk like a boy sometimes, you know that? No, you talk like a *man* sometimes."

Maybe, Catherine thought, but the only men she had known were priests and a handful of drunken uncles in New Orleans. She wasn't sure what to make of the priests, since being a priest sometimes seemed to contradict being human; as for the uncles, all on her father's side, she actually liked all of them but one. And there was no doubt about her uncles being human.

Her father, Francis Michael McCain, was killed in 1862 in the battle for this god-forsaken town, run through with a Yankee sword while fighting on the grounds of the Magnolia Cemetery. There his bones remained, poorly protected by a cheap pine coffin. Without fail, Marie McCain visited the cemetery once a month. Catherine tried to get out of going, but last month her mother insisted.

"The Yankees killed your daddy right over yonder, and I like to think he's still fightin' them now, has them in his sights, takin' his revenge. He would, you know. Take his revenge. Your Daddy Frank was a man, young lady. A real man." Catherine sometimes had blurry dreams of a man or a man's face, an outstretched hand, and a clear, kind voice. But she was only three when he was killed.

When she realized that she and Gabe had turned the corner and were almost at her house, Catherine stood taller, anticipating what was to come. Marie Fleurot McCain, when sober, was lethargic and self-pitying, often waiting in the porch swing until her daughter came home from school. She generally finished her first tumbler of cognac about the time Catherine arrived. Now, Catherine remembered it was the anniversary of her parents' marriage. Marie McCain would be well into the second tumbler by now.

She grabbed Gabe by the arm. "Go, quick!" On the porch Marie rose unsteadily to her feet, supporting herself with one hand on the railing. Silently, Gabe turned and walked rapidly toward Florida Street, merging with a curious crowd around a wagon carrying the latest thing in town: blocks of manufactured ice, shipped up the Mississippi from a new company in New Orleans.

Catherine walked straight to the front steps, put down her book satchel, and folded her arms. She knew her mother wanted her to speak first. Catherine fixed her gray eyes on her mother's. The left corner of her mouth rose, almost as if to smile—a sign of disdain that her mother failed to observe.

"So is this what you do now, missy?" her mother said, slurring her speech. "This is what I get for laying out good money for that school? So much for those sisters teaching you how to behave. Now you've taken to walkin' with the darkies? Why, your daddy is out there writhin' in his grave! They been tryin' to run things around here ever since the war, them and the Yankee soldiers, but you know what, missy, their time is done. And you know what else, you prideful child? You will be goin' to confession, and you will do a stiff penance. You hear me, girl?"

"I've been hearing you for almost eighteen years, Mother. I stopped listening when I was ten. I figured I'd heard plenty about never being good enough, or pretty enough, or smart enough, so I decided to listen to myself instead." She picked up her satchel and walked straight up the front steps.

Her mother lurched toward her, trying to grab the heavy bag, but lost her balance and fell backward into the swing, causing it to bang against a front windowpane. "Now look what you made me do!"

"Sorry. What did you say? I need to go in and get supper ready. Like always."

* * * * *

"Hmm. Cather*ine*, I wonder where Marcel might be?" Louise said mischievously the next week, nudging Gabe to the side as he joined them near the boys' academy. "Oh, and hello, little Gabe. You do not speak to Louise; you are too good for Louise? We should speak French, you know. It is, how you would say, more in*teema*te." She giggled and slapped him playfully on the shoulder.

Gabe gave her a derisive look. "You speak the French of the woods and swamps. Your people stay always in their little boats, or in their dirty shacks on stilts. Your people eat those big swamp rats; you eat the ugly gator, those mean and nasty beasts."

"Bah! It is *your* people who butcher the *langue française*. Your people, with the voodoo potions and drums. And you have seen my house. It is a fine house, with very short stilts. And it is not so far from the church, close to the house of God."

"The *langue française*, it is lost to you people. As for the Catholic Church, I go to their school," Gabe said, cocking his head toward Louise. "But let me tell you, little Louise—God has many faces, but many more faces have those priests. I doubt you could comprehend such a thing."

Catherine broke in. "What he means is *comprendre*, to understand a thing more or less completely. In other words, he thinks the priests are shifty."

"You foolish Gabe! Blaspheme at your, your—"

"Peril," said Catherine.

"*Oui!* Silly Gabe."

Catherine scowled. "I hate this town."

"I love it!" Louise said. "It is my true home, and I love it! And it is as well the home of my spirit, and the church that I love." She cut her eyes at Gabe. "You should spend more time in the chapel and less time seeing faces that are not there. Silly Gabe."

Gabe ignored Louise and succeeded in getting close enough to Catherine to whisper in her ear. "We should leave together, you and I." They were about halfway to her house. He was almost skipping along, trying to keep up with her. "Not far from here now, just beyond that lamppost—"

"I will leave alone." She looked over her shoulder at Louise and gave her a little wave.

CHAPTER 3

Early in the fall term, Louise asked, "Did you sit for your portrait, Catherine?"

"No."

Louise had grown an inch or so since the summer, and she was almost as tall as Catherine now. They were heading home from school. Louise was walking more slowly than usual. She kicked at some loose leaves. "I miss Gabe. He was so much a rascal, yet he was, would you say wise? I think he was wise. I hope he is safe."

"Almost all have gone. From the orphanage, too. I heard they tried to hunt down Gabe's father. He had some power, you know, for a while. Not only with his own people but with most of the other freedmen in town. He was friendly with the soldiers, too. Now the soldiers are gone. Another Haitian man was painted with hot tar and covered with feathers. They said he stole some chickens. I did not see Gabe before he left." She paused for a moment. "You know, I really liked Gabe." Catherine was surprised to hear a mix of emphasis and revelation in her voice.

"*Mon père* hates the Black people. He is glad they are leaving. He is drunk now more than before. He says he is so happy now. He makes everyone else unhappy." Louise took two more steps and stopped. "But he has always made me unhappy."

Catherine paused and stared at Louise. Never had she heard her friend say anything critical about either of her parents.

They walked two more blocks. Louise said nothing. She stopped and pulled a wooden ruler from her satchel. "Here is your ruler, Cather*ine*. I hate geometry. I don't know how you do it. Even Sister Brigid has given up on me. Why should I care about it, huh? Why should I care?"

Catherine took the ruler. Louise had scratched her initials—"LP"—on the back. Annoyed, Catherine drew a breath to say something but decided against it, for Louise did not seem to be herself today. Catherine had finished geometry with ease almost two years ago, but for Louise, the complexity of mathematics seemed at odds with her natural playfulness, a consistent trait unless she was hearing Mass in the chapel. Usually Louise joked about math, apparently unconcerned with what Sister Brigid or anyone else might think. Her outburst today was visceral, emotional, serious, so unlike Louise.

Catherine touched Louise lightly on the shoulder. "What's the matter?"

"Nothing." But less than a minute later, Louise blurted, "Do *not* sit for your portrait with Father Jean."

"Did he use you for a model again?"

Louise shook her head emphatically.

"What happened, Louise?"

"He asked me to meet him again at the rectory. He was alone. He said it was time he explained my portrait—I mean to say, my face in the portrait of the Blessed Virgin. He told me I too was blessed. That more blessings would come. And he told me the birth of our Lord was a miracle. I said yes, I knew very well that it was, and yes, I was ever so grateful for such a blessing. He told me there was nothing holier than to be the mother of Jesus, that the Blessed Virgin Mary was without stain, that God's grace had kept her so in the act of conception, that I was chosen—"

Louise began to cry. Catherine guided her to a grassy spot beneath a sprawling oak. "Chosen?" Catherine sat down and motioned for Louise to do the same.

Louise managed to nod. "And that for me to be like the Virgin, to be ever free from stain, that my, my first act must be holy, that the body of Christ was the church, and that, that the church was its priests, the apostles of the Lord himself." She took two deep breaths and wiped her eyes. "He spoke of his mission, to see the *sweetness* within us—Oh God!—to sanctify it forever."

Catherine stroked Louise's hair. The fury that filled Catherine glinted in her eyes. "That son of a bitch."

Louise's eyes were closed as she waited for a sign that what the priest had done would be excised from her being, buried in a place she had not known before and would never have to know again. But when she continued speaking, more rapidly than usual, her voice sounded flat, far away. "He told me to get on my knees beside him and pray. He mumbled something in Latin, and then he touched me on the leg and leaned against my body. I was afraid and didn't know what to do. It could not be real, it could not be happening. Not from a Priest! Then it *was* happening. He put his right arm around me and tried to. . . Oh, Catherine! I felt sick, so sick, like my whole body, my whole—everything—my heart, my soul, was rotten, ruined, dead. I could hear him giving me a blessing. The next time, he said, I would follow the Blessed Virgin, the full grace of the Lord would fall upon me." Louise looked up at the encircling oaks, the swirl of cirrus clouds above, her eyes eager for a sign that God would easily erase such a short span of time and restore her former self. Yet now, whatever signs there might have been in the past seemed suddenly, irrevocably gone. All she could see was the face of the priest. Soon she slowly raised her head and was able to meet Catherine's eyes. "That was two days ago. I have heard nothing since. Sister Francine watches me though. I don't know why."

Less than a minute later, she grabbed Catherine by the arm, holding on so tightly that the much stronger Catherine could not have pulled free had she tried to do so. "Oh, Catherine! I cannot stop thinking about it! I want to disappear, or die. I feel—it's all I *am* now. There is nothing I can do." And seconds later, very quietly, "No one else will believe me. Only you."

* * * * *

"Catherine, Father Jean will see you now at the rectory," said Sister Francine.

"I have to study. It is my library time." Catherine's voice was unemotional.

"You must go. Now."

Catherine picked up her papers and placed them in her satchel, along with three books Sister Brigid had given her, and left the classroom. Outside, she shouldered the satchel and walked steadily down Main Street toward the rectory. The door was ajar. She did not knock or say a word.

A man spoke from within. "Enter."

She did so. Father Jean was standing before her. A white canvas rested on an easel near the only window in the room. The room was too warm. It smelled of body odor and beeswax candles. He gestured toward a chair by his side. "You may sit."

"I will stand."

His dark eyebrows rose above his wide blue eyes. His graying hair, what remained of it, was cut short, and when he turned toward her, light from the window shone on his balding head.

"You will sit."

She did not move. She stared at him the way she often stared at her mother, her gray eyes hard and unblinking.

"You are willful," he said, with a gentle smile. "That is why I chose you, Catherine. Yes, it can be said that you have a pretty face and that your hair, in a certain light, falls about your shoulders like an auburn veil. Ah, but your eyes. They embrace shadows; their grayness when you are angry becomes darker, yet straight from them comes a blazing fire. As now. A fire of rebellion. But the Blessed Virgin Mary was a model of obedience to God. Perfect obedience, you might say, yes, perfect obedience, so absent in this land. Your friend Louise Pennette was perfect in action but later consumed by doubt. It has come to me that the face of the Virgin today should reflect an obedience won over, not given quietly. In this there are precedents. The great painter Caravaggio used courtesans as models for the Virgin Mother, Martha, and Mary Magdalene, and in their faces one can see the emergence of obedience, regretting only its tardy arrival. But it must be said that they lacked . . . sweetness."

He paused. Seconds passed. "You may sit."

"I will not."

He moved to the chair and let his hands rest on its back. Behind his smile was a hint of impatience. "My dear, you must know that to defy the Church and its priests is to open the gates of Hell. Here, in this place, I am the Church, and the Church is the body of Christ. Now come; sit."

"I will not."

"You will not. Ah, but it is your will that is the problem, girl. It is willfulness that gives rise to evil. What does your catechism say, your Bellarmine? 'For evil Christians, there's eternal death, replenished with all misery, and void of all good.' And recall the catechism of Trent: 'Obey your prelates, and be subject to them; for they watch to render an account of your souls.'" He crossed his arms over his chest and smiled.

"But that's not the end of it," Catherine said to herself. Sister Brigid, her favorite at the school, taught the catechism along with running the library. Knowing full well how much Catherine resisted authority, Sister Brigid had required her to write a paper at the end of last term with the simple title, "Obedience." The result was not all that Sister Brigid might have wished.

Catherine stood as straight as she could, her head held high. "And what does St. Thomas say?"

"You dare to query me!" The priest leaned forward across the chair, perspiration gleaming in the space between his thick lower lip and chin. "He says disobedience is a mortal sin. It is as simple as that."

"Not if obedience would itself be a sin! You are the evil here!"

At first, Father Jean did not reply. He feigned sadness, and then showed disgust. "The sin of pride, it corrupts you."

She smiled scornfully. "Corrupts? You should know, Father."

A snarl transformed his face. "You need a lesson, and I am the one to give it." He removed the rope cincture from his cassock.

When he came close, she grabbed her satchel with both hands and smashed it against his head. He staggered backward and his face turned red; when he tried to talk, nothing came out but spittle.

"You goddamned son of a bitch!" she screamed, striking him one more time and knocking him to the floor.

* * * * *

She knew where Marie McCain kept the money that one of the drunken uncles had given her. It was the same drunken uncle—Connor—who showed up in Baton Rouge every couple of months and brought Marie a case of cognac. He alone among the uncles contributed nothing for Catherine's schooling. During his most recent visits, Connor had begun to stare at Catherine and smile for a change, giving his face a strange, unnatural look.

The hiding place her mother had chosen was exactly where Catherine guessed it would be: a hollowed-out space in the wall, hidden by a framed color lithograph of the Holy Family. There she found two hundred and twelve dollars in bills, plus five double eagle gold pieces. She only took fifty dollars in bills, leaving the rest of the paper money behind. The gold pieces, she knew, were brought by Uncle Connor in person. A hundred dollars in gold from his dirty hands would now belong to her.

Her mother was at the academy, meeting with Sister Francine. Catherine went out on the porch and sat in the swing, which was badly in need of painting. When she rocked back and forth, it squeaked and tried to move sideways. She sat there, rocking unevenly, until Marie McCain came home.

Catherine was surprised to see that Marie was sober. Her mother was walking briskly, leaning slightly forward, her head thrust out and her jaw set tightly. "Well, missy, you've done it now," she said, panting as she came up the steps. "They don't want you there no more."

"I'll bet they don't."

"And to a priest—what in the world were you thinkin'?"

"What was I thinking? Hmm. I was thinking the priest is a nasty pile of *merde* who forced himself on Louise and would've done the same to me. I was thinking he would do it again and again. And he probably will."

"A priest! Sister Francine said you tried to—to—touch Father Jean, and when he tried to calm you down and get you to follow him in prayer, you lit into him with that big bag of yours."

Catherine smiled; the smile turned to a wide grin; the grin gave way to a harsh, high-pitched laugh.

"You've gone stark raving mad!"

"Tell me, Mother, would you—even you—touch that slimy little bastard if he was the last man on earth?"

"The thought would never cross my mind. And I don't like your language, missy!"

"Well, anyhow, I'm leaving. I'll say goodbye to Louise and go. I'm going to . . . Haiti." In fact, Catherine had no idea where she was going, but she felt certain no one would follow her to Haiti.

"Like hell you are. You always was one to lie. And you can't see Louise; she'll be in school. They'll run you off, sure."

"I will see Louise. She's my best friend." Catherine had packed a valise and still had her satchel, with the three books from the school library. Going down the steps past her mother, she said, "I took fifty dollars and the gold pieces. You won't have to pay for my schooling anymore. So thanks; I know how you came by that gold."

Catherine did not see Louise outside the school, where she would normally be waiting for friends. She must be with Sister Francine, Catherine thought. Then Catherine saw Sister Brigid outside the small chapel.

"You don't need to say a word," Sister Brigid said when Catherine reached her. "I have heard enough." The sister closed her eyes for a few seconds. When she opened them, she held out her arms. Her small face seemed surrounded rather than shielded by the white wimple, worn tight, as always.

Catherine bent down so Sister Brigid's arms could encircle her shoulders. "I didn't do what they said."

"I believe you. And hear me, dear girl, do not be carryin' a sin that isn't of your makin'."

The lilt in her voice comforted Catherine. Unlike the other sisters and Father Jean, Sister Brigid was Irish, as was Catherine's late father. A lot of Irish immigrants had settled in the parish since the Famine. Sister Brigid had an older brother, still in Ireland, a Capuchin Franciscan with whom she often corresponded. Once, after Catherine had told her about a dismal Christmas with her mother and Uncle Connor, Sister Brigid took the risk of confiding in Catherine.

"Think on this," Sister Brigid said, "and know that what I'm about to be sayin' is between us, and is, one might say, at odds with our Saint Augustine"—she lowered her voice to a whisper—"and to much of our creed."

Catherine nodded, hiding her surprise, and Sister Brigid continued, "My brother believes that Christmas has occurred every day, aye, since the moment of Creation. He says our Lord was born with the universe, lass, though he only appeared to us later on this earth, at that time we call Christmas. God has loved us and his creation from the beginning. He did not send his beloved son in the flesh to be killed long afterward, but to be an example of his love, an example we humans ignored. The death of our Lord was not in payment of our debt to God for our sins, no; it was ourselves who killed him in the flesh, and only after killing him could we begin to see the one we had pierced. What the chalice holds is the blood humanity spilled, yet he still loves us, my girl, despite the grave, stupid suffering we imposed. Now it is for us to repay *our* debt by seeing what we refused to see before. He suffered, yes, and so must we; but in suffering we must also love, accepting both, as did our Lord. To remember the stain is to know what we killed and to see what we owe: Our duty to accept and love in return. Our salvation lies in knowing how to remember."

Since Catherine's own creation, not one Christmas was worth remembering. And now, it was impossible to replace the image of a dear friend abused with that of a loving God remembered, although a sharp lance in the fat belly of Father Jean would have suited Catherine's mood.

"What will you do? Where will you go?" Sister Brigid held Catherine at arm's length but did not let go.

"I don't know. I could teach, don't you think, Sister?"

"Oh yes, but you must not teach in *their* schools! They tell lies about us Catholics. And what the Protestants say about us Irish is worse." She stood back and held Catherine by the shoulders, giving her an appraising look. "You're eighteen now, I believe, your mother havin' been tardy gettin' you into school. But you can easily pass for older, dear girl, early twenties for sure, what with that posture, your height, that confident stride—and those strong and steady, some would say hard looks you can give. Aye, girlish is not a word one would use to describe ya." Sister Brigid eyed the satchel. "How many of my books are in there? Tell the truth."

"Only three. You said the two readers were worn, so I could keep them. History and geography. And I kept some notes, from the readings of Saint Teresa. The ones you had me memorize."

"My brother, with his training in Salamanca, he kept urging me to read her works, not so long before I came over here. I knew you were not to be takin' the faith at first sight. I thought the saint might help you to see. I know full well, young lady, that you will be rememberin' one thing the good saint left to us."

Catherine knew which saying Sister Brigid meant. "'To have courage for whatever comes in life—everything lies in that.'"

Sister Brigid smiled, although her eyes were sad. "I think you were born knowin' that one, lass."

"Yet . . ." Catherine hesitated, but with Sister Brigid, especially now, she must be honest.

"Yet, what?" The smile had vanished.

"I was only going to say, Sister, that you helped me to learn courage, but it was not with courage that we discussed Saint Teresa. You did not want Sister Francine to know."

"Aye, that is true. Sister Francine would not love a mystic, nor was I trained to do so either." She paused for a moment, reflecting. "Well, my dear, here is another thing you will have written in that little notebook of yours, and wise it was of the dear saint to write it centuries before you did: 'I do not fear Satan half so much as I fear those who fear him.' Sister Francine is a hard woman because she is afraid—afraid of the Devil, afraid of breaking one small vow, afraid of that, that man who calls himself a priest. She sees the devil everywhere but where he is, lass. See him, my dear girl, where he is, always." She patted Catherine tenderly on the shoulder. "Now—what is the third book of mine that you are keepin'?"

"*Bessie Conway*, that silly and sentimental book you told me to read."

"Well now, Bessie was an Irish lass alone, in New York City no less, vulnerable to violence and abuse. Good enough reason you should know her. She might as well have been an orphan with her poor parents starving in Tipperary. It was her steadfast faith that saved one and all—and converted that dandy Mr. Herbert from the Protestant maggot he was into a right Catholic worthy of her hand. A fine woman she was, for not seein' him as an instrument of the devil."

"I am not to be about saving any man," Catherine said, stiffening a bit. "I have no need of one. I suppose I might teach. Can't say I'm exactly cut out for washing clothes or picking cotton. I tried that last summer for Uncle Connor. Now, I'm sorry, but I have to leave you." She halted briefly, caught off guard by the sudden emotion she felt for Sister Brigid. "And—and I appreciate all you've tried to do for me, I really do. No one else has done as much. But I have to see Louise. Please tell me where she is. I must say goodbye and tell her what really happened. She needs to hear it from me. I think it would help her." Catherine peered through the branches of the big magnolia, anxious to see Louise.

Sister Brigid slowly shook her head. "Louise is gone."

CHAPTER 4

Tascosa, 1939

So here Frenchy was, about to turn eighty and still living in a town left drawn and quartered on the prairie after the railroad turned northwest from Amarillo. Two miles of deep sand separated the town from the line of track, and no pack mules, much less wagons, could make the trip. What the railroad didn't kill, the barbed wire did, leaving Tascosa cut off, imprisoned, and bereft. Forty, no, fifty years had passed, and the town never came back, though she had sworn it would. Not that she had planned for her life to work out this way. What happened was that she had spent some of her prime years escaping from men who would do her harm, and once she was shut of them, she wanted to stay put where she'd landed. So she did. But truth be told, escaping wasn't exactly the right word.

Her happiest years were with Mick, a good man for an Irishman, as only his friends might joke, no others daring to do so. But she lost him all those years ago. After he was gone, she couldn't bring herself to leave him behind and, when she was able, visited his grave outside of town every week. And anyhow, she couldn't afford to move elsewhere. Later, her persistence became something more difficult to define. She couldn't sort out how much of it was from pure stubbornness or from a mysterious loyalty to what she had decided to call the presence, and not one that required a raised chalice in order to seem real.

There wasn't one plot of ground in the whole town that she did not know, with or without the houses, businesses, and saloons that originally occupied the space; not one person who had lived in the town had she forgotten, though she knew many of them only by the made-up names they'd used to scatter dust over their trails; and not many screams in the night, shouts of joy, songs sweet or bawdy, or gunshots fired to kill a man or graze the stars could she not recall, at least in her restless dreams. They all made up her presence, and she figured she would dwell in that for the remainder of her days.

So far, she had managed to mostly ignore the modern world and new-fangled things. She hadn't read a newspaper since the Great War ended; she had only heard rumors that newsreels existed. She had no radio but knew the country was in a Depression. It didn't change her life one bit. Her own little library occupied her well enough, the books recommended by Doc Shelton, long departed, who had set out to become an author instead of a doctor on the frontier. She ordered them from Topeka or St. Louis, and weeks later, they arrived with the freight from Dodge City, or more recently from Amarillo, all of them now dog-eared, pencil-marked, and barely holding together. They included *The Call of the Wild*, *The Deerslayer*, *Jane Eyre*, *The Red Badge of Courage*, *Ethan Frome*, *Oliver Twist*, and *Kim*—and a book by a peculiar fellow from back East, Henry Adams. She must have read Mark Twain's *Life on the Mississippi* eight or ten times over, relishing his stories of the river that had changed her life. She also read *Hamlet* and *King Lear* before Doc moved to Amarillo, hoping to catch him misquoting the Bard.

All was well until she went to that damned picture show.

The home sent one of the boys to her place with an invitation. His name was Tommy, and he was probably the one who had pestered the people over at the home to invite her. He beat on her door and would have loosened the flimsy hook latch if she hadn't hollered at him to stop. When she opened it, there was Tommy's beaming face. "Somebody done gave us a projector! Come and watch the picture show. You have to! I got the buggy outside."

She grunted and said she thought not. Tommy shook his head. "I sure do wish you would!" She had taken to him, but not that much. "They baked up more than a hunnerd cookies," he added, narrowing his eyes and smiling at her. Sometimes he brought her cookies, old-fashioned tea cakes, and she loved to eat them when she had her coffee, relishing the sweet and buttery flavor and the texture that was both flaky and soft. Some folks liked to dip them in their coffee or tea, but she preferred them just as they were, with all of their ingredients distinct and intact. Although Tommy knew how much she liked them, he would never know all the reasons why.

Tommy was around sixteen years old but wasn't too sure of his age. Whether he knew his parents, or knew of them, she had not heard, but the forthright need for connection that she saw in his blue eyes was of a searching kind, betraying no obvious pain from the callous or intentional denial of love. He was kind enough to deliver her mail when she had any and liked to stop and talk. Weeks would go by without her talking to anyone else. If she still prayed, it might be for Tommy. Hell, he had almost made her feel motherly a time or two. Anyway, grandmotherly.

He was watching her closely, the smile still on his face. Well, I won't have to bake the damn things myself, she thought. She hated cooking. The next thing she knew, she was pulling her coat off the rack. When he tried to help her into the buggy, she shoved his hand away, regretting having done so when she felt the pain in her knees. "You'd think we was in Amarillo!" he blurted, popping his whip at the old mare pulling them along. They went east on Court Street and turned right toward the river, passing vacant houses and businesses in different stages of decay, as if a giant predator had ambled through town gobbling up some places almost whole, nibbling away at others, and spitting out the pieces it did not like. Amarillo, it was not. What it was: a town with one old woman and a bunch of boys who need looking after. Bless their hearts, sent out here to the middle of nowhere with nothing to call their own and nothing but hopelessness in the places they left behind.

Tommy was in such a hellfire hurry because they were late for the show. The place had three shelves with barely enough books to have lasted Frenchy a week when she was a girl back in Baton Rouge. She was amazed when she saw the picture show cowboys wearing fancy shirts and shiny boots, some of them carrying a silvery pretend pistol on each hip. They rode their big horses hard, bright spurs a-flashing, and shot off their pistols at a full gallop, not that any man alive could hit a double outhouse that way. Yet the Indians they were chasing obligingly dropped off their ponies or surrendered on cue in a rugged box canyon.

She thought the whole thing was some kind of joke and couldn't help but laugh at the way they rode and the damn silly things they said. The boys scowled at her, and the man in charge, the boys' teacher, told her to shush. She glared at him, and at the boys, who glared back. "Shush, yourself!" Tommy glanced at her and looked away. Surely, she thought, they can't be taking this seriously.

In the picture show was that so-called sweetheart who had come from back East to teach school, a skinny blond who wore frilly blouses and petticoats. Frenchy never saw her do much of anything but look scared or cry or, at the end, all but swoon when the tallest of the costumed cowboys kind of mumbled that he might be ready to settle down. He allowed that he loved to ride the range when it was wild and free but the day of the cowboy was passing. Such observations should have been the end, thank you, Jesus; but soon they were kissing in the moonlight, their closed lips stuck together like they'd been brushed with horse glue. As the picture faded, it was the woman's blond hair that was the last to go.

The worn clapboard walls trembled from the loud applause and stamping of feet as the credits flashed on the screen. The younger boys pulled imaginary pistols from their frayed overalls and went about imitating the sound of a pistol popping off as they pointed their index fingers toward their friends, and then toward Frenchy, whose contempt for the film was fresh in their minds. About as much spittle as explosion came from their mouths. She recoiled from them, her occasional sympathy for their plight turning into revulsion.

"Oh, this can't be," she whispered. This present foolishness had cast a spell on these boys, and all their wild whooping and hollering told her where they, and the world, were headed. That it was happening in this place, the same old Jenkins and Dunn Saloon where she had practiced her trade and known joy and sorrow and a rawness that could be nothing else but real, was an assault on the world she had known, leaving her with a sense of loss she would not have felt elsewhere. The feeling was similar to a nightmare, but without the latent consolation submerged in most nightmares that the damn thing wasn't real. There was no waking up that would send it away. The decaying of the town had seemed almost natural, as much as she regretted it, like the deterioration of the human body before it expired. But the old saloon had been for her a kind of temple and this—this profanation—struck at her soul. How dare they point their dirty fingers at her, the little snots, in this town, her town, whose sole occupant she had been since the twenties.

She was about to stand up and have a go at them, but she felt a heavy hand on her shoulder. It was the same man who had told her to shush, now saying there weren't enough cookies to go around. "It *is* time for you to leave."

Well, maybe it was. Living the last twenty years in what was practically a silent ghost town had actually worked to keep her recollections sharp. Seeing an empty doorway, a faded sign, or an overgrown lot where the Jinkenses or Siernas once lived always triggered her memory of real people, reinhabiting the space she saw. But now, she would never see the saloon as it once had been. That was bad enough. Then a deep, cold fear rushed past the sadness and set her wondering about what else she wouldn't be able to see.

Tommy grabbed up half a dozen cookies and took her home. Frenchy ate two cookies on the way. She didn't feel much better—and tea cakes had always made her feel better. She wondered if the picture show was a sign that the time to leave Tascosa was finally at hand. She had an acquaintance over in Channing, since 1898 the headquarters of the XIT Ranch northwest of Tascosa. The widow Blackwell now had a wood-framed house, whitewashed, and had been after her to move there for five years and more. Channing wasn't much more than a ghost town itself. The land was the same as in Tascosa: fit for antelope and rattlesnakes and okay for sheep and cattle if the prairie grass came out. There were no buffalo left to eat it. Some of the nesters around Tascosa said she should move to Amarillo instead. Damned if she would move there. It wasn't a wide space in the road when Tascosa was the light in every cowboy's eye between the Southern Rockies and the winding Sabine. Only last month, Louis Homan showed up from his daughter's house north of Vega to see how she was doing, though mainly he wanted a drink. She had saved three cases of Jesse Moore Double-A from when the saloon closed down, making it some of the oldest whiskey in Texas.

Homan was set on drinking it all. That day he had his teeth in and was sober enough to be understood, and he swore that Amarillo now had fifty thousand more or less human souls. Good God Almighty, who would want to live in such a place as that?

* * * * *

In her dreams, the flickering images of the picture show returned; worse, she dreamed that the boys were surrounding her, yelling louder and pointing real pistols at her face. But when she shouted *"No!"* in the kitchen that first morning after the show, she promised herself that it would take a hell of a lot more than a bunch of screaming boys and a stupid picture show to get the best of her.

CHAPTER 5

A few weeks later, a reporter from the paper in Amarillo parked his Model A coupé on the other side of the narrow creek bridge and made his way unheard to the path leading to Frenchy's house. She had been drawing some water from the well and saw him out of the corner of her eye. "Who the hell are you?" she said, irritated but unafraid. After his initial retreat, he explained that it was "a human interest story" that she had settled in Tascosa, back when it was the craziest cowtown on earth in the early 1880s and stayed on for decades after everyone else had died or otherwise departed. He was struggling to look her in the eye. "And . . . and they say you're the last of the golden girls of the Old West. Is that right . . . ma'am?"

"Listen here, young fella, by the time I got here I wasn't a girl, and I wasn't golden except on one occasion, and that's none of your damn business."

Hastily scribbling some words in a notebook, he didn't look up when he asked, almost meekly, what she thought about the new boys' home?

By then, Frenchy had made peace with the teacher over there, a man named Jim, who had brought her not only fresh tea cakes one Sunday afternoon but a whole peach cobbler, saying that, as a good Christian, he didn't want to hold any grudges against her and hoped she felt the same way. Given her past dealings with church people, she doubted his sincerity at first, but the man was reassuringly direct, a trait she greatly admired.

"I have to tell you, Miz Frenchy, I didn't like that picture show either," he told her. "I grew up in Vernon and did a little cowboyin' myself before college. No cowboy I ever saw would dress like that."

"I'm sorry for the way I behaved, Jim. I can be a tad too direct sometimes."

"Yes, ma'am."

She couldn't really pay him back for the cobbler, but she was the only person outside the boys' home to attend the next play they put on, performed at the renovated schoolhouse north of Main. The place now housed their library; the Jenkins and Dunn Saloon had been erased by a windstorm, all but her memories of it. Her applause at the end of the play was loud and extended as she recalled a time in her past when education, believe it or not, had been at the center of her life.

"It's good they're here, good for the boys," she told the reporter, and meant it. She decided to go ahead and tell him a story or two about the old days and found out later that the paper had run a long article about her and the town. Some of the ranchers nearby told her it made for better reading than the usual stories about drought or those fools who still drilled for oil in Oldham County. It had a picture of her and ancient Louis Homan, the only picture anyone had ever taken of him during his entire contrary existence. He had come by to trade a pair of skinned rabbits for a bottle of Double-A whiskey. She didn't bother to read the article, and Homan couldn't.

Two mornings later, Frenchy sat on the front porch and waited for the sun to creep up from the east, relishing the tones of the blue hour and the warm orange glow before sunrise. A time of peace. She returned to the kitchen and stood at the window, sipping black coffee out of a large tin mug with a strip of deer hide glued to the handle to keep it from burning her fingers. She wondered about the path of her life, starting out near an orphanage and now going out near a remote home for boys. It wasn't long before she was, yet again, watching the boys head out for work. No cradle scythes today, so it was likely they'd be digging postholes and setting fence, yanking the barbed wire tight with leather-gloved hands, seasoned tough and hard despite their youth. Oh Lord, the wire, and all the trouble it had brought.

Frenchy drank the last of the coffee and decided she wanted some more. That meant going outside and drawing water from the thirty-foot well Mick and some new friends had dug before they built the house. "No use in a house without water," he had said, and there was no arguing with that. He also made a porch roof of timber that sheltered her when she went outside, and off to the left, only ten feet or so, was the well. It had its own small roof, so she only needed a few steps to get from one covered area to the other.

The well pump was rickety but still gushed with good water after only a half-dozen downward pulls. Mick used to fill a five-gallon bucket that would last them all day and more; now it was all Frenchy could do to fill up half of a three-gallon milk pail. It didn't take too long. She finished and watched the sun rise higher, revealing more of the hard country, cut at odd angles by dry creek beds and runoff channels from the iron-red, often sluggish Canadian a short mile to the south, its color rising from broken rock formations below. Toward the running creek, to the east was a stand of prairie cottonwoods, and to the north were three bur oaks, some patches of prickly pear cactus, and jagged lines of yellow broomweed marching up a rocky hill in a quest for decent soil. She took a deep breath and exhaled. It wasn't much, but she liked it. She didn't want to leave.

With the second cup of coffee made, she sat down at the kitchen table. She picked up a pencil that still had a good point and opened the notebook with the ruler. She didn't like to think about Arkansas; she might skip over that time. But she knew she could not. It was there that she met Mamie Jackson. And not long after, she learned what had happened to Louise Pennette. Frenchy wrote:

> *All I knew when I left Baton Rouge was that Louise was gone. She wasn't at her house and no one else came to the door. Sister Brigid couldn't find out where she went. I didn't know if she was dead or had escaped like me or was hiding out in Baton Rouge. I was sure Sister Francine would have shamed her, and I was sick with worry. Louise had said she wanted to die. I hoped that if she was alive she had gone upriver.*

Every young person in town longed to take a steamboat trip up the Mississippi. The river more than anything else brought out the adventurous side in me. My best memories of Baton Rouge were the walks to the Florida Street landing with Gabe and Louise to watch the boats come in. None of us knew then where the river could take us. Down the gangplanks came a stream of humanity that could have come off the ark. Most of them got off only to stretch their legs or see what little there actually was of the town. There were gamblers and planters and boat captains, along with some women dressed in the latest fashion with their faces caked with rouge. The poor souls with deck passage—they were last off the boats and always in dirty ragged clothes. The children were usually barefooted, some sucking on cut sugar cane, frightened, gaping, or hollow-eyed. The steadiness of the stevedores fascinated me but Louise even more. Maybe because she could be so flighty outside of church. They rarely moved fast but they never stopped. They loaded and unloaded bales and barrels and crates, back and forth across the groaning gangplanks, some of the men hollering or singing as they worked. Gabe used to shout at them or try to sing along. They paid him no mind. It's odd that the sound from the dock that I still hear most clearly was the odd range of whinnying from a dozen or so mules—the ones that were not only stubborn but loud.

The boats from St. Louis were the best. They carried more passengers, more life, good and bad. No place on the river called out to us like St. Louis, a city that we had heard was bigger than New Orleans. It was the true hub of a country spreading out across the West.

She touched the tip of the pencil to her lip, thought for a moment, and put the pencil down. She pictured herself as she had been, tall, straight-backed, lean but strong. *I was not afraid.*

Mississippi River, September 1877

Leaving her drunken mother behind, Catherine felt rich with the hundred and fifty dollars she had taken from Marie McCain, finding special comfort in the solid weight of five double eagle gold pieces in the inside pocket of her coat. At first confident that she had enough to pay her way to St. Louis with money to spare, she was shocked to find it would cost a whole double eagle and part of her cash to reach Helena, Arkansas, a town smaller than Baton Rouge. She sat down on a hard bench outside the ticket office, watching the intermittently idle stevedores as they talked, smoked the occasional pipe, or spit streams of chewing tobacco while glancing at the big clock outside the office, now showing only a half hour till noon when the next boat from New Orleans was due.

She had taken all the ham and fresh bread, baked with her own hands, from the house when she left. So she decided to eat and figure things out. Two hours later she was still on the bench, but in her hand was a ticket to Helena, on the same boat that had docked, its cargo and passengers still being unloaded ahead of reboarding. "I'll stay in Arkansas a little while," she whispered. "Find work, save some money, and go on up to St. Louis." The adrenaline that shot through her body as she ran from her mother's house had by now worn off; she was full of thick bread and ham. She yawned, congratulating herself on paying for a small cabin all the way to Natchez, about halfway to Helena. She would sleep, and sleep long, free, and on her own. Once she was rested, she could stand sharing a room for the last leg of the trip.

And for five full days she got her fill of sleep and food, often joining a table of young women in the dining room, most of whom were traveling with a "matron" named Sally O'Neill. Unable to carry many clothes, Catherine began to feel dowdy and thought that Matron O'Neill was watching her closely, even judgmentally. Two nights before their scheduled arrival in Natchez, Catherine joined the matron and her group for an early dinner. She was a few minutes late, and when she appeared at the long dining table, the young women stared at her in embarrassment. At breakfast Catherine had heard one of the girls, Suzanne—returning from New Orleans to her home in Natchez—talk excitedly about the evening when the main cabin would be transformed from a dining hall to an elegant saloon filled with music, merriment, gambling, and drink for all aboard. The girls would be allowed to attend. Matron O'Neill, of course, would be present; the visit would be only for an hour or two; the young women would be in their cabins by ten, tucked in, prayed for, and longing to be back in the saloon.

"Oh, you are not dressed!" Suzanne reached out and, reluctantly, touched the sleeve of the plain brown frock Catherine was wearing.

Catherine felt her face turn red, and the surge of shame that came with it was all the more shocking because she was so unused to it. When she turned to look at Suzanne, the girl drew back her hand so quickly that she knocked over a crystal water glass. "I believe you are mistaken." Catherine fixed her eyes on the other girls at the table, each in turn. "I trust Matron O'Neill will attest that I am clearly not naked." As her eyes found those of the matron, Catherine was surprised to see not alarm or condemnation but an obviously half-hearted effort to stifle a laugh.

"Well," said the matron, after briefly surrendering to a chuckle, "I would say, young ladies, that given the expanse of carefully bared cleavage I have observed at this table, Miss McCain is, in fact, *dressed* to a greater extent than any of you dears." The matron took a sip of water and cleared her throat. "Not to mention that Miss McCain is coming to my stateroom after dinner for a fitting of very fine clothes that arrived for her by packet only yesterday." Her face took on a look of command, clearly often used and never questioned, as she caught Catherine's eye again. "I am sure you have not forgotten our appointment, *have you*, Catherine?"

"Oh, I am sorry!" This time, Suzanne touched Catherine's arm out of tenderness.

Later, showing less cleavage but more elegance than the young ladies displayed, Catherine emerged from Matron O'Neill's stateroom arm-in-arm with her new benefactor. The dress Catherine had on was, in fact, a never-worn spare belonging to the sweet but spoiled Suzanne, who had forgotten all about it. "I see something special in you," the matron whispered as they joined the group. "You are older than your years and oh-so-smart. You will prevail, my dear."

For the next two hours Catherine tried to remain close to the matron's charges, but they would rattle past her in pursuit of the next grand lady or splendid young man while she gazed at the heavy chandeliers, rimmed with burning candles, the ceiling like a sky magically filled with both sparkling stars and lambent daylight, shining through the haze of tobacco smoke that hung in the air. From every quarter came the clink of heavy glasses, the loud laughter of men, the clear musical mirth of women—happy in their finery and free of the curtained ladies' lounge at the dark end of the room.

But most of all, she watched a few other women who were dressed well but smiled only briefly, their hands and eyes almost a blur of movement, all business, dealing what she heard a man beside her say was "the best faro game on the river."

Just then, one of the women Catherine had been watching left the faro layout set up two tables away from the end of the saloon's long walnut bar. "You're damn right it's the best game on the river," she said brusquely to the man next to Catherine. The woman strode up to the bar, waiting impatiently for two men to move aside so she could reach her waiting mug of cold beer. Intrigued—this woman was unlike any she'd ever known—Catherine followed.

The woman must have felt that someone was watching her. She turned abruptly. "Who are you, and why are you standing behind me?" She paused, considering. "And you're too damn young to drink."

"You're a woman—"

"Now, ain't you brilliant." The woman took a swig of cold beer, wiping her mouth afterward with the back of her free hand.

"I mean to say . . . you are in charge of that—" Catherine nodded toward the game board.

"It's a layout. A faro layout. I'm the dealer." The woman glanced toward the restless men gathered near the table, where the layout was being guarded by a man who was motioning for her to get back over there. "George, I'm gonna have another, so you sit tight!" She turned quickly to the bar and picked up another cold mug that was waiting for her. When she faced Catherine again, almost half the second mug of beer was gone. "Hot work, honey, hot work."

"I'm Catherine. I am curious—"

"Killed the cat, they say." The woman gulped more beer.

Undaunted, Catherine tried again. "What is it like? To do what you do?"

"You're a persistent one, ain't you?" The woman's words were brusque, but Catherine saw a hint of humor in her face. "I'm Jules."

Catherine understood her to say "Jewels," and the name seemed to fit, given the string of pearls hanging from her neck.

"Honey, it's not a bad life. I make more money than half of the men in this room. But it ain't easy. I know what you're thinkin'. You remind me of me twenty years ago, 'cept I was purtier."

That was likely true, Catherine thought. "But I want to know what it's *really* like, the game, the life."

Jules shrugged. "You look around, say, at that table over there. Those men are big shots, planters, as they still claim to be, like they was before the war. They've mostly taken to poker, and like to show their steel by bettin' too much and actin' like losin' five hunnerd bucks don't matter. There's a few who lose the whole shootin' match and next thing you hear, they've done blown their brains out or thrown theirselves into the paddle wheel back yonder. In another hour, those other men across the room, they'll all be drunker'n shit. By the time we close, one of them will win big and buy drinks for the house, standin' up and bowin' and actin' like he does it every day." She drank half of the remaining beer and lifted the mug so George could see it.

"Faro ain't so personal. You can have some big winners and losers, all right, but they ain't goin' at one another so much as they're bettin' against the house. Takin' a chance, but not puttin' their whole selves on the line against somebody else. That wasn't the reason I took to dealin' faro, though. It didn't matter a whit to me if some stuffed shirt son of a bitch jumped off the boat or got mad and threw a drink in someone's face across a poker table—but poker required too much patience, and it was almost entirely a man's game. Part game and part pissin' contest."

"So how do you play faro?"

"You put thirteen cards at a time on the table, burn the first card from the deck, deal the banker's card, followed by the player's card, and keep at it till what they call 'the turn'—the last three cards. Punters who have put their money on the banker's card, they lose. Money put down on the player's card wins. The big money goes to the punters who peg the order of the last three cards. Bets get bigger as cards are removed. A casekeeper keeps track of the dead cards with abacus buttons in an open case the punters could see if they took the time. So there it is."

George was beckoning again, the muttering of the players audible across the saloon as they milled about. Jules set the empty mug down sharply on the bar and waved both hands back and forth above her head. "George, here I come!"

* * * * *

Tascosa, 1939

Now, more than sixty years later, Frenchy remembered Jules and that evening so clearly, feeling for a few moments that she was back on the riverboat, standing near the bar. She wanted to forget almost everything else about the trip to Arkansas, but forgetting wasn't her way. If anything, in old age she held on to the trouble in her distant past more than she welcomed the parts that were good. Each day, when she thought about the time before Tascosa, she had to face down the worst before she could move on to the best, and the older she got the harder it was to make the move. Sister Brigid had been emphatic about the specific memory that was critical to salvation. But, Frenchy wondered, what about the swirl of other memories, some of them bearing their own lasting stains, and all hovering, hiding, stalking, and abruptly reemerging in defiance of her will or reason?

She set her mouth and squinted. "There's things I wish I could change, about people who are gone now." When she herself was gone, those people would be lost even to memory. She would be washed away as well, flowing into a place without time, and so without memory. The last woman held the last memories.

CHAPTER 6

Helena, Arkansas, September 1877

The Mississippi hemmed in Helena from the east, and to the north and west was Crowley's Ridge, covered with hickory, oak, poplar, and ash, rising two hundred feet above the flat delta land so often prone to flooding. To the south was mostly swampland, a few crude levees, and what remained of the shacks built by escaped slaves, called "contraband," during the late war. There were four private schoolhouses, but two of them were at the point of closing down. Most schools opened and closed so fast that it was the rare student who could start and finish at the same place. Catherine quickly found a boardinghouse, owned by a spinster, Miss Baird, two blocks west of Cherry Street. She joined two other young women, one of whom was Mamie Jackson.

They met at suppertime on Catherine's first day. Catherine arrived early for the meal, and so did Mamie. Catherine had skimped on her food after Natchez, where the matron and her group had disembarked, and her stomach had been growling for an hour. She didn't know where to sit.

"I reckon that's your place over there, closest to the kitchen. As the new boarder, you'll help to serve. My name's Mamie." And suddenly, two big front teeth appeared in Mamie's pretty face, alarming in the way they transformed her appearance. When she wasn't smiling, the crooked teeth were mostly contained because she had a way of pursing her lips very slightly to compensate for their outward thrust. Everything else about her was pretty—that is, all but her clothes. The white collar, buttoned under her chin, was dirty in a couple of places and the dull gray dress, full length of course, had dark smudges on the sleeves.

"I'm Catherine." Catherine only nodded at Mamie, who had seemed inclined to come forward for a warmer greeting.

"You have a really small waist!" Mamie blurted. "You ain't wearin' a corset, are you?" Mamie wasn't fat but could have been considered plump. Her own corset seemed too tight. She had a bosom like a much larger woman. She wore no cap and her blond hair was curled high on her head. Whether from excitement or the heat in the small dining room, her face was turning pink, or rather more pink, as her natural complexion appeared to have such a tinge.

"It's just the way I'm built. But I wouldn't wear one of those damn things anyway."

Mamie glanced anxiously toward the kitchen, where they both could hear the mistress of the house brandishing utensils and pans. "That old maid don't like cussin'," she whispered. "You get one warnin' and then you're out. I've done had my warnin' and prob'ly won't last here much longer." Again the broad smile, the big crooked teeth. "You know, I like you, Catherine. I can tell."

"All right."

After only three days, Catherine got a teaching job, taking over from a young woman who had run off with the purser on the *Natchez*. The best part of the job, as far as she was concerned, was the small two-room house built on to the school, extending from a tiny office behind the chalkboard and the main classroom. The door to the office was always open, but there was a heavier door leading to the living quarters. The lodging came with the position, a considerable perquisite, and the space was hers alone.

The bad thing was, now she had to cook. Every time she picked up a pan or kneaded dough, she thought of her mother sitting half-drunk at the table and demanding that her supper be served. Another thing she didn't like was having to use the same three-hole privy that the students used, set up about twenty feet west of the schoolhouse door. She told the students that the hole on the far right, next to the girls' place with a painted crescent moon on the wall, was hers alone. For all the good it did. With her first month's pay, she bought herself two chamber pots at the general store on Fifth Street.

The school had a bell tower that appeared to be a truncated steeple. Catherine found out that the place used to be a church, but the congregation had outgrown it. The preacher now had a church in the main part of town. His younger brother ran the schools, and if he hadn't been so hard up for a teacher, Catherine wouldn't have been hired.

His name was Rainey. Last name, Harper. "You can call me Mister Harper," he said when they met the first time in the schoolhouse.

"All right."

He waited several seconds for her to say more. She didn't.

"Your landlady Miss Baird says you got your education from a bunch of nuns down in Louisiana. Baton Rouge, that right?"

"Yes."

He looked down at a letter she had brought with her. In it she had listed the books she had read, along with all the readers by level and subject, and her marks at St. Mary's. "So do you in fact know your tables through the rule of twelve, long division, and, uh, so on?"

"I mastered Ray's Practical Arithmetic up to and including fractions, percentages, and proportions. After that, I learned plane geometry. You might know it as the geometry of Euclid."

"Hmm. Ewe-clid, you say. I do not know him."

"He is long dead."

"You can write a good hand—that's clear enough. I see you can spell," he looked up and smiled, "or whoever wrote this letter can spell."

"I wrote it. You want me to write another one, right now?"

"No, I was only making a little joke, you see."

She stared at him and waited.

"Now I reckon Miss Baird at the boardinghouse told you that in our schools we do teach the Bible and the word of God along with everything else?"

"Yes."

"And by the Bible and the word of God, I don't mean any of that hocus-pocus you picked up down in Baton Rouge?"

"I know the catechism backward and forward, but that doesn't mean I can't forget it." *As it was strictly taught.*

He leaned back, his eyebrows pinched together as he considered her remark. "But y'all did look into the Bible while you were learning this, this cat—cat-a—"

"Catechism. Sure. I have some of the Bible by heart."

He was pleased; his face relaxed. "How about a verse or two now?"

After a brief pause, Catherine said, "Well, there's 'Do unto others' and so on. And the one about the meek inheriting the earth. And in Romans it says, 'Do not be overcome by evil, but overcome evil with good.' And in the Old Testament there's the Commandments. Ten of them. Now some of those are a little strange—"

"Yes, the Lord works in mysterious ways, Miss McCain. Catherine. May I call you Catherine?"

"Mister Harper, call me whatever you like as long as you pay me on time."

"I'll take that as a yes. Ten dollars a month it will be, payable on the first, or thereabouts. And your nice quarters at the school, of course. Now, Catherine, if you need ideas about religious, uh, instruction, I will ask my brother Campbell to pay you a visit. He is quite the preacher, Campbell. Once our mama thought we'd both be preachers, the lights of her life; but Campbell, he has the gift. Our Lord speaks through him like no other I've ever seen." His voice trailed off as he finished the sentence. "Like no other," he repeated quietly. "Smart he is, went to college, down in Clinton, Mississippi." He looked away for a moment. "But this here is my mission. This small school and another one like it, closer to the river, they are my purpose on this earth!"

"I see. Yes, I can surely see that they are. Now, when do I start?"

* * * * *

There were twelve of them on the days when they all showed up, but on most days only seven or eight made it to school. One of the girls, Abigail, was almost as old and as tall as Catherine herself. Abigail was a good reader, well-behaved, and after a week or two became a kind of assistant to Catherine. Catherine noticed that when Abby, as she was called, became her helper, she started wearing shoes or, rather, old lace-up boots, probably worn previously by her mother or some relative who had died. All of the other students were barefooted most of the time. But only once did any of the students get a splinter in their foot from the puncheon floor. That was Little Jim. He was only seven and had been sickly since birth. Between Jim at seven and Abby at sixteen, the other students ranged in age from eight to fourteen. Only four were boys.

Outside of Abby, Catherine favored Millicent, or Millie, who was twelve, and Henry, who was the fourteen-year-old but small for his age. Freckled with ginger hair, he nevertheless reminded Catherine of Gabriel Celiot, maybe because he was always flirting with Abby or trying to get her attention. Millie was the best reader and had the best head for numbers; she liked to show off, to read aloud as fast as her mouth could move and to finish first at the chalkboard when math was the lesson. In her right hand the chalk was a weapon, striking the board loudly and sometimes even breaking, causing her to exclaim, "Tarnation!"

At this, Julia, also twelve but very prim, would scowl at Millie. One day she stuck a plump index finger in Millie's face, saying, "That's a bad word! My mama said so!"

Catherine moved between the two girls. "Julia, have you finished dividing 431 by 23? Hmm. No, I see that 431 sits all alone with no numbers below it. Now, would you rather finish the problem on your own or would you like for Millie to show you how to do it?"

"And she says worse than that!" Julia whimpered. "She says 'dang' and 'Good Lord' and—and other words, too."

The readers Catherine used were remarkably similar to those at St. Mary's, except the many references to Christianity and the Bible now identified with Protestantism exclusively, implying that all Protestants were one, and all set against popery, superstition, and drunken immigrants who would destroy American liberty. Catherine did not care. She had a job to do, and she needed to save some money. Sometimes, when she was tired of explaining fractions to Henry or sentence diagramming to Julia, Catherine would read some of the morality stories to the class, often seeing Julia's face light up when a virtue to her liking was associated with God's will.

One morning, Catherine read aloud from the *Eclectic Primer*. "'God sees and knows all things. He sees me when I rise from bed. He sees me when I go out to work and play, and when I lie down to sleep. If God sees me, and knows all that I do, He must hear what I say. Oh, let me speak no bad words, nor do any bad act; for God does not like bad words or bad acts.'"

When Catherine looked up, after fighting back a sly grin, most of the students were staring out the window or drawing in their notebooks. Julia, however, had been listening intently. She gave her teacher a sweet little smile.

* * * * *

The look on Rainey Harper's face was equal parts superiority and regret. "I would have come to you sooner, uh, Catherine, but the girl's mother talked to Campbell first. That's why he's standing outside, waiting for all the students to leave."

Catherine continued to gather papers from her small desk at the front of the classroom. Holding them in her left hand, she picked up an eraser and wiped away most of the fractions remaining on the board. When she turned around, Campbell Harper was standing in the doorway. His brother stepped aside to let him walk up the narrow center aisle, but Campbell remained where he was. Catherine had seen him around town when she was shopping with Mamie. More than once he had walked straight past them without speaking or tipping his hat, often gazing straight ahead, as if whatever it was out there in front of him was all that mattered or anyway was all he could see.

Catherine lifted her chin and was ready to meet Campbell Harper's cold stare when it came. "Sir, you might want to take off your hat now that you're inside the school."

Rainey saw this as a good time to step into the aisle himself. "Catherine, I mean Miss McCain, this is my brother, the Reverend Campbell Harper." The reverend's black hat, wide-brimmed, stayed on his head, pulled slightly forward. Outside he had been facing the sun, which now cast the reverend's shadow up the aisle.

Catherine walked around her desk and marched down the aisle, forcing Rainey to step back among the small student desks, and making sure to keep her eyes on his brother. "You want to sit down or stand, Reverend Harper?"

"Miss McCain, I will not be long." This struck Catherine as humorous because Campbell stood several inches taller than either Catherine or his brother. He had a long and thin nose, rising to a space between intense dark eyes. The afternoon light projected and distorted his already elongated image.

"You are amused?" He cocked his head to one side, clearly unamused.

"It is nothing."

"In that I suspect you are correct." For a tall man, he had a fairly high voice, but it was clear and penetrating. "We, that is my brother here and myself, have received a complaint from a parent. A Mrs. Brumley, her daughter is Julia Brumley."

"She would be the one." Whatever amusement Catherine had felt now disappeared.

"You are aware that our mission here is to provide a sound Christian education?"

"I am sure about the Christian part, and I have no quarrel with that."

"No quarrel! Why, I should hope not!" Rainey took a tentative step into the aisle.

"My brother tells me that you are not a Protestant." Campbell offered a sad little smile.

"I am as much a Protestant as I am anything else."

Campbell glared at his brother. "Well, Miss McCain, however it was that you were hired for this position, the fact is that we have this complaint, and now I do not wonder at it. Not only do you ignore blasphemy among your students but you, you yourself, take the name of our Lord in vain, in plain hearing of those whom you would attempt to instruct."

"Is all this about Millie saying 'tarnation'? It's a sight better than saying other things. I know what it means, all right: 'damnation.' But it's not 'damnation' that she's saying, is it? And besides, we all get a little wrought up from time to time. Millie is a fine young woman, sharp as a barber's razor, smart enough to teach one day herself and do it well."

"And what do you say, Miss McCain, when you are 'wrought up'?"

"I'm not sure I'm stuck on any one expression. I might have picked up two or three from some uncles of mine. They are given to drink and can be colorful at times."

"Here's what you went and said." Rainey stood up straighter and seemed to be gathering his thoughts. "For one, you said 'Goddammit to hell and gone' when you were at the back of the schoolhouse last Thursday. Two days before that, you twisted your ankle on a rock in the schoolyard and hollered 'Jesus, Mary and Joseph, who put this damn rock in the middle of the schoolyard!' And finally, you once told Abigail Armitage, and I quote, to 'get that shit off those boots, young lady, before you come into this schoolhouse!'"

"So I did, but I called her a young lady." Catherine returned to her desk at the front of the room and put the papers down. "And I do remember that rock. I had a nasty sprain and it hurt like—the dickens. Can I say 'dickens'? Now about that one last Thursday. The only time I might have used the Lord's name in vain was when I went to the privy and found that some of the boys had pis—urinated all over the seat and on what rags were left out there. So put yourself in my place—"

"I beg your pardon!" Rainey said.

"I need my own privy," said Catherine.

"Enough!" Campbell stomped his right foot on the floor. "We have no other teachers at hand right now, so here is what we will do. Beginning this Tuesday, Rainey will come here for one hour each afternoon and conduct Bible study for you and your students. If necessary, I will come myself. If I hear any more complaints about your conduct, Miss McCain, I will, or rather, Rainey will, require you to stay in your quarters for a full week, with no pay. Do you hear me—no pay? And one other thing. It looks bad for one of our teachers not to attend church. In this case, *my* church. I expect to see you there every Sunday morning unless you are injured or near death."

"What do you have to say for yourself now, Miss McCain?" Rainey asked.

It had been a long day, and Catherine had begun to tire, of the day's work, of the silliness of these men, and of the hard reality that she needed this job. "All right, I'll be there." *I guess I have to try to behave.*

* * * * *

After three weeks Rainey had decided he was a preacher, too, maybe better than his brother. He didn't seem to notice that Catherine was often busy whispering threatened punishments in Henry's ear if he didn't pay attention or glaring at Abby and Millie when they yawned too loudly. Catherine tried to catch Rainey's eye and nod when he looked up from his reading, but she was concerned that he might see the gesture as a sign that she admired him or, worse, that she saw him as potential suitor.

By early December, Rainey, with the full support of Campbell and Campbell's wife, Hannah, had charged Catherine with preparing a Nativity play for Christmas Eve.

Henry was stuck with playing Joseph. Millie wanted to play Mary, but the part went to Abby instead, much to Henry's delight. Julia was furious, and so was her mother when Julia had to join Millie and Little Jim as wise men. But Catherine agreed to use Julia's favorite doll as the baby Jesus. Nobody had a sheep; an ox or a donkey was too big for the schoolhouse; and anyway, hooves would damage the wooden floor. Rainey wanted to dress up his half-crazy coonhound to look like a sheep. It fell to Catherine to explain Aesop's dog in a manger fable to Rainey, who seemed unable to grasp it.

They ended up staging the play in the schoolhouse, despite its small size, and nobody came but the students and their parents. That filled the place up, though, and as Mamie and Catherine watched from the back, Catherine actually felt proud. Henry was so pleased with his role that he behaved during the two rehearsals and, aside from almost losing his fake mustache and beard, played his part perfectly, finding a lower voice range than Catherine thought was possible. Henry could see that at last Abby appeared to acknowledge his presence. Julia had a pouty look the whole time and glared at her doll as though it were a traitor. No one could hear her lines, even in the small space of the schoolhouse. Once, Millie prompted her in a stage whisper that caused the audience to titter.

Campbell and his wife were among the last to leave. The brothers lingered by the schoolhouse door. Catherine heard Campbell's voice rise in its sharp clear way. "Brother, you must never show yourself again in this condition!"

Rainey went outside for five or six minutes. Making little noise as he returned, he fetched the broom and swept up some cookie crumbs and took down the red and green bunting around the windows. He and

Catherine bumped into each other as they were moving some small hay bales and chairs that had made up the set for the play.

"You look beautiful tonight," Rainey said. "Your hair, it's—"

"Like an auburn veil?"

"Why, yes, come to think of it. Just like that." He reached out and let his fingers feel the hair on her shoulder.

"You need to go home." She retrieved the broom from its place by the chalkboard.

"Oh, I'm sorry. I might have had a nip or two, Christmas Eve and all." And with that he turned crisply, picked up his hat and coat, and walked out into the night.

"Ah, yes," Catherine said to herself, thinking of Sister Brigid back in Baton Rouge. "It's Christmas every day."

* * * * *

Catherine sat near the back of Campbell Harper's church, resuming the practice she had used while attending Mass at St. Mary's. She knew Mamie went to church most Sundays but discovered that she went to Campbell's church, usually sitting four or five rows in front of Catherine.

Catherine always arrived at the last moment. It was easy for her to spot Mamie because of her blond hair, partly covered by a white lace cap when she attended church. There was a lot of singing in this church, much more than Catherine had heard during any Mass. She only mouthed the words or muttered along. But Mamie had a strong, clear voice, some kind of soprano, Catherine guessed, with the limited knowledge of music she had. But she could tell it was a beautiful voice, standing out but deservedly so. At the end of some of the hymns Catherine could see the Reverend Harper give Mamie a slight nod of recognition.

At least with the Catholics, you didn't necessarily know what the priests were saying, their backs to you and their voices pronouncing or chanting the ancient language, mostly incomprehensible but sometimes beautiful in its echoing way. The Reverend Harper erred on the side of enthusiasm. At the beginning of his sermons the sharpness of his voice was not offensive to Catherine, but as he went on, it carried an urgency to match the fears he meant to arouse. Catherine was not used to this kind of preaching, or to much preaching at all. Or church. Maybe if she had gone to Mass with her family, if her father had lived, if her mother had cared for anything beyond herself, the Mass could have made sense or, more likely, have been a mysterious refuge, safe, dark, and candlelit, like a hidden pathway through the endless tunnels of the world. On the other hand, there was Father Jean.

As she waited outside the church for Mamie, who was talking to some women in the choir, she remembered all those times she had waited for Louise in the courtyard with the big magnolia. Here there was only red dirt or mud underfoot and no trees or flowers nearby. Then Mamie was standing beside her on the wide front porch.

"Oh, I'm so full of the spirit I could fly!" Mamie's face shone with joy. "They want me in that choir, they do. Soon as somebody dies off, I'm in!"

Catherine was relieved that the service was over and wanted to change the subject. "How's your work at Clymer's?" Clymer's was a dress shop and millinery. Mamie was a seamstress there.

"Miz Clymer says I ruint another piece of silk and she cain't have that. And listen, that old lady Baird said I would have to pay another dollar a week to stay there. Now Catherine, I ain't got no extry dollars."

"What about Dale? Wasn't he sending you money from Little Rock?

"He says he's done sending me money. He says the papers is done, and me and him are too. I cain't hardly argue with him, now can I? He's wantin' kids, and after what happened, I cain't have none. Dale never beat up on me too hard, generally treated me good. But without me givin' him a child and no chance for another one a'tall, he's got to go out and find him another woman. Remember now, he give me fifty dollars, almost all he had, and loaded me up in the buckboard and took me to the train. And he sent another ten dollars before Christmas. Anyhow, the papers is done."

"It's not like it was your fault." As Catherine recalled, Mamie had come close to dying herself. Catherine took Mamie's elbow, and they walked toward Cherry Street.

"It might not have been so bad if the baby hadn't of died right in front of him, right after they took our little boy out of me. All stained with blood and stuff and blue-white dead. I know I'll never forget it. And come to find out the doctor had ruint me, too. After that, Mama said I was damaged goods and I'd better look out for myself. Anyway, she couldn't help me if she wanted to, which she don't."

"How much money do you have left?"

"I have four dollars and three bits. Period. And Dale give me a .22 derringer pistol, for protection, he said. I could sell it. Don't need much protectin' around here."

"Let's hope so."

CHAPTER 7

Helena, 1878

Abby continued to help Catherine during the spring term. She had grown taller, but Henry had shot up, too, and found a normal voice that matched the one he had discovered while playing Joseph in the play. His shins and calves above his bare feet were now sprinkled with curly light red hair, visible when he sat down and crossed his legs. He spent most of his time watching Abby, especially when she was helping to write lessons on the board, and the steady movement of her right hand caused her whole body to move beneath her calf-length dress.

Henry soon volunteered to walk Abby home, carrying her satchel (much smaller than the one Catherine had used at St. Mary's) and taking every opportunity to show off. Catherine took little notice of all this. By now she had almost won over Julia Brumley, having made her a kind of room monitor, with the main task of tattling on students who misbehaved during Catherine's brief absences for office work or personal necessity. Julia still had it in for Millie, she of the "tarnation," but Millie was so busy with geometry that Catherine, a bit rusty after three years, had to work to keep pace with her.

One day, Henry, again in the manner of Gabe Celiot, tried to persuade Abby to accompany him in search of a quiet place near the river where, he said, they could go on Saturday for a picnic. Abby was having none of it. Henry was insistent, moving ahead of her and getting louder and louder as they headed south toward her house near one of the levees. Her older brother, Albert, was a new deputy sheriff, tall like his father's side of the family and heavily built for a young man of twenty-one. He had swung by the family home on horseback for a routine patrol and heard Henry carrying on. When Henry noticed that Abby was looking past him at something on the dirt road, he turned and saw Deputy Albert Armitage glowering down at him.

Albert nudged the horse forward until Henry had to retreat. Abby had come around to the left side of Albert's horse and was trying to tell him everything was fine, she was almost home, and besides Henry was harmless. This bothered Henry more than the big horse and rider in his way. "I ain't harmless!" Henry tried his best to look tough.

"Is that right? So I reckon I should rope you up right now and pull you on over to the jail. How's that sound?"

Henry's people—the Ryersons—were in the saloon business and ran some freight to Little Rock on the side. They mostly avoided running afoul of the law but had no love for the sheriff or his crowd. Albert Armitage had been known to rough up a few of the Ryersons' best customers for no more than an occasional street brawl. Many of those happened when the steamboats were in, and the sheriff always sided with the passengers and crew when they got crossways with the saloon crowd.

"Well, I reckon my people might not like that." Henry cut his eyes at Abby, hoping to see in her eyes some support. There was none.

Albert gave the big bay gelding a gentle kick with his boots. The force of the horse's motion was just enough to move Henry backward about three or four feet without knocking him down. Albert leaned forward on the pommel. "Henry, why don't you get your skinny little ass on out of here."

The following Monday, Albert changed his patrol route to include a stop at the school when it was letting out. Abby came out with Millie, saw her brother on his horse, and hurried out to the playground. Henry was held after school for pestering Abby, yet again, and for interfering with her extra math work. Catherine was tired of putting up with Henry and told him to go on home. When he reached the schoolhouse door, Catherine was right behind him. "I've about had it with you, young man!"

Albert Armitage, not a churchgoer, had never seen Catherine up close before, but Abby had talked about her a lot at home, proclaiming,

"Miss McCain knows about everything there is to know." Albert was all set to say something sharp to Henry, except he couldn't stop staring at Catherine. He looked odd up there in the saddle of the big bay, the picture of horse-borne power, suddenly struck dumb.

Catherine grabbed Henry by both shoulders and turned him toward the steps. "Now go on home and behave yourself, and you best leave Abby alone!"

"That's right," Albert backed his horse out of the way to let Henry pass. "Yeah, you best leave." He never took his eyes off of Catherine. Henry went straight out to Abby and her friend.

Catherine turned her attention to Albert. "Now, can I help you?"

"Ma'am, I mean Miss, I am Albert Armitage, that is, Deputy Albert Armitage, and I came out here on—on a patrol to make sure all was well out here and, so I will be back. On patrol, I mean to say."

"So you must be Abby's brother. She's told me so much about you."

"She has?"

Catherine thought Deputy Armitage was for the moment not the most alert or competent officer of the law she had ever seen. "Anyhow, that Abby is a smart one," she said, and immediately realized that she might appear to be contrasting Abby with her brother. "I mean to say . . ."

"Yes, miss. She is." Albert had regained a little composure by now. He tipped his hat and, finding nothing else to say, turned his horse and rode off.

Abby was fifty feet down the road, trying to keep Henry from pestering her. "Albert! Brother, surely you can swing my book satchel up on that big horse and take them home for me!" Abby tried hard to look ill-used and a bit pitiful, but she was not able to bring it off.

"Official business, little sister! You get on home now, hear?"

* * * * *

The following Sunday in church, Catherine became aware of another late arrival who was making his way down the pew in search of a seat. On most Sundays now Catherine had an empty space next to her, or several empty spaces. At first Catherine didn't give her new isolation a thought; she figured the congregants saw through her, sensing that she was not sufficiently or transparently pious, and so they instinctively avoided her. Or maybe they had heard about her supposed lapses at the school. Either way, she didn't care.

The pew creaked and sagged a little as Albert's big frame settled in beside Catherine. Only now did it occur to him to take off his broad hat, and as he did so he gave her a nod and a shy smile. She barely moved her head in response. Soon the choir began the first hymn. Not only was it obvious that Albert was unfamiliar with the hymn, but Catherine could also see that he had difficulty reading the verses and no talent whatsoever when it came to carrying a tune.

Catherine was surprised that she felt something—kindness, sympathy—for the hulking young man beside her. No longer aware of the singing, she was thinking that, given Abby's above-average ability in school, the problem with Albert was probably not that he was stupid but that, like most boys and young men, he had simply not taken to school or lacked the time to go.

Outside, as Catherine waited for Mamie, she did not object to Albert standing quietly beside her. Then Rainey Harper came out of the church—he had been an usher, and was somewhat tardy making his exit—and seeing Catherine and Albert, he quickly joined them, taking care to fix his hat on his head just so.

"A glorious service, wasn't it?" Rainey said, a little too loudly and with an exaggerated smile. He looked at Albert, having to throw his head back and gaze upward to see Albert eye to eye. This caused him to have to reposition his hat, as a good breeze had come up. "I don't believe I've seen you here before, Deputy."

"Likely not."

"I suppose that evildoers, they don't stop for the Sabbath and so they keep you busy," Rainey said, rocking back and forth on his heels. "Too bad for you, I'm guessing. I'm sure you would be here more often if you could." Rainey smiled, trying to project generosity in providing a ready excuse for the deputy's lack of attendance.

Two days later, Rainey was concluding his Bible lesson, on Corinthians, at the end of the school day instead of earlier, as before. "I hate to say it, Miss McCain, but I have to head out to the other school. Problems with the levee again." The younger children were already outside when the lesson ended. Henry and Millie raced to the door, while Julia remained seated, trying to show how much she was devoted to the lesson.

Catherine gave her a look that should have been sufficient to cause her to leave, but Julia now seemed absorbed in prayer. "You need to go, Julia. Now."

Abby grinned, pleased to see Julia depart. "Will you be needing me anymore today, Miss McCain? I have already erased the board and taken out the trash." Abby had begun to rush through her chores of late.

Turning to Rainey, Catherine said, "I will see you to the door."

There was little he could say, although it was clear he wanted to stay a bit longer. But he tried: "Now that we have been at these lessons goin' on a year, I thought perhaps we might confine future lessons to ourselves. I mean, I would say that we could go deeper, that is to say, we might be able to—"

"Ah, but that's why we go to your brother's church on Sundays." The door was left ajar. Catherine opened it and went out on the porch. Rainey came along behind her. He was unaware that Albert Armitage was also on the porch until he saw him standing there tall and straight.

"Well, hello, Deputy," he said, his voice indicating vague suspicion. "What brings you here?"

Albert ignored Rainey and touched the brim of his hat. "Hello, Miss Catherine."

"Afternoon, Albert." Catherine gave him an especially warm smile, pleased that Rainey would witness it. Abby slipped quietly past them, and turned, smiling, to watch the pair interact.

Seeing Catherine's smile, Rainey stiffened. "I'm sure most of the misbehaving in this town would be over by the river."

Catherine tilted her head toward Albert. "Trouble can be hard to predict, isn't that right, Deputy Armitage?"

* * * * *

By the time fall arrived, Albert was driving a buggy over to the school on Sunday mornings to pick up Catherine for church. After another month, Rainey's Bible lessons at the school ceased. He hardly spoke to her at church. On a calm, mild Sunday in late October, Albert walked

Catherine to the front door of the school, but she was curious about his family and wanted him to stay for a while and talk. His parents and grandparents both lived in the house he grew up in, on the south side of Helena but not too close to the cypress swamps. His family operated a leather goods store. Besides Abby, he had two more sisters and two younger brothers. Catherine was fascinated by the way he spoke of them all, with few negative things being reported, and those most often presented humorously. She was content to listen, aware that she was curious to learn what a family life could be as opposed to what hers had been.

Of course, she knew Albert was sweet on her—very sweet, in fact. On that Sunday, as he stood at about the same spot where the Reverend Harper had stood on his first visit to the school, but with no lengthening shadow in the hour before noon, she quickly adjusted her heavy shawl, stepped directly in front of him, and gave him a kiss. It was only on the cheek but he was taken aback at first. "Why, Miss . . . why, Catherine, I don't know what to say."

She took his hand and they stood in the doorway, talking quietly in the bright sunshine with only a light north breeze and some wispy clouds floating across the clear blue sky. She moved a little closer to him and placed her head on his arm, below his shoulder. Albert leaned down and kissed her firmly on the mouth, at the same time cradling her head in his big hands. Catherine threw her arms around his shoulders. "I knew you would be trouble, Albert."

Fifty yards away, hidden within a grove of pecan trees, Rainey Harper let out a gasp so loud that he thought for an instant Catherine and Albert might have heard. They did not.

CHAPTER 8

Campbell Harper waited for all the students to leave before appearing at the schoolhouse door. Catherine was about to close it for the day. "I regret the necessity of this visit, Miss McCain. My dear brother has despaired of reaching your soul, and now he tells me he has learned you were carrying on with a man in this very schoolhouse, a place dedicated to teaching in the light of our Lord. It is a sacrilege, Miss McCain, and I—we will not have it. Please consider this to be your final warning."

"I can promise you that I have done nothing to bring dishonor on this school, Reverend Harper."

"That is not true, Miss McCain. I have it from an eyewitness that you and Deputy Armitage were, as the witness described it, 'locked' in a passionate embrace on this very spot in full view." He moved backward a foot or so, having realized he was standing on the "very spot" he had mentioned and found it to be unsettling.

"In full view of no one. There was no one here. Besides, Albert is a gentleman, and he would not 'lock' me into anything." Belatedly, she realized that, as a deputy, Albert could in theory actually lock her up. She suppressed a smile. How was it that when this stern and unrelenting man confronted her, she kept encountering these silly thoughts? The last time it was the word "long" that had set her off.

In any case, a hint of humor served to lighten the moment for her and give her courage. "Yes, I am unaccompanied here, but I am nineteen years of age. Albert did kiss me, yes, right where we are standing, but it only happened after I kissed him first."

"You kissed the man first? Why, no wonder he felt free to grab you up in a surge of passion!" Harper shook his head quickly, repeatedly, trying to rid himself of something so distasteful that he could not speak until he had banished it.

"I'm sorry you are fretful, Reverend. And all over nothing. I will not allow Albert into the schoolhouse again, and I will not so much as hold his hand when he comes out here."

"Oh, he will not be out here again, Miss McCain. I have spoken to the sheriff, and your Deputy Armitage will be lucky if he still has a job tomorrow. And in any case, teachers in our schools are not allowed to marry, unless my brother and I grant an exception. Therefore, courtship would be a waste of time." With this assertion of his power, the Reverend Harper regained his composure. He moved closer to Catherine and leaned down so far that the brim of his hat almost touched the top of her head. She wanted to back away but refused to let herself do so. Recalling the flat gray-eyed stare that had served her well with her mother and Father Jean, she fixed it on the reverend's dark eyes. But he did not blink or waver, and the word to describe the intensity in those eyes was the very one he had used himself: passion.

* * * * *

Mamie had to move out of Miss Baird's boardinghouse in November because she couldn't afford the cost. She had long since violated her probation for swearing, but Miss Baird let her stay on for over a year because Mamie was so sweet otherwise and attended church every Sunday, sitting in the same row where Miss Baird had recently staked out a seat. Mamie had been fired from the dress shop and was living on money she had borrowed from Catherine.

"I can't let you stay with me for very long," Catherine told her, after they had talked Albert into helping Mamie move into Catherine's quarters at the school. "The Harpers are giving me fits as it is. And I'm not much good at sharing a bed. Never had to, except with some cousins of mine in New Orleans. Told I'm given to kicking in my sleep." Catherine cut her eyes at Mamie.

"Honey, ain't I got the bruises to prove it. Anyhow, there is a man I know from church, a Mister Washburn, and he says maybe he can help me find some work. He says he owns part of the New Southern Hotel, you know it I'm sure, right about where Fifth crosses Cherry Street."

"That's a nice building. I've gone into the drugstore right next door." Catherine had seen the young man at church, often sitting beside or near Mamie. He could hardly be called handsome, with a face so ravaged in his youth that Catherine could see the deep pitted spots half a block away. In church he had to struggle against nodding off. "What kind of work would you do for this Mister Washburn?"

"Wallace, Wallace Washburn is his name. He says he needs help in the drugstore and maybe at the front desk in the hotel. The same folks own both places. I cain't see me workin' in no drugstore. All them medicines and things has got some funny names, and I cain't read or spell worth a shit. I s'pose I can say 'shit' around you."

"Probably best you don't while you're staying here," Catherine said. "I've begun to think this school has eyes and ears of its own." She thought for a moment. "What about the front desk at the hotel? Can you write out the names of the guests?"

"Wallace, he don't know I cain't read and write real good, but he done told me that the desk clerk, she only has to turn the—the—"

"Register. The guest register." Catherine sighed. She had always struggled with being patient if someone else's brain did not seem to keep pace with her own.

"The clerk turns the registry around so's people can sign in theirselves. Then it's only the keys and such that you give the people before taking their money and givin' change if you have to."

Catherine hesitated a moment before asking, "But you can count money, make change, all that?"

"If it has a number, I have it. And you'll never guess what else?" Mamie held her head up proudly and showed her big teeth.

"What else, then?"

"Along with my pay, I'll get my own small room in the hotel and one full meal a day in the dinin' room. Well, not in the dinin' room but right by it, near the main pantry. I can start in a week."

"That is wonderful!" Catherine was greatly relieved that now, after trying to ignore Mamie's snoring, she could finally get some real sleep.

Catherine's kicks in the night were often intentional, but Mamie never woke up. The snoring began with a loud and almost desperate inhalation, followed by a delay and a whistling sound through those big front teeth.

A few weeks later, Mamie reported that Wallace Washburn was so pleased with her work that he let her fill in at the drugstore when the regular helper was out sick. The only problem was the druggist had to point out exactly which bottles and patent medicines to bring to the customers because Mamie couldn't read well enough to sort them out for herself. By the end of the first day, the druggist was allowing Mamie to deal with the customers and make change while he picked out the medicines. He decided that this was a better way to operate, since he often had to leave the main counter anyway to measure out prescribed doses. This he had not wanted to do previously because he didn't trust anyone else to receive payments; he already suspected that the helper who was supposedly ill had been stealing patent medicines all along. As it turned out, after the first time the druggist showed her the medicines, Mamie remembered exactly where they all were and what their bottles or cartons looked like. Often it was she who had to tell the druggist where the item was located.

"I wish I could use you over here all the time," the druggist said after a couple of weeks. "But Wallace says the best he can do is let you work here on the slowest days in the hotel. He's busiest over there when the circuit court is in session and when the biggest steamboats come into town. Lots of folks lay over a night or two before taking the train to Little Rock. I'll talk to Wallace and work something out."

It turned out that Wallace thought it would be better to let Mamie work most mornings at the drugstore and cut the hours of the unreliable worker. The mornings were pretty slow in the hotel, and if things really got busy, Mamie could run next door and help out.

* * * * *

Early December, 1878
It was a Friday evening, and all the students had finally departed for home. Albert had come by for a quick visit but didn't get off his horse. That was the deal he had to make with the sheriff in order to keep his

job. The restriction did not apply to Sundays, when he still picked up Catherine for church, or on any day when he went with her to a rare social function downtown. "I told the sheriff that I have every right to escort you—I mean, to downtown and such."

"Preacher or no preacher putting ideas into his head, the sheriff can't find another man in this one-horse town who has the sense and the honesty and, by the way, the brawn and manliness that you do. I'd like to see him knock some heads together down at the saloon and pull those drunks apart when they're mad as hell. I don't give a damn what he or the Harper brothers think."

Albert was smiling. "You do have a sharp tongue." By now, he was used to the way she talked when the students weren't around. "Manly, am I?"

"Don't let it go to your head." *Or anyplace else, for now.* Catherine was still trying to banish the encounter with Father Jean from her memory.

After watching Albert ride away, Catherine set about sweeping the schoolhouse floor and cleaning up around the blackboard. Abby and Millie were not as reliable on Fridays as on other days when it came to cleaning up. Catherine had her back to the door, closed most of the way now that the evenings had turned chilly. The change in the weather brought to Catherine's mind the specter of another Christmas pageant and with it a determination to avoid staging one ever again.

There were still some coals glowing in the new Bridge & Beach potbellied stove that was Catherine's pride. She had helped to raise money for the stove and had donated five dollars of her own toward the purchase. It was a big improvement over the small stove she had inherited and much larger than the ornate but inefficient parlor stove in her quarters. The Bridge & Beach held a lot more wood, so much that Catherine had to keep piles of kindling and logs on hand. The schoolhouse felt especially cozy this evening; the big black kettle was still steaming on top of the stove. Catherine poured some tea into a cup on her desk and sat down with a satisfied sigh, paying only cursory attention to the papers strewn across the surface. She took a sip of tea and told herself that this was the happiest she had ever been in her life, Harpers be damned.

She was sitting there still when she saw the schoolhouse door slowly open fifteen minutes later.

"Who's there?" Catherine put her teacup down on her desk. She stood and walked toward the door.

She was only halfway down the center aisle between the student desks when she saw the face of Rainey Harper peering around the door. He immediately removed his brown bowler hat, and as he closed the door behind him, he held the hat near his chest, as if he had removed and positioned it for a salute. "Good evening, Catherine," he said huskily, not using "Miss McCain" as he did most of the time.

"What do you want?" Catherine stood her ground in the center of the aisle, about five paces from the door.

"It's been awhile," Rainey said, moving closer to her. "I know Campbell has visited with you a time or two, but I thought this would be a good time for me to pay you a special visit."

"Special. In what way?"

He placed his hat on a desktop near the aisle. "Now I'm here to let you know—"

"So he's going to fire me, is that right? After more than a year, after all the progress I've made with these students, he's going to fire me? Not to mention putting up with his hellfire and brimstone sermons every Sunday."

"He would, yes. But that's not why I'm here, Catherine. If I may . . . call you Catherine?" He took another step toward her, and she noticed he was somewhat unsteady on his feet.

"Have you been drinking again, Rainey?"

"You mean, 'Have you been drinking again, Mister Harper'? Maybe so."

"You must go."

"I guess I won't."

"Say what you have to say and then leave."

"Campbell wrote to your school down in Baton Rouge. What was it? Oh yes, St. Mary's. And only today he received a letter in response. From a Sister, uh, Francine. And do you know what this Sister Francine had to say about one Catherine McCain, a former student at St. Mary's?"

Catherine walked over to the stove, extending her hands to warm them. "Whatever she told you is a lie."

"Now, here's the problem, Catherine. Who would believe you over a Catholic nun, though granted she *is* a Catholic, but it's not the nuns who do the damage, is it? It's that Pope and all the priests who go around spreading nonsense about—"

"Christianity? Religion? Jesus? The Bible?"

"Take your pick." He reached inside his coat pocket and pulled out a flask. He took a sip from it, then another. "Anyhow," he began, but for a while said nothing more. Finally, he started up again. "Here's the long and short of it. You went and grabbed the private parts of a priest, and they ran you out of Baton Rouge. And you just a girl. Campbell, he says he's going to run you of out of Helena now. I figured I'd get here first. I got the letter from Campbell's desk at the church. Here it is." He took a letter from his side pocket.

Her fists clenched. "It's a lie."

He ignored her. "Now you and me are gonna have a little understanding. I'm gonna take this here letter and put it in that fire over there, but not till you and me do what we should've done months ago."

"What about your brother?"

"To hell with him! These schools are my dream. They are mine, period! I'm tired of him pushing his way into every nook and cranny of my life because he's a preacher, and he thinks his shit don't stink."

"I don't care what you do with that letter, but you'd better get out of here. Now."

Rainey slipped the letter back into his pocket. "I reckon not. I gave you this job, and I'm gonna save you this job, but by God you're gonna be nice to me now." He threw off his coat and rushed her, grabbing her by the shoulders. He tried to force a kiss, but she pushed him partly away. He ripped some of the buttons off her blouse, and when she turned from him, he shoved his hand beneath her dress collar and began dragging her toward the school office. "Come on now, teacher gal, let's go into your quarters and seal our bargain. I'll make sure you stay as long as you like, if you come on—"

Her right hand closed around the handle of the teakettle and she grabbed it off the stove. With all her strength, she twisted out of his grip and slammed the scalding bottom of the kettle into the side of his face. Screaming, he released her for a moment and came at her again, this time slugging her on the cheek and pulling at her hair. Still gripping the kettle, she held it against his left ear, hearing his flesh sizzle in accompaniment to his renewed screams. Furious now, he jerked up her dress and began to pull at her underclothes. He tried to clap a hand over her mouth, but she bit him so hard that he began to bleed and she had to spit out bits of his flesh. He butted her in the head and continued to rip at her clothing until he could see her bare legs.

"Damn you to hell!" Rainey knocked her down and threw himself across her body. She felt his powerful hands between her thighs and the scraping of his fingernails as he ripped at the seams of her drawers.

Catherine bent her right leg and pushed off the floor, shoving him off to the other side as she grabbed a hatchet that leaned against a stack of kindling near the stove. When he recovered and stared at her, she brought the hatchet down on the left side of his skull and split it open.

CHAPTER 9

She didn't remember getting up from the floor. Finally, she was aware that once again she was sitting at her desk. The hatchet was still in her right hand. Thinking she needed to button up her dress, she carelessly laid the bloody hatchet down on a small stack of penmanship papers turned in that day. Henry's was on top, his best effort to date. What a shame to smear blood on his good work, she thought. Henry was trying so hard to do better. He might as well have not made the effort. After staring at his paper for almost a minute, she studied her dress. The imprint of her own red-stained hands stood out clearly, but on her emotions there was no impression. Most of the buttons were ripped out or dangling by a thread. She fastened those that she could and then sat motionless in the chair.

How much time went by, she could not say. She was neither frightened nor surprised when Campbell Harper appeared at the door. Barely taking note of her, for several moments he stared at the body of his dead brother next to the stove.

Odd, he doesn't look surprised either. She watched the reverend come up the aisle. He stopped about five feet away when he saw the bloody hatchet on the desk. "He tried to rape me. He was drunk and he tried to rape me."

Campbell kept his eyes on the hatchet. "I wouldn't be surprised if he had something to drink, all right. He was sick when he read the letter. He fancied he was in love with you, you know that? He could hardly have known what kind of woman you are." The preacher walked over to

his brother, leaning down to inspect Rainey's awful wounds more closely. His manner was clinical. "Hmm, disfigurement too. And he always
wanted an open casket."

"In love with me! He tried to rape me! He might have killed me."

Campbell studied the burned places on his brother's face and ear.
Yes, the burn scars would remain. He was quiet for several moments,
considering. "No, Miss McCain. My brother came out here to tell you
that your time in this town was over, that he knew about your evil ways
back in Baton Rouge and that you must go. You knew he was completely
taken with you, God knows why. He confessed to me that you seduced
him last Christmas, after he had taken too much Christmas cheer. Only
two nights ago I found him in the gutter near the church and would have
rebuked him had he not chosen that opportunity to confess. He could
not rid his mind of the sinful occasion, try as he might with the help of
whiskey to do so. He was sure he could bring you to repent. I am sure
that this very evening he tried again, and you would have none of it. He
had let you stay here long after it was clear that you were not worthy
of this post, or of being in our town. Tonight he showed you the letter
from Baton Rouge, hoping you would swear to change your ways, and at
last, yes, repent. But you, a vain and sinful woman, tried to seduce him
once again, hoping to save your job in the only way you knew how. You
attacked him after he spurned you, burned him with that big kettle, and
when he tried to fight you off, you split his head open with that hatchet."

"No! He tried to rape me! I would never think of seducing Rainey,
never. I loathed your brother, as I loathe you!" She tried to collect herself. "The only man I've ever cared for is Albert. I've never been with—
it's none of your business."

He thought about this for a while. Then he knelt beside his brother's body and pulled Sister Francine's letter from Rainey's pocket. "You
would have thrown the letter into that stove and done God knows what
with Rainey's body. But I have the letter now. Who will believe that a
woman who tried to seduce a priest in his own church, for God's sake,
would not do the same to a fine, eligible man such as my dear brother?"

"I am no whore. I am—untouched." As soon as she spoke the word,
she was furious at herself for disclosing so much to this awful man.

"Is that so? Well, Dr. Whitmire is a good friend of mine. He will say if you are as virtuous as you claim to be. The letter gives good reason to doubt it, and my brother's soulful confession to me confirms your true nature."

Catherine moved her hand toward the hatchet and thought about making a run for the door. Four years ago it had happened, on Uncle Connor's farm. She had learned to ride like a man would ride, astride a western saddle. The big colt didn't throw her, although he tried; but for a few seconds as he bucked, her body shifted toward the back of the saddle, and she came down hard on the edge before she could re-center herself. She didn't feel much of anything, but later she saw a few drops of blood. It was not her time of the month. One washing and the stain was gone. She had given it little thought. Louise Pennette and two other girls at St. Mary's told her what it meant. "It's my word against yours, Reverend, and you weren't here."

"Your word! A woman who tried to seduce a priest?"

If only Albert were here, he would believe me. She stood up, leaving the hatchet on the desk, and took a deep breath. "Are you in your buggy or do you have the wagon?" Sometimes he drove the latter when he was picking up supplies for the schools or the church.

"The wagon. Why do you ask?"

"If you need help getting Rainey into the wagon, I will do what I can. You can leave me with the sheriff."

* * * * *

Harper left the wagon, with Rainey's body in the back, outside the sheriff's office on Main Street. There Rainey lay, uncovered on the way there, and uncovered still. The sheriff came outside, and he and Harper half dragged Catherine into the office.

Albert had been at the saloon breaking up a fight when he heard the news of Rainey's killing from a teenaged boy who had stopped to pester the sheriff for a job, only to be sent to fetch Albert. On horseback, Albert outraced the crowd down to the sheriff's office. Glancing inside, he could see the sheriff and Reverend Harper talking at the sheriff's desk. He could not see the cells, for they were down a hallway off the main office and usually closed off to keep out the noise of prisoners misbehaving or relieving themselves. Albert had heard that Catherine, or rather, "that teacher gal," had been arrested for killing Rainey. The saloon crowd was gathering—loud, drunk, and demanding.

"Look what that woman done to him!" yelled Raymond Wilkins, whose appearance at any place other than the saloon was remarkable. "Look at his head, God Awlmighty. It's split like a melon, I swear."

"She ought to be hung," said another.

"You cain't hang a woman, by God!" Raymond slapped the side of the wagon. "Can you?"

"They hung a woman for helpin' to kill Lincoln," someone said.

"Well, they shouldn't've hung her." Raymond spat on a wagon wheel.

Albert walked out to the gathering crowd. He rested his left hand on the muzzle of the old horse still hitched up to Campbell's wagon. He stared straight into Raymond's eyes. "Here's one thing y'all need to know. None of you can hang anybody, not man nor woman nor child, God forbid, because you are not and will not be the law."

"You would say that," Raymond muttered, but loudly enough for many to hear him.

Albert stood half a head taller than any of those gathered and was broader and thicker besides. He walked directly to Raymond, who was standing at the back of the wagon and had begun to shiver, and not only from standing in the cold without a proper coat. Raymond grabbed the top of the rear wheel as Albert came toward him, finding that he required something other than his own frail will to hold him steadily in place.

Albert stood so close to Raymond that he was essentially pinned against the wagon. "I'm guessing you have nothing else to say." Seconds went by. "That's what I thought. Now the rest of you go on home or back to the saloon."

When they had gone, Albert entered the office without knocking. "Since the reverend here has left his dead brother out in the chill for all to see, I'm wondering, Sheriff, if we might have an old blanket to at least cover up the man's body. It's a sight . . . sir."

Sheriff Rawlings was an unlikely sheriff. He seldom wore a badge and hadn't made an actual arrest in more than a year. People in Helena liked him, so they elected him. He was a Mason, he went to church, and he could hold his liquor. They knew he didn't do much, but they knew Albert could handle the real trouble. Mostly bald on top, the sheriff wore heavy, graying sideburns and let what was left of his hair grow long and wild. "Evenin', Albert," he said, and immediately found some papers he needed to shuffle on top of an old cabinet behind his desk.

Campbell stood and faced Albert. "I have made my statement, but I am not leaving until Judge Phillips gets over here and formally charges that woman with murdering my brother."

"And how about Catherine? Has she made her statement?" Albert heard the sound of a cabinet drawer closing behind him.

"I done heard it," Sheriff Rawlings said. "Took some notes too."

"Mind if I see 'em?" Albert knew the sheriff hated paperwork; signing warrants and citations seemed to unsettle him.

The sheriff handed him a single sheet of paper. "You didn't write this, Sheriff."

"No, but it says what she said."

"So the reverend here wrote this down?"

Campbell nodded. "I did so, as a public service to Sheriff Rawlings here."

Albert began to read the notes, but his eagerness to know the contents outpaced the level of his literacy. He handed them to the reverend. "You wrote it. Now read it."

"Well, it says Rainey tried to rape Catherine, and she killed him in self-defense. What you don't see in those notes is that my brother had come under the spell of your, uh, *friend*, Catherine McCain," Campbell said, looking somewhat uneasy. For a moment he couldn't find the words he needed to go on. Clearing his throat, he looked toward the ceiling, certain that whatever came next would reflect the wishes of the Almighty. "The sheriff here has heard this tawdry tale, but I see you will not be satisfied until you have heard it too. I am ashamed to say that my dear, late brother was seduced by Miss McCain last Christmas, his true and innocent desire for her having been twisted into lust. God bless him, he did open his heart to me two nights ago, confessing the sin and not denying that the worst evil had occurred. Tragically, this evening, after receiving evidence about her depravity that even he could not overlook, he walked to the school to tell her she must repent with all her heart or leave at once. She obviously went into a rage, attacking him first with a scalding iron pot before laying his head open with a hatchet. He no doubt attempted to defend himself, to take hold of her and cast her away, but the hatchet did fall, Deputy, and he was killed."

"What evidence? And how do you know what your brother was doing there?"

Campbell, now completely sure of himself, pulled a folded letter from his coat pocket. "You may read this."

Albert's confidence in Catherine's innocence had been strong, but as he read the letter very slowly, too proud to ask the reverend for assistance, his lips moved hesitantly at times, and his shoulders became more rounded. Toward the end, his hands began to tremble. He quickly laid the letter on the desk and wiped his open palms on his coat. "I cannot believe it." Albert's voice was barely audible. "I know she would never do what that letter claims she did, and there is no way she would kill Rainey or anyone else unless she had to."

The sheriff excused himself to go look for an old blanket. He found one and went outside.

"You know it? Don't you think it's strange that she never told you why she came here?"

"Why, no, I assumed she had finished school in Louisiana and wanted to teach somewhere else. She is a wonderful teacher; the students love her. I also know that her mother was, I would say, a hard woman to abide."

"And what of her virtue?" The reverend was mindful enough to remove himself to a safer place behind the sheriff's desk.

It was a good thing he did so. Burdened with anger, doubt, and despair, Albert at first responded angrily. "She was—is—pure! We were going to marry!" His eyes moistened, and he paused to take a deep breath. "She loved her life here, no thanks to you and Rainey, and loved the kids and the school. I never asked her about her life before Helena, but one Sunday on the way back to the school after church, she touched me on the arm and said, 'You are my only man, Albert. I guess I've been waiting for you without knowing I was waiting for you.' I will never forget those words, how I felt, and how she moved closer to me in the buggy seat and let her head rest on my shoulder."

The sheriff returned, to get out of the cold and to flee from the awful proximity of Rainey's corpse. Campbell gave Albert a few moments of quiet. "Yet after she told me the same story about her virtue, what do you suppose she did when I said Doc Whitmire could settle this once and for all after a brief examination?"

"That's what done it for me," Sheriff Rawlings said. "She said no."

Albert took off his hat and ran his long fingers through his hair. He let his head sag and stared at the floor. Then he snapped up Sister Francine's letter. His eyes moved slowly across the lines, as he sought reassurance where none existed. He let the letter drop from his hands.

"You want to see her?" The sheriff's voice was less gruff that usual. Albert didn't move or respond. "I say, do you want to see Miss McCain?"

As fast as he had picked up the letter, he now retrieved his hat, fixed it firmly on his head, and hurried outside to his horse, hitched next to Campbell's wagon.

CHAPTER 10

Judge Phillips didn't appear until the next morning when, hungover and unsteady, he officially charged Catherine with the murder of Rainey Harper. A trial was set for Monday the next, five days away.

Mamie heard the news from a customer while she was working in the drugstore, wrapping up a bottle of Brown's Iron Bitters, a dusty bottle like the rest of the stock that hadn't been selling since a new product had come in with a higher alcohol content.

"This cain't be," she whispered to herself, when the customer had departed. Mamie could see that maybe Catherine could take a man down if she put her mind to it, but there wasn't any way she would kill somebody unless she had no choice. Mamie took some comfort in the thought that if anyone had to be killed, it should probably have been Rainey Harper. The nasty little man had tried to take liberties with Mamie more than once, including a time back in September when he showed up drunk at the hotel front desk and said he'd take the best room in the house if Mamie would join him later on. Wallace Washburn heard Rainey's loud talk and came out of his office with his eyes on fire. In an angry tone Mamie had never heard from him, he told Rainey that he would throttle him with a cane if he didn't get out and do the same if he ever came back.

After that, Mamie began to consider Wallace in a different light. He complimented her often, especially on her ability to handle money, a surprise to him given her near illiteracy. Aware of her front teeth, yet not extremely self-conscious about them, Mamie nevertheless took notice when a person she was talking to kept glancing at her teeth or studiously avoided looking at them at all. Wallace did neither; what he did instead was gaze into her eyes like they were blue sapphires set into her face just so he could admire them.

Mamie had come to prefer the drugstore to the hotel front desk. She came to really know many of the townspeople who came in regularly for their medicines and learned when the busy and slow times would be during the day. She was trying to learn to read more than a few simple phrases; Catherine had given her a copy of the first reader used in the school. During the slow times, she worked her way laboriously through the reader. After eight weeks, she was still on lesson three.

After hearing the horrible news about Catherine, Mamie rushed next door to find Wallace in his office. "I have to see her, and now!" Mamie said, after telling him what had happened and not at all doubting that Wallace would let her do as she pleased.

He nodded. "I can cover for you, and the new druggist will come in by noon."

At the jail she had to knock repeatedly before Sheriff Rawlings, who had been dozing, got out of his chair and opened the door. "My name is Mamie, and I'm a friend of Catherine's, who's in your jail. Is there any way I can talk to her?"

"Supposed to be no visitors." The sheriff tilted his head back and squinted at Mamie in case she might challenge him. "And besides, I was . . . restin'."

Despite wearing a warm coat, Mamie managed to shiver and said, "Brrr, it's freezin' out here." The sheriff moved back a step. "I'm so sorry, Sheriff, to have woke you from your nap. You must be tired, what with all the—the crimes and fightin' and stuff that goes on around here. I want you to know, Sheriff, that all the God-fearin' people of Helena appreciate you and what you do for us."

The sheriff looked surprised. "I don't get a whole lot of thanks around this town." The lines of his mouth and his eyes reflected the unfairness of it all. "So thank you, Miss . . ."

"Mamie. And I figured you and them other boys workin' out of here might be wore out from all the goin's on, so guess what?"

Sheriff Rawlings was gradually shifting into full wakefulness and was aware of an unaccustomed sense of happiness upon doing so. "Don't know. What?" He leaned closer to Mamie.

"Do you know that I work at the New Southern Hotel, and do you know what else I do there? Here's what I do: I help the cook bake cookies! Ain't that grand? And the cook, he give me two dozen fresh tea cake cookies right out of the oven not fifteen minutes before I left out of there to come see you. I love a tea cake cookie, don't you, Sheriff?"

"Yes, ma'am, I do."

"Now you go on back to your desk, and I'll take this here sack of tea cakes out of my big carryall and fix you a nice fresh pot of coffee. You'd like that, I'm guessin'?"

"I like tea cakes and coffee. I sure do."

The coffee freshly brewed, Mamie poured a mugful for the sheriff and a regular cup for herself. She put the cup down near the sack of tea cakes. "My, that shore does smell good, don't it? I reckon you won't mind if I pull up that chair yonder and maybe have a cup of this coffee and only one tea cake, if that's all right with you?"

By the time Mamie was settled at the right side of his desk, the sheriff was on his second cookie. Crumbs from the first lay on his desk. He eyed the sack jealously as Mamie took out a tea cake for herself. "Only one," she said, giggling. "Us ladies have to watch our, well, you know we cain't go about eatin' whatever we want when we need to keep purty for, well, for our jobs and all. Now you men, y'all git so much exercise with all the work you do, chasin' down them bad fellers out there, that y'all don't have to worry none about eatin' whatever you want."

With three tea cakes down and an empty cup, the sheriff held the mug up and tilted it so Mamie could see it was empty. Mamie took the mug over to the square-topped stove. She filled the mug slowly and stole a glance at the sheriff. "You know, this smells so dang good, I shore do feel bad about not maybe takin' a cup in to Catherine. She loves her coffee. Cain't see how that could hurt, Sheriff Rawlings." Mamie went ahead and poured an extra cup before taking the sheriff's mug over to the desk.

The sheriff sipped from the fresh mug, as if his answer might depend on the taste of the coffee. He put the cup down and reached into the paper sack for his sixth tea cake. "Naw," he said.

Startled, Mamie struggled to think of a new approach.

The sheriff swallowed a mouthful of tea cake and coffee. "Naw, I cain't see that it would hurt a thing. But mind you, don't tarry."

Catherine, still in her torn and bloody clothes, was alert and standing at the door to her cell, both hands tightly gripping the bars. She was almost but not quite tearing up. "Thank God for you, my dear friend. I heard it all and, yes, I did smell that coffee, and God how I want a cup."

Mamie handed her the cup through the bars. Catherine drank from it eagerly. "And here's six tea cakes for you." Mamie parceled them out from the side pockets of her long dress. Catherine ate three of them almost as fast as Mamie could pass them to her.

Mamie let her be until Catherine slowed down and seemed to relax a little. "I cain't help but ask what Albert had to say? I'm guessin' he gave 'em what for."

Catherine took a small sip of coffee and looked away.

Mamie had seen something unusual in Catherine's eyes and realized that her friend might be tearing up after all. She had never seen Catherine cry. Nor would she now, for Catherine composed herself and tossed some loose hair away from her face.

"I haven't slept for thinking about it. He came back last night, late, to take over the office from the sheriff. We talked for only a few minutes before the sheriff told Albert to lock up the main door and stay in the office till the saloons closed down. He was beside himself, all right, but Campbell—your sainted preacher—filled his head with nonsense. Campbell had a note from Sister Francine in Baton Rouge saying I tried to seduce a priest. I think Albert might have believed I would be with Rainey Harper, if you can imagine that. I stayed awake hoping to talk to him again. All I heard was the sound of him locking the front door when he left."

"And by seduce, are you talkin' about knowing a man, in the Bible way?"

"I mean sex, Mamie. Sex. And no, all I did to that priest was knock him on the head."

"Gracious sakes alive! You didn't kill him too?"

"Of course not." Catherine closed her eyes and took a deep breath. "As I said, I've been thinking about it, and here it is in a nutshell: Albert is a man who looks at life such that right is right and wrong is wrong. He can't take anything in between. That's why he's a good lawman, I suppose. But Campbell filled him with so many lies and cast so much doubt on my . . . my character that Albert couldn't find enough certainty in what I said to offset the lies. See what I mean?"

Mamie appeared to be thinking hard but said nothing.

"It's like this. I let slip to Campbell in trying to defend myself that I had never been with a man. But that wasn't good enough for him, and it wasn't good enough for Albert, either. You know what Albert told me? He said all I needed to do was let the town quack come in and check out my genitalia and say I was a virgin, leaving 'no doubt' that I had not been with Rainey Harper. Damn stupid men, all of them. Any woman could tell them a doctor can't always be right about such things."

"I'm gonna guess that word you used, ginny-tail-ya or somethin' like that, means what most folks call the private parts?"

"Specifically, the hymen. It's what often breaks the first time and maybe bleeds some too."

"My goodness! Mine done broke years ago without havin' any of that sex."

"Same with me, while I was on a damn horse."

"I was chasin' a dang old cat up a hackberry, and the next thing I knew I was straddlin' a limb. Yep. Scared me, it did, but Mama done a good job of makin' me understand what happened. Mm-hmm. One good thing she did. I reckon maybe the only good thing she did."

Now Catherine was angry. "I told Albert he could believe me or he could forget me, but I wasn't having any half-drunk hick-town sawbones going near my vagina. Very near. And that's what did it for Albert. He left and slammed door."

"Well, I think I've heard of that v-word you said." Mamie had known what she wanted to talk about before she saw Catherine, but now she had to collect herself before she could remember it in full. "Now here's what I been thinkin'. You're gonna be hung for shore. I hear more news than anybody in this town, and you will be hung, prob'ly on Monday, right after the trial. So here it is. I ain't got it all in my head, but you can round it out. I found me some stuff in the drugstore that'll knock the sheriff plumb on his butt for hours when we decide to use it. But after that, I don't know."

Catherine sat down on the cot near the back of the cell. She munched on the last tea cake and drank more coffee. When she had finished with both, she jumped up and handed the empty cup through the bars to Mamie. "I'll need money and a disguise. I'll need to look like a man, so get me a hat and trousers and a man's shirt, and a black tie and a pair of brogans, about size eight but no smaller. The money is hidden under a light-colored board about a yard to the right of the parlor stove in my quarters at the school. There's a clasp knife in a cream cup on the mantle. Use that to lift the board. The gold is in two leather pouches. Use some of the money to buy me a steamboat ticket to St. Louis. Come back when you have it all ready, and speak up so I can know you're here. You might have to wait for a St. Louis boat, but there should be one by Saturday, by way of Memphis." She took a deep breath and added, "Mamie, you must know they'll come after you."

At first Mamie seemed surprised. In her excitement about the plan she had hatched, she had given no thought to the consequences for herself. She was quiet for a while, her brows drawn close together as she absorbed the undeniable truth of what Catherine had said. Then: "How much is half of that gold of yours?"

"Well, half of the gold would be exactly forty dollars, but if you take all the bills, too, half would be seventy dollars, give or take." Was that right? Catherine wondered. Yes, close enough.

"Hmm. I make six cents an hour times ten hours a day times six days a week, and with three hunnerd sixty-five days a year minus fifty-two Sundays and Christmas that means I would work, let's see, three hunnerd and twelve days at sixty cents a day, which comes to one hunnerd and eighty-seven dollars and change for a year. So that means seventy dollars is, let me see now, that's about four and half months' pay right there. You sure that's all you got?"

"You lost me early on, but I guess I'll take your word for it. I see why Mr. Washburn appreciates your head for numbers. And yes, that's all I have."

"I reckon I might go with you. You did say St. Louis? It ain't like I'm broke, you know. I got nine dollars and twenty-five cents stuck under my mattress."

Catherine tried to set aside the excitement she was feeling. "But I thought you and Washburn were sort of getting together."

"I been thinkin' on that a lot lately, before, you know, you kilt Rainey. It won't do. Wallace loves me, and I can see he does. But I can tell for shore he don't really love the Lord."

"Well, then, best by far if you can get tickets for an evening departure." Catherine paused, trying to picture what else they would need. "Does the store carry any hair dye? Plain black would do, and you'll need some too. Oh, and Mamie, bring some scissors and a paper bag."

They heard footsteps followed by the sheriff's loud knocking on the door to the jail hallway. "That'll be enough!" he shouted, and at first they feared he might have overheard. But then he said, "And now, Mamie, I'm thinkin' we'll need another pot of coffee."

CHAPTER 11

Two evenings later, a Friday, Mamie and Catherine—the latter dressed in a brown woolen suit and knee-length overcoat taken from Wallace Washburn's closet, a black bowler hat with a fake satin band, and mud-spattered brogans a size too large—left Sheriff Rawlings sound asleep and snoring with his head on his desk. Next to his head were tea cake crumbs and half a cup of spilled coffee. After walking in the shadows for only a block, Catherine spotted Albert on his horse heading their way from the south end of town. She and Mamie ducked into an alleyway and were relieved when he turned off to the west to finish his patrol.

For several moments, Catherine watched as his broad body, uncharacteristically slumping to his right, receded with each dutiful step of the bay. She could see him living his life that way, not inert or desperate but simply going on, following orders and routines and summoning the cursory physical control he would have to apply periodically to the drunks and rowdies of the town. She felt sorry for him now, her admiration and respect for him, once pronounced, giving way to what she saw in his future. Taking one last look at the man whom she had thought she could marry, she nodded once, emphatically, now sure that one day she would have left him behind regardless, sadder and worse off than he was now.

Mamie looked at Catherine with concern. "He was a nice feller. He treated you nice and would've stood strong by you if he hadn't been so dang stupid."

"It's not that he's stupid. It's—it's men, what they think this world expects of them, that they alone must know all the answers, even when they don't."

"I see that. Mm-hmm. So they ain't stupid, they're just plumb wrong and cain't see it."

While they were in the alley, they divided up the money, putting most of it in their copious shoulder bags. Mamie had cut Catherine's hair, and they put the scattered clippings into a paper bag, stuffing it behind a loose board next to a rusty drain spout. Catherine retained as much hair as possible on top, covering most of it with the bowler, tipped back toward her neck.

They had an hour before the steamboat *Natchez* would embark. Mamie had with her two bottles of Batchelor's Liquid Hair Dye, black, from Washburn's store. Catherine wasn't too concerned about applying it to her hair as long as she was wearing a hat and still pretending to be a man, but Mamie would need to cover her natural blond curls. "It would be best if we could slip into the hotel and color your hair." Catherine had an idea how Mamie would react.

"No, ma'am! Wouldn't have time to dry, and besides, I ain't goin' to rur'n my hair with that stuff."

Catherine had little patience with Mamie's vanity. But Mamie's hair was exceptional, and Catherine suspected that, consciously or not, Mamie might feel that it offset the appearance of her front teeth. "People searching for us will be giving out our descriptions. We don't want to look like ourselves."

Mamie stopped and took something out of her valise. Quickly she pulled a dark brown wig over her hair and stood statue-like, glaring at Catherine. Some blond hair peeked out at the edges, but Catherine reluctantly agreed that it might do the job.

"It's a Batchelor's wig, same company as makes the dye. Wallace, he sells a lot more of the dye; he won't miss the wig or the dye for quite a while, I'm thinkin'. I guess you should go ahead and put the dye on now so's it'll be set when we git on that boat. And while we're on the subject, I'm sayin' you need to work on that walk of yours. You ain't none too prissy as it is, but you might try to throw them toes out and stride a little longer. Good thing you ain't got a big old butt." Mamie thought she was done, but one more thing occurred to her. "We could pull that cinch a little tighter up top, though, I mean for hidin' what little there is to see."

CHAPTER 11

Catherine was growing annoyed with Mamie's instructions. Instead of answering back, she satisfied herself by thinking it wouldn't hurt Mamie to do some cinching up too.

There was a decent dock in Helena, and they were able to board without getting much more mud on their clothes. Their tickets were for one stateroom on the larboard side of the boiler deck, a short distance from the "holiday deck" that passengers used for strolling and sightseeing when the weather permitted. The day was mild for early December and people were about. Mamie was frightened by another term, "boiler deck," until a smartly dressed junior officer patiently explained that the actual boilers were below in the boiler room.

"Well, sir," she replied, "bein' as we are right above your 'boiler room,' that means if somethin' goes wrong down there we'll be blown sky high!"

The officer was direct in his reply. "Miss, if the boiler room explodes the whole vessel will be, as you say, blown sky high. This river is littered with the remains of boats large and small. But it's way safer than the Missouri."

The officer left them near the stairs to the boiler deck. Mamie was shaking her head. "If I'd known all this, I'd have stole me a horse. We could git off this thing in Memphis, ain't that so? By the way, I didn't know they was so proud of these dang tickets. We ain't got all that much money left now. I didn't figure on no thirty dollars apiece."

"Memphis isn't far enough away. Maybe St. Louis isn't, either. Don't worry, we'll make do."

As they left their stateroom, they paid more attention to the painted panels at either end of the large stateroom deck. Indians, war dancing on one panel, bowed down in sun worship on the other. Mamie looked at them warily. She and Catherine went to the next deck down, moving forward with a sizable group toward the main dining room. Catherine had taken off the overcoat and now carried it folded across her left arm. "I hate these clothes. If could find me a couple of decent dresses, I could go back to being a young woman again." *Being a woman again. Be careful what you wish for.*

They let the larger groups pass them by. Catherine heard a loud, clear voice, somehow familiar. As she and Mamie moved ahead, she gave up trying to place it. Soon she heard it again, closer, ahead and to the right, fluttering out of a porthole open to the relatively mild air for late fall. "Oh, look at you, *Mademoiselle*! You need to find one of the *artistes* on board, I think. If he is at his very best, he might capture enough of your beauty that you would not be too dissatis*fied*."

"Good God Almighty!" Catherine walked quickly to the porthole and removed her bowler hat to get a better look. Inside, Gabriel Celiot was shaking a young lady's freshly cut hair from the scarlet chair cape she had worn, tied at her neck. He smiled at the happy customer as she walked past him, dropping a shiny coin into his open palm. As she left, Gabe glanced at the porthole. An instant before Catherine could see her name form on Gabe's lips, she recognized his smile, and was filled with the most spontaneous joy she had ever felt. "Gabe! Oh, Gabe, it's you!"

Mamie closed her eyes and let out a deep sigh. "Now what?"

Gabe motioned for Catherine to turn around and enter the salon from a door off the deck. Mamie followed. Catherine threw her arms around Gabe's neck and they hugged each other tightly. Mamie jerked her head around to see if anyone was watching. The salon was empty, luckily, as most passengers were intent on reaching the main dining room as early as possible.

Holding each other at arm's length, Catherine and Gabe regarded each other for several moments, both with big smiles. "What have you done to your hair?" Gabe asked, affecting strong disappointment. "The most beautiful hair I have ever seen! And what are these clothes? Oh, I see now. You have done something bad, Catherine McCain."

"That ain't the half of it," Mamie said.

The joy left Catherine's face so quickly that Gabe's affected disappointment turned quickly to genuine concern. "It's a long story, Gabe." She removed the bowler hat and let the considerable hair she had retained tumble down.

"Much better! And who is your friend?" Gabe walked around Catherine to engage Mamie more closely. "That is not your hair! You . . . you are a blond, correct? You have beautiful skin."

He started to reach out and touch it, but Mamie stepped back. Initially, she'd felt annoyed that he had detected the wig; now she was blushing at his compliment. She promised herself a nice long bath after she escaped these two. "Yep, a real long story," she muttered.

"Gabe, please meet Mamie. She is my dear friend. Among other things she has just saved my life."

"I am delighted to meet you, Mamie."

She smiled, but not so widely that it revealed her front teeth.

Catherine grabbed Gabe's arm. "And what about you, Gabe? I was so worried. So was Louise."

"Ah. Louise." A shadow crossed Gabe's eyes.

"Have you seen her? Oh, Gabe, is she all right?"

＊＊＊＊＊

"I will close the salon for the rest of the day, Catherine. We must talk."

"You can do that?" Mamie still felt unsettled around this young man with ebony skin, so confident in himself.

"Yes. Now, as it is dinnertime, please tell me what you would like to eat. We can eat in my anteroom. I will have the food brought in."

"Now hold on." Mamie eyed Gabe suspiciously.

"It is this way. I have this salon and a large cabin and anteroom. To assist me I have two cabin boys, one to clean up and another as an apprentice and helper with errands, supplies, other little things."

"And you as black as—"

Gabe smiled at Mamie. "Yes. Blacker than Catherine's bowler hat, and far more lustrous, I believe."

"Lust-er-us?" Mamie's stomach growled loudly.

"It is like this. My father—Catherine will remember him—he became a steward on a much smaller boat, a boat on that oh-so-nasty Missouri River."

"I already heard all about that river." Mamie drew her shawl tighter around her shoulders.

"This was after we escaped from Baton Rouge. He came to know the owner of this boat while he was in Memphis. The man needed a steward, and now my father is, I would say, the boss man to all the cabin staff, waiters, kitchen helpers on this very *Natchez* boat. And the chambermaids, of course." At this, his eyes brightened. "This is actually the *Natchez Seven* boat. The others are—"

"Let me guess, all blowed up or sunk?"

"Well, not quite all." Gabe had the daily menus from the dining room in his salon. Perhaps Mamie would feel better after eating. "We will have none of the greasy pork or mutton. Ah! Let us have the catfish! It is fresh and tasty! We will have *patates frites* and fresh corn. And a bottle of champagne. *Voilà!*"

Once the food came, Catherine and Mamie ate greedily and so rapidly that Gabe was only half finished when they were enjoying their fresh custard pies. Trying not to be too pushy, Catherine had forced herself to avoid asking about Louise Pennette until they were done with dinner. She was about to bring up the subject when Mamie said, "This stuff here is kinda fruity, don't y'all think." She held up her champagne glass, already emptied twice over. She burped, but not too loudly. "Pardon me, I'm sure," she said primly.

Gabe put his plate aside and declined to take a custard. He poured more champagne all around, sat back, and sighed.

"About Louise," Catherine began.

Gabe took a breath. "I saw her only once. We had docked in St. Louis and the pilot took sick. He didn't want any other pilot taking his place, and since he has a stake in the boat, nobody could tell him what to do. The hands and crew had liberty for three full days. The white men from the boat could go anywhere; most of the blacks could not. But I could, and went to hear my Uncle Baptiste play in a saloon on Garrison Street. Well, I must say it—a saloon and burlesque house. All of the patrons were white, including four or five from the *Natchez*. I came through the back door and took my place in a chair near the stage. I was only five, six feet away from Uncle Baptiste but hidden by a curtain. He knew I was there, of course. He called for beer after beer, but between songs he would come behind the curtain and give me a beer too.

"I was there more than an hour before I saw Louise. She came onstage with four other people. I could not believe it was her! It was a burlesque, you see, and I could not imagine Louise like that. They had a juggler and a fire-eater, and some man throwing knives into a box, a box that had a woman inside, you could only see the woman's head and her eyes. What eyes she had!"

"Oh, no." Catherine set what was left of her custard on the table.

"Louise was on the end of the stage closest to Uncle Baptiste and the piano. The women, they did their own dances as they removed some of their clothes, tossing first their scarves and then their sashes and . . . and that's when she saw me, there in my chair offstage. She stared at me for two, three seconds maybe, before clasping her bare arms across her chest and running straight past me and down the steps, toward the dressing room near the back."

"Who is this Louise?" Mamie's tone revealed her disgust.

"Another dear friend, Mamie. But Gabe, when we get to St. Louis, I must find her. You can take us there? Please do it for me."

"Sorry to say, I must remain on the boat and help my father with the inventories of fresh supplies. But I will tell you how to find the saloon. Now, my old friend, about your long story?"

Catherine found herself struggling to begin an account. She was still thinking about Louise.

"So here it is," Mamie said bluntly. "Catherine here up and kilt a man who needed it when we was in Helena, Arkansas, on this here river. That man, Rainey by name, tried to, well, I'd say he tried to have his way with our girl here, but she wasn't havin' no part of it."

"That is certain."

"You see that man, Rainey, he got aholt of a letter sayin' our Catherine had tried to grab the private parts of a priest back in Baton Rouge, and so Rainey and his preacher brother thought she should be fahred from teachin' 'cause that ain't Christian, but Rainey wasn't goin' to fahr her if she give him what he wanted. Which she didn't, 'cause she split his head open with a hatchet. Now, there warn't no truth to the story 'bout the priest. You should know that part."

"Yes, I remember that priest. I had heard something of his ways."

"And Catherine was a fine schoolteacher in Helena, with the young'uns who adored her, and there was a big strappin' sheriff's deputy who thought he loved her and she thought she loved him, too, but she don't no more on account of he believed all the lies they told on her. I guess that says it all."

"It says enough." Catherine was ready to change the subject. "Later on this evening, after supper, I want to take Mamie to the main saloon.

She has never seen the inside of a saloon. Besides, I love to watch the faro tables. Mamie, you will like it, I'm sure."

"Why not? I done wrapped myself up in all kinda sins and crimes as it is. Lord help me."

"But I do need at least one more dress. You brought only one, from my quarters at the schoolhouse, is that right, Mamie?" One more dress. For a moment she thought of Matron O'Neil, her first benefactor. But now Catherine had friends. Real friends.

"Yeah, and I brought that one on my own. You didn't say one thing about no dresses."

Gabe took a sip of champagne. "Ladies, I can easily take care of that."

CHAPTER 12

Tascosa, 1940

Frenchy had lowered her head and rested it on her arm at the kitchen table, thinking she simply needed to rest her eyes. But sleep came on—until insistent knocking on her door caused her to open her eyes, still only an inch or so from the red checkered tablecloth. After pushing away her now cold cup of coffee, she stood and placed both hands on the table to assist in steadying herself once she was more or less vertical. Annoyed, she went to see who'd stopped by to disturb her, not that there could be much doubt.

It was Tommy from the boys' home. Before she could say anything, he blurted out the news: "There's a war on, Miss Frenchy! We ain't in it yet, but ever'body says we will be. It was on a newsreel we got from Amarillo. I'll be signin' up whenever Uncle Sam says fight."

To Frenchy, it seemed like the Great War had ended only about five years ago instead of more than twenty. "After what happened in that last one, I wouldn't be in too big a hurry," she muttered. At the time, there were only a dozen or so men of fighting age still left in Tascosa. Four of those were killed, not living long enough to see their hometown die off too. The ones who weren't killed didn't return to town after the fighting. "That one was supposed to end all wars."

"But I want to go. The other boys too. One said we could go ahead and join somethin' called the National Guard right now. Anything's better'n bein' stuck out here on these plains." The next instant, Tommy looked sheepish, standing silently in front of an old woman who belonged only on those plains.

"I don't suppose you've ever been to Arkansas."

"Why, no, ma'am, I ain't never been out of Texas, nor even east of Clarendon."

Having told his big news, Tommy jumped up on the bareback ranch horse he'd ridden out to Frenchy's place and headed back to the boys' home. Frenchy's mind had gone, reluctantly, back to Arkansas.

She returned to the table and took up her pen and paper. Avoiding recollections of the horrible night before her escape from the Helena jail, she tried to think of something, *anything*, that was pleasant, aside from meeting up again with Gabe.

> *It's not like me, but I was so pleased with the damn dress Gabe picked out for me that I actually enjoyed prancing around the boat, especially on the nights when the faro dealers were busy. That was the prettiest dress I've ever worn. It was deep green satin with white frills on the collar and on the bottom of the three-quarter sleeves. And believe me when I write that it had no damn bustle. Gabe claimed the latest styles back East and from Par-ee, as he said, didn't have any bustles, so I'll say it right here and now that the French have something going for them besides their food and language.*

* * * * *

Steamboat Natchez, *early December, 1878*

When Catherine and Mamie walked into the saloon, resplendent in their new finery from Gabe, Mamie's face was so flushed with excitement that her eyes would have matched the picture in Wallace Washburn's imagination: blue sapphires. Her dress, dark blue and also made of satin, selected by Gabe, was the perfect complement.

Catherine led the way to a faro table not far from the end of the bar, having guessed correctly that a smart faro dealer would pick a spot close to a ready supply of liquor and beer. Not only did alcohol fuel the desire to gamble, but the short round trip to the bar and back allowed for more time at the table.

Enough of the men moved aside to let them get close to the layout, several ogling Mamie's bosom as she walked past. Mamie, her head slightly bowed, almost smiled at the attention, but made the subtle movement with her lips that helped to hide her protruding front teeth.

"Mamie. Mamie! Now watch, watch the dealer. And watch the man at the end of the table. He's called the casekeeper. Watch what he does."

"Why, would you look at that dealer's hair! Piled up there like a coil of rope."

"It's called a pompadour, Mamie."

"Don't look like no kinda door to me."

"Would you please try to focus on the keeper?"

And Mamie finally turned her eyes to the casekeeper, a gray-bearded man much older than the woman dealer. He had a case a bit larger than a foot square. In the case were thirteen thin horizontal rods, six on one side and seven on the other. Each rod had four sliding abacus buttons, fifty-two in all. Each time a card was dealt from the spring-loaded dealing box, the keeper was supposed to move a button for the card's name or number to the right on the thin rod so people could see which cards had been played. The cards weren't tracked by suit, only by number or name, such as four, six, ten or king, queen, ace, jack. At first, Mamie looked puzzled. But after ten minutes or so, Mamie was nodding as the keeper moved the buttons. "Mm-hmm. That'd be right, I reckon. Mm-hmm. Now do that one, yeah, that's it."

For another half an hour, Mamie didn't take her eyes off the man. Then she nudged Catherine. "There's gonna be a jack comin' up pretty quick. Two of 'em still left."

Catherine frowned. The case showed three jacks had been dealt. "How do you know that?"

Mamie shrugged. "I remember every card that's got dealt so far. I see 'em in my head. All them punters, they're too rushed to keep up with the changes. But I'm not. That there case-keeper, he just slid a button down for the third jack, and it ain't been dealt yet."

As Mamie spoke, the casekeeper reached up and scratched behind his right ear, while keeping his left forefinger on the thin rod for jacks.

One of the punters promptly bet on a jack and won. Did he know it was still in the deck, Catherine wondered, or was it simply a lucky guess?

The game resumed, with the punters placing fresh bets. "Now watch this," said Mamie. The casekeeper moved his hand. "Look! He done the same thing with that deuce. He slid the button over to show three of 'em have been dealt, but there's still a pair of 'em in the deck, I swear. And see, he's scratchin' behind his ear again. He's tellin' somebody that he's hid that card so they know which one is good odds to bet on."

The same man who had bet on the jack also bet on the deuce. He might have been a clerk, a shopkeeper, a deacon of the church, neatly but plainly dressed, a faded brown bowler pushed carelessly back on his head, revealing a shock of reddish hair. He smiled frequently, talked up the men nearby, and acted totally surprised when he won. Mamie glared at him, twisting her lips back and forth over her front teeth. "That ain't right," she said, barely controlling her anger. "Them cards don't lie, but they been made to lie. I won't stand for it when things don't add up."

Catherine moved in front of her, determined to keep Mamie from getting involved. A man wearing the fanciest clothes in the whole room began to swear in French. To Catherine's ear, the gist of what he said was that the game was run by crooks and he would have every one of their heads off if he didn't get his money back.

"*Oui, vous avez raison!*" Catherine yelled. For a moment, the man appeared to forget how furious he was. He strode over to her and wrapped her in his arms, thanking her for saying he had good reason to be angry, and in his own language to boot. Next, he tried to tell the dealer and the saloon manager what had happened. In response to their bewildered looks, Catherine spoke up in English, and after some hemming and hawing, the man got his money back. A small crowd had gathered and now applauded the outcome. Mamie told her side of it as well, going into way too much detail. But by the time she was done, her indignation had melted away. The casekeeper had been dragged out of the saloon by two brawny crew members.

The Frenchman bought them a bottle of champagne and another for the onlookers. He asked Catherine what her name was, to thank her properly. Knowing that she should not use her real name, Catherine hesitated. The Frenchman nodded in a knowing way. *"Ce n'est pas important. Vous êtes Frenchy!"*

Catherine raised her glass and smiled, not wanting to spoil the man's delight in having bestowed a new name upon her. But the name itself? At first, she associated "Frenchy" with her Cajun French mother, from whom she was now completely estranged. So, no, it did not strike her as a name she would want to use. After two more gulps of champagne, it occurred to her that her mother would be more likely to resent the name than to consider it as any sort of tribute. Although Catherine preferred the Cajun dialect to standard French herself, she had often used her academic knowledge of the language as a weapon of sorts, bluntly correcting her mother's usage when a drunken Marie McCain berated her in Cajun French, as she often did.

Frenchy. Hmm. Yes, it will do. The name would remind her always—always—to stand up for herself, as she had done with her abusive mother.

"Merci, Monsieur. C'est mon nom!" The French gentleman raised his crystal glasses and clicked it against her own before turning and bowing to the crowd as he made his grand exit.

"Now what was that all about?" Mamie was annoyed at all the foreign talk.

"That nice man called me Frenchy, and now it is my name."

"Well, I'm happy he got his money back, but one thing for shore is I ain't gonna let no furriner change my name."

"You should go by Molly instead of Mamie, in case anybody asks. I guess Jackson is such a common name, you can keep using it."

"So I s'pose I'm supposed to thank you for lettin' me use my own dang name?"

They spent as much time as they could in the saloon after that, always welcomed by the saloon manager, who provided free champagne. Taking Mamie aside, he said, "I'll bet you can tell me the last ten cards before the final draw on that first night."

"Why, shore. Seven, queen, ten, king, five, seven again, ace, nine, five again, and deuce." She paused, picturing the sequence to make sure she was correct. "Yessir. That was it."

"Amazing!" The manager clapped his hands.

"Well, I seen them, didn't I? I remember 'em clear as rain."

From that night on, Mamie toured the faro tables in the manner of a visiting royal.

Almost three weeks later, they docked in St. Louis. Gabe had made sure that Catherine and Mamie were well dressed, telling them they could keep the clothes when they reached the city. "If someone told me to give them back to the assistant steward of *mon père*, I would refuse to do so. No other women could possibly wear them *pour un effet magnifique!*"

By now Mamie was so taken with Gabe's easy flattery that she hated to leave him behind on the *Natchez*. "Why, I don't think I ever knowed a-a man that was colored, I mean to say dark, like him, that was so—"

"—a *Black man*, Mamie. Gabe is a Black man."

"Anyhow, ain't he the nicest thing you ever seen?"

* * * * *

They had enough money to pay for a cheap room and board in St. Louis for only one week. The room was eight feet by ten, with two hard cots and a washstand. It was about a quarter mile east of Almond Street, where women stood shivering on the corners, trying to keep their cheap clothes clean enough to get a man to pay for sex with them in a back alley or dark doorway. The old man running the boardinghouse fed his lodgers bread, beans, onions, root vegetables, and potatoes, mostly, with sausage, pickles, eggs, and cheese on occasion. Breakfast was weak coffee and oatmeal. The old man was curious about them and asked a lot of questions whenever they saw him in the weedy back courtyard, where there was a well they all used.

"Mamie, we need to keep our distance from him and be very careful what we say." Catherine had seen something other than curiosity in the man's eyes. She was wary of whatever it was.

Gabe could not stay over because the *Natchez* had to turn around and steam back down to Memphis as soon as the new stores were aboard. Before leaving, he drew a detailed map showing the way to the Bosse Saloon on Garrison Street, where his Uncle Baptiste played the piano, and sent word to Baptiste that Catherine and Mamie would show up.

CHAPTER 13

After resting for a day and trying to figure out the best way to walk to the saloon, Catherine and Mamie set out in midafternoon, careful to avoid the splashing mud from passing carriages and cabs. They wore stylish dresses beneath their overcoats—and while not the fanciest in the wardrobe Gabe had given them and less visible than they would have been in warmer weather, the clothes still made them feel conspicuous in the Almond Street neighborhood for the twenty minutes it took to reach a different part of town. Another twenty minutes and they were at the front door of the Bosse Saloon. A doorman told them to wait while he sent for Baptiste. Piano music drifted in from another room in the back. Suddenly, the music stopped.

A few seconds later, a tall man, as dark as Gabe, met them at the door.

"You are Baptiste?" Catherine asked. The man did not reply. "Gabe sent us. Louise Pennette is an old friend of mine from Baton Rouge, and we must see her."

"Yes, I am Baptiste." He took a quick drag on his long, ready-made cigarette. "Does she know you are coming?"

"She doesn't know. But we have to see her."

"You cannot be standing outside this door!" His eyes were nervous, bloodshot, and in his face Catherine saw anxiety and sadness. Cigarette ashes dotted the lapels of his sleek black coat and the edges of a black cravat. "You must wait—over there." He pointed to the doorway of a vacant building half a block away, across Garrison Street.

Guiding them away from the saloon, he threw the cigarette stub on the steps and crushed it with one of his scuffed, unpolished brogans, always tapping unseen beneath the keyboard during his performances. "She might see you, she might not. She should be here soon. These days, I never know. So, you must wait." With that, he quickly lit another cigarette and hurried back to the saloon.

At first, they tried standing ten or so feet away from the front door, but by now, men were arriving at more frequent intervals. A few were already drunk, or nearly so. One beefy man, with a wide black hat and a white shirt so tight on his neck that the flesh hung over the collar, walked right up to Mamie, stared boldly at her bosom, and said, "I do like the look of those!" Moving in closer, he whispered, "How does one silver dollar sound, my sweet?"

Three other men had arrived, and they paused to see what was going on.

Mamie was speechless. After being treated like a princess for days, she now faced this red-faced oaf who had decided he could buy her.

Catherine pushed her way between the fat man and Mamie. "I'll tell you what you can do with that silver dollar!"

The three new arrivals came closer, grinning, one of them saying, "I think Frank might've bit off more than he can chew."

Frank eyed Catherine up and down. "Well, I guess you'll do."

"You can take that silver dollar and go buy yourself a sheep because that's the only female animal that *might* have anything to do with a stupid bastard like you!"

"A sheep!" one of the men yelled. "Yeah, Frank, go get you a sheep." They all began to sing, "Baa, baa, baa, where is my Frankie?"

Frank raised his right hand to slap Catherine. She took a strong position and grabbed the small purple bulb on the end of a six-inch hairpin she often wore now, tucked in alongside a French comb that kept her rapidly growing hair in a twist. The pin was not needed to keep her hair in place, but given her experience, she had been quick to see its potential as a weapon if another man ever attacked her again. Frank's eyes widened as she began to withdraw the pin, and he shoved his way past the others and into the saloon, slamming the door behind him. As the other men followed, the youngest of them, with thick black hair sticking out from under the brim of his hat, said, "You're a feisty thing, you are." He was well beyond her reach when he passed.

Catherine and Mamie moved farther away from the front entrance after that, finding a refuge or sorts at the vacant building Baptiste had pointed out. They tucked themselves inside a covered doorway with spiderwebs spanning the space above their heads. Frenchy was continually peeking out to see if Louise was in sight.

Mamie's eyes widened. "Sheep! My goodness, I never would've thought." They stood there quietly for ten more minutes.

Catherine saw Louise as she came around a corner crossing the street to Bosse's. Recognizing her face, Catherine still had to convince herself that the woman she was looking at was actually her old friend. When Catherine had last seen Louise Pennette in Baton Rouge, Louise was five foot five or six at the most and had yet to fill out. Her hair was dark brown and curly and had hung in rings down to her shoulders. Like her red-haired brother, she had freckles, but they were smaller and darker and sprinkled under her green eyes. Now, her hair was up in a pompadour like the faro dealer's on the *Natchez*. Under Louise's overcoat Catherine could see lots of white frills and a splash of bright red where the coat was loose around her legs. She had filled out, though she was not as bosomy as Mamie. And she was as tall as Catherine now, five foot eight.

Her walk was different too. In Baton Rouge, Louise was bright and chatty with a quick step. When she talked to you, it seemed her whole body was involved, especially when she was walking. Somehow, she turned the top half of her body toward you and gestured with her hands while she jabbered, and still kept up the pace. Today, her hands were at her sides, and she walked progressively slower as she neared the front of the saloon.

Hearing Mamie cough, Louise glanced at them, but showed no recognition. With Catherine's hair put up and dyed dark, it was understandable that Louise had ignored her. Louise's shoulders were stooped as she turned to enter the saloon. Then she stopped abruptly and let the valise she was carrying drop to the front step. She turned toward Catherine and Mamie, closed her eyes for two or three seconds with her head upraised, and began to cry.

"Louise! Louise! It's Catherine! Oh, Louise!" Catherine ran to her old friend, who opened her eyes and tried to smile. Mamie followed, slowly.

Louise didn't move from the steps. Three more men heading for the saloon door hollered at Louise to get out of the way. Catherine grabbed her shoulders and pulled her aside. At that, Louise called out, *"Catherine! Catherine!"* while half smiling amid the tears. Catherine felt then that her heart had recovered part of itself, and now was not only mended but reinforced, even as it filled with a sense of overwhelming relief and love for her old friend. Mamie was quiet and let them be.

* * * * *

In all the excitement, they managed to agree very quickly to meet the next day at Faust's Ladies' Restaurant on Elm Street. It was a place Louise knew, where three women could sit and talk without being bothered.

Arriving a little early, Catherine and Mamie watched as Louise moved gracefully among the waiters and tables to join them. She was wearing a full-length charcoal dress, a black tunic, and stylish lace-up shoes, along with what appeared to be real pearls and silver earrings. She had clearly dressed with care, and no one would take her for a young woman who worked in a saloon. When she reached them, she deployed a sophisticated, slightly skeptical smile and raised an eyebrow toward Mamie.

Catherine could see that Mamie felt out of place. After greetings and hugs and a brief exchange with a waiter to order champagne, Catherine said, "You know, Louise, I wouldn't be here today if dear Mamie hadn't saved my life."

At that, Louise's whole appearance changed. She reached for Mamie's hand and squeezed it tightly. "Bless you, dear soul!"

Mamie beamed. "Well, I guess I need all the blessin' I can git, runnin' with this here gal!"

"But what happened? Why are you in St. Louis, Cathe*rine*? Have you seen Gabe? I haven't seen him for months."

"He is well, and he's the same old Gabe. He had to go back down to Memphis right away and couldn't come along with us today. As for why we're in St. Louis . . ." Catherine glanced at Mamie.

"You tell it," Mamie said, no doubt sure that Catherine would deliver a version of the story that lauded Mamie's heroic role more than she could have done herself.

Catherine did not disappoint her. She told the story from start to finish, praising Mamie as much as Mamie could have wished. "And after coming up with a plan to get me out of jail," Catherine concluded, "what do you think our girl here decided to do? Well, she decided in a trice to leave her beau and jump on a riverboat with me."

"A trice?" Mamie looked a bit puzzled, but she figured it had to be a good thing, and the tale as a whole pleased her.

The champagne arrived, and the waiter poured for them all. "A hatchet, you say?" said Louise, when he was out of earshot. "Ah, so it had to be. The animal had it coming!" The green in her eyes looked darker, and she seemed distracted for a moment. She took a breath and sighed. "I'm so glad you saw Gabe, Catherine! He is still such a rascal, you know." She took a sip of champagne and started to put the glass down but quickly lifted it again and drained it.

Mamie downed some champagne herself and managed to suppress a burp. "Why, I think that Gabe is right nice, what they call genteel."

"Yes! Yes, of course, Gabe est tres gentil." The waiter came by and poured a fresh glass of champagne for Louise. She quickly took a sip. "Well, now that I know, dear Catherine, that you are a bloodthirsty axe murderer, it is much easier for me to describe my work. I take off a lot of my clothes in front of a room full of howling men. But, you see, I do it so tastefully."

From Catherine and Louise came giggles, soon transformed to loud laughter. After two glasses of champagne, Mamie was tipsy but unsure how to react. Then she got into the spirit of the thing, chuckling at first before quickly succumbing to the wave of good cheer.

Louise was much more at ease now. "Ooh, what would Sister say, Catherine?"

"Maybe we could show her our 'inner beauty?'"

"And you could tell her you became a teacher, at a Protestant school!"

Catherine raised her glass. "But I do miss Sister Brigid. To Sister Brigid, Merry Christmas!"

"Christmas ain't here yet," said Mamie, drinking anyway.

＊＊＊＊＊

"By the way, Louise, we're broke as hell. We need work." Catherine put down her glass and frowned.

Louise shrugged. "I know what you mean. It was the same for me, when I came here almost two years ago. But you see, women like me don't have to go to bed with any filthy man who comes along, though I could probably make more money if I did. There are women on Sixth Street and in the fancy hotel district who make a hundred dollars a month, sometimes much more. And I dare say, few are as attractive as we are."

Mamie shifted in her chair at this. Louise seemed to know that she had slighted Mamie and turned to her. "And it is sure, Ma*mie*, that no woman in all of St. Lou*is* has a figure as majestic as yours, *ma chèr amie.*"

Mamie smiled, showing her front teeth. She didn't seem to notice the change in Louise's eyes. "It is strange, you know," Louise went on after the briefest pause, "but I speak almost as much French here as I did in Baton Rouge. It is a different French, better I suppose. I use it in my performance, you see. I look well enough, but it is the French I use and the dancing that make my performances, I would say, special."

"Mm-hmm, right special." Mamie raised her eyebrows.

Catherine noticed. "Speaking of French, here's another story, Louise. I put my French to good use on the *Natchez* coming up here, and a Frenchman, a gambler, gave me a new name—I suppose it's now an alias. It's 'Frenchy.'"

Mamie yawned. "Yep, and I have one of them pretend names too. It's Molly. I hear it's a Irish name. But I ain't really used it."

"But when we are together, only us three, I can use your real names, no? Around others, we can use the other names. But otherwise, let us be who we are, *please!*"

"Agreed." Catherine could see how important the matter was to Louise.

"So, if you don't mind telling us," Catherine said after a few moments, knowing that to some extent the champagne was speaking now, "just how much do you make from your, uh, performances?"

"Ah. It is eighty, ninety dollars a month, average. But, you see, I only perform three or four nights a week. And Cather*ine*, that is two or three times more money than many men can make—and five or six times what a seamstress gets paid." She looked at Catherine with one eyebrow slightly raised.

"Not to mention schoolteachers."

Mamie brightened. "Goodness, that's a right smart amount of money! And you ain't workin' half the time."

Three hours and two more bottles of champagne later, two old friends and one rustic heroine, now jabbering almost nonstop at their table in the town's most respectable ladies' restaurant, had come up with plans for their own joint "performance." Louise had worked it out.

"Catherine will come out first. We will be after the knife-thrower but before the new act with the beer-drinking bear. Poor thing, he gets so drunk. Catherine will do some dancing, do some cartwheels—I know you can, I remember! And next, speaking a little French, you will take a bow and give them a glimpse of your breasts. A glimpse, mind you."

"You ain't talkin' buck neckid here, are you?" Mamie's speech was a bit slurred.

"Oh, no, no, no, no, *no*! They would tear down the stage and rip off what's left of our clothes if we did that, dear Mamie. They will see your black garters, Cather*ine*, when you do your cartwheels. But it is nothing, no?"

Louise told them that she would follow with her usual act, which included some fancy footwork and high kicking, some flirty-sounding French, lots of fluttering eyelashes, and some extra deep bows allowing for a view of much of her bosom, larger and more shapely than Catherine's.

"And next, Cather*ine*, you will come back out and appear to be arguing with me about who has the prettiest bosom, and our Mamie here will rush out from behind the curtains and shove us aside so she is in the middle. She will glare at you first and kind of smirk?—yes, that is the word—and then at me, showing the audience what I would call a haughty look." Now, with a nod to Mamie, "You will pull out the silk belt holding your red tunic in place and show the men who is who when it comes to bosoms. You will not lift or remove your chemise, oh, no, no, no, no. But you will strut up and down the stage, and nod your head while showing how superior you are!" Louise paused, thinking. "And we will call ourselves, let's see—'The Nymphs du Prairie.' *Voilà*!"

Catherine looked anxiously at Mamie, half expecting her to refuse. "Well, I s'pose I cain't call it good work, but for shore there's good money in it." Mamie was slurring her words more than before. "And all that free time." She nodded, at the same time blinking away any concerns she had. "I reckon I'll have to do a bunch of extry prayin' though."

Relieved, Catherine turned to Louise. "So when do we start?"

CHAPTER 14

They asked for $270 a month and they got it. Catherine had to admit it was kind of fun for a while. It was playacting, allowing them to improvise and tease each other on stage and off. It was the spirit of the thing.

She figured that sooner or later Mamie would begin to feel guilty—but Mamie seemed to be doing fine for almost three months. Never once during that time did she go on about how God was going to strike them down for showing some of their bodies. It occurred to Catherine that the burlesque show was the first time in Mamie's whole life when anyone other than poor Wallace Washburn in Helena, Arkansas, had focused only on her and thought she was fully attractive.

For Louise, those few months they were all in St. Louis had to be her happiest time since she had run away from Baton Rouge, with only a hundred dollars from her parents. They were ashamed of her and no wonder why. They'd gotten the same story Catherine's mother did about what happened with Father Jean and were as quick to believe it.

Far more deft than her partners with the precise manipulations of bodices, garters, and stockings, Louise had found a way to think of her work as a performance that was not without artistry. Her renewed friendship with Catherine and a growing camaraderie with Mamie brought back some of her natural joy and ebullience. When they met at cafés or went shopping together for the fancy clothes they wore, Louise's animated walking style often reappeared. Mamie loved her new-found freedom, nice clothes, and the money she brought in. She and

Catherine talked often about moving to better lodgings but never did, always choosing to keep banking their money.

So yes, Catherine thought for a while if it was fun, or mostly so. Some of the men when drunk would shove their way forward and break into scuffles when a garter or cheap glove flew into the crowd. But only once out of thirty-five or forty appearances did a man reach the stage itself, in what proved to be their final performance. He was the hulking chief mate from the engine room of a dirty packet boat from Cairo, Illinois. Drunk when he arrived and out of his mind near the show's end, he vaulted up beside Mamie just as she completed her part of the act. Fixated on what he had just seen, he managed to pull away her red camisole, for the first time actually baring her bosom until she could cover it up. Her lace underwear, garters, and stockings were fully exposed, and the whole audience went into a frenzy.

Mamie let out a scream, her face contorting with shock, her big front teeth now all too visible to the throng. Jeers, catcalls, cigar stubs, and pennies came flying at the stage. One man threw a beer mug that shattered on a piano leg, not three feet from Louise. Two bouncers, one almost a head taller than the chief mate, grabbed him up and threw him back into the crowd, putting an end to the misbehavior.

"You two go on without me," Mamie said after the show. It took her almost an hour to leave the dingy dressing room behind the stage. Catherine and Louise had waited for her to finally join them outside on Garrison Street.

"If you're out, I'm out." The fact was, Catherine was tired of granting glimpses of so much of her body to a bunch of yahoos, regardless of the money she was making. She knew exactly what she wanted to do next.

Louise shot her a look of alarm. "Oh no, you cannot leave!" She reached for Catherine's arm. "Where will you go? You cannot make this much money anywhere else unless you move to a fancy house on Sixth Street. That you *will not do, ma chèr amie!* We must stay together, you and I. We cannot be separated again. Mamie, dear Mamie, you can find another job—in a drugstore or a hotel, like before—or at that new store, that department store they call it, yes, Nugent's, selling clothes and perfume. We can all share our money. It will all be so fine, it can be . . ."

Catherine held Louise as she began to cry, having seen that her friends were not persuaded. "But, Louise, you can come with us. I've had an itch to deal faro ever since I saw my first layout on the steamboat to Helena. I know how Mamie and I can make it. Working at Nugent's or any of those other places, Mamie wouldn't make more than four or five dollars in a whole week. That's not fair to her. You could learn to deal faro, too. You're prettier than we are. The men would flock to your table. And dealers don't have to sell themselves to men. I hear they can get fired for flirting with a punter. Everybody knows that the women who sell themselves are upstairs in the cheap saloons or in their little thrown-together cribs or walking the dirty streets and alleys. And no more taking off your clothes. We can make enough money to do what we want, go where we want. We can be free. Nothing can follow you if you go far enough out west." *Let's hope so, anyway.*

Louise pulled away. "In Par*is* it is an art," she said, thrusting out her chin.

"This ain't no Par-ee." Mamie's feelings were still raw from the attack on the stage.

"You are jealous!" Louise pointed her right index finger straight at Mamie's face.

"So you're purtier than me, so what?"

"No, no, no, it is not that!" Louise was standing tall now, with her hands on her hips. "You are jealous because Catherine and I, we are like sisters, we have a . . . a special feeling for each other. It is true—you know it is true! Isn't that right, Cather*ine*?"

"Here's what's true. I have what you call a special feeling for both of you. They might not be exactly the same, but they are equal, or I guess Sister Brigid would say equivalent. And anyhow, I don't like it for anyone, not even one of you, to go about telling me what I feel. Now, it's clear to me that Mamie and I are leaving this town and more than likely going to Dodge City. I don't see either one of us thinking what we do is art, but I can see what you're getting at with your beautiful danc-ing. Mamie and I are both small-town girls at heart, and St. Louis is too damn big for us. Dodge City is full of cowboys, and cowboys from the big trail drives have a lot of money to spend. I aim to get them to spend it on faro."

Her voice softened. "There is nothing I would like more than for you to come with us, Louise. We have shared so much, you and I, things no one understands but ourselves. I love you for that and for the return of the happiness we shared as girls in Baton Rouge. No matter what, I will not forget that. I'm not given to begging and I'm not going to beg now, but I know as sure as I know I hate a preacher in Helena, Arkansas, that we will all be happier if we do what I say. How about it?"

Louise turned and walked away, heading toward her new lodgings in a decent neighborhood to the north. At the first corner, she stopped and turned to look at them. "We can meet at Faust's at noon tomorrow. I will tell you then."

* * * * *

The next afternoon, Catherine and Mamie had been at the table for fifteen minutes before Louise arrived. They and most of the other women in the restaurant stared at Louise as she made her way through the crowded dining room to the table Catherine had selected near the back. Catherine had never seen Louise look so beautiful. She wore a green day dress of the latest style, with a fitted, deep blue bodice of lattice design that revealed some green beneath the blue. She carried herself in a way that complemented her dress; she might have been famous or wealthy, or a royal personage on the fringe of the frontier. She smiled—generously, not quite condescendingly, Catherine thought.

"You look beautiful, Louise," Catherine said, a fact that was obvious to anyone looking on.

"Oh, the dress. Maurice selected it for me this very morning. I barely had time to change before I left for our lunch meeting today."

Mamie sipped some water and set her glass down abruptly on the linen tablecloth. "Who's Maurice?"

"He is a special friend." Louise gracefully took her place at the table.

"So how special is he?" Catherine affected a girlish curiosity to cover the degree of concern she actually felt.

Louise shrugged. "One might as well ask if love itself is special."

"Worth askin'," Mamie picked up the water glass but only took a sip.

"Yes, he is *very* special. I have not mentioned him because I did not want either of you to think I was planning to leave the act and settle down. Maurice is a man of the world. With him, I can be who I choose to be. He will love me as I am." She was wearing fine gloves, soft gray in color. She carefully removed them and picked up a glass of water.

Catherine closed her eyes and sighed. "If Maurice played no part in your life, would you still choose to remain in St. Louis?"

For a moment, Louise seemed to lose some of her self-assurance. "I love St. Louis. This city, it has everything. To say it is full of life is to diminish the intensity of the life that is all about us. People from all over America come to St. Louis—from all over the world. So yes, *mon amie*, I would stay in St. Louis without my dear Maurice."

"Kinda odd, ain't it, that you haven't spoke of this Maurice fellow till now."

"Maurice likes his privacy, Mamie," Louise said curtly. "Besides, I've already told you I didn't want you to think I might leave the act."

"So are you two goin' to get hitched someday?"

"Maurice is a man of the world," Louise repeated, somewhat defensively. "We do not talk of such things. That may be hard for you to understand, but—"

"Oh, I reckon I understand all right. Your Maurice is married, ain't he?"

"Mamie! That's enough!" Catherine was on the edge of real anger, hating to be in the middle of this fight.

Louise shifted in her chair. "I think it is time to order."

Catherine reached across the table and gripped Louise's hand. "I can't begin to express how much I will miss you. I will write and let you know where we are so you can join us anytime you want. If you don't come to us, I'll come back to see you. I promise. We will never lose touch again." *Never.*

After a moment, Louise gently squeezed Catherine's fingers. There were tears in her eyes. "Yes, he is married. I know he doesn't love me. But you see, I don't want him to love me."

Mamie got up from her chair. She moved to stand behind Louise, put both hands on her shoulders, and bent down to kiss the top of her head. "I'll be prayin' for you, honey. From my heart, every day of this world."

CHAPTER 15

Helena, March 1879

"So, Sheriff Rawlings, you are telling me you cannot or will not take any further action to find the woman who killed my brother?"

For Sheriff Rawlings, this was the fourth confrontation he had endured with the Reverend Campbell Harper. He had hoped that after three months, the reverend would focus more fully on his flock and forget about the loss of his sorry brother.

On this occasion, the sheriff would have remained at his desk, mostly silent, except that after taking a sip of coffee, he had found that the sustaining beverage was tepid, if not downright cool. Slowly, he got up and took his mug to the pot sitting on the new parlor stove. He filled the mug, took a sip, nodded with satisfaction, and ambled back to his chair, recently fitted with a nice soft seat cushion. Yes, the reverend was likely to bust open with frustration, but to hell with him. The sheriff took another sip and considered how nice it would be to have some of those cookies that Mamie, the woman who helped that schoolteacher escape, had brought to him. On the other hand, the last batch had put him to sleep, a state he preferred to achieve at least three times a day on his own.

"Like I done told you, Reverend, I contacted Marshal Parker before the first of the year and asked him for his best deputy—"

"You have known all this time that I will not accept a—a *Black* deputy marshal to go in search of that woman and her accomplice! Who in God's name would reveal information to such a man, especially since his inquiries would be about white women?"

"Bass Reeves may be as black as a piece of charcoal, but he's the best deputy marshal within five hundred miles," the sheriff said. "You said you wanted the best. Well, I give you the best, and you went and turned him down. Marshal Parker ain't inclined to do you no more favors, Reverend. Period. And I cain't spare Albert Armitage, and if I could, what use would he be tryin' to run down the woman he was so dewy-eyed in love with that he's been useless as a rudder on a duck's ass ever since she excaped." This was quite a speech for the sheriff, unused to calling to mind even one colorful description across the span of a whole week. Or a month.

Reverend Harper pointed a long bony index finger straight at the sheriff's head, causing the latter to lean back a little farther in his chair. "You, sir, are an embarrassment to your profession. If I were not a man of the cloth, I would whip you here and now."

Sheriff Rawlings was lazy, but he was no coward. He grabbed the reverend's finger and stood up quickly, holding the finger so tightly that the reverend could have no reasonable thought of wresting it away. "You want me to break your goddamn finger and stick it in your damn mouth to shut you up? *Reverend*." For emphasis, he pulled the finger toward him, causing the reverend to move with it.

Harper tried to appear composed as he was wincing. "I shall report you, Sheriff Rawlings. Now release my finger or I shall be compelled to—"

"To do what? Pray? Well, go right ahead. Say us a little prayer."

"I pray you will meet your maker and be sent to hell!"

"I s'pose that's not exactly what I was hoping for, but you ain't much of a preacher so I reckon your prayers aint' worth a shit. You best git on out of here now. Raht now!" Sheriff Rawlings released the reverend's finger but stood where he was.

"Know this, Sheriff, your days in this office are numbered!" Two strides took him to the door where he paused long enough to tear a partially hidden WANTED poster bearing Catherine's likeness from the wall.

The sheriff watched him leave and kicked the door closed behind him. "Now, maybe I'm finally shut of that son of a bitch."

* * * * *

When the Reverend Campbell Harper returned to his tidy parsonage, his wife, Hannah Winslow Harper, heard his footsteps on the front porch and greeted him at the door. She had seen her husband when he was in a study and when he was out of sorts, but never in their eight years of marriage had she seen his face so contorted with rage, even after his confrontations with his late brother. Instinctively she backed away from him and let him stomp into the fashionable front parlor of which she was so proud.

"That sheriff is the most incompetent wretch I have ever known!"

Hannah moved to be near his side. Something kept her from touching him just now.

"I have a name and a place of honor in this community." Campbell was trying to be more resolute now than angry. "I cannot in good conscience allow the murderer of my dear brother to go free. How can I preach of the final judgment that will come to us all while that vile and satanic woman lives? What prophet of righteous justice can be believed against the triumph of such raw injustice?"

Hannah took his hand. He was a preacher and he was preaching now, an activity that banished his troubles and carried him to a place of conviction and power. "Pure evil, she is," Hannah whispered, with a hint of sadness that any human being could, in fact, be so far beyond redemption.

"Perhaps," he said, sounding like a new revelation was on its way. "Perhaps this is the voice of God telling me what I must do! Here is my new path, if I will only take it. My blood is my brother's blood. It courses through my body, calling me to vengeance."

Hannah released his hand; he did not seem to notice. "And what must *I* do? And what of the church and your congregation?"

Campbell stared at her as though he had just realized she was beside him. Her transition from an audience symbol to his wife had escaped him. "Why, uh, you must do as you have always done—and done so well, my dear—take care of our beloved children and keep up our home until my return. We have been prudent and my flock generous; there is money enough to live on during my special mission, and live well, especially with the inheritance we will receive from your dear mother."

The "dear mother" had been at the point of expiration for three weeks after dominating their household for much of the previous year, claiming to suffer from "a nervous condition" that kept her from living in Little Rock on her own. The ten-thousand-dollar inheritance, substantial as it would be, was in Campbell's mind, insufficient compensation for the havoc Matilda Winslow had brought to the parsonage. Not least among her offenses was her continual correction of what she insisted were errors in his scriptural interpretations. But at last he would have the time and energy to pursue justice for his late brother.

And for something grander.

"I now know my true mission!" Once again, he was back in his preacher's realm, alive with a new conviction. "I shall preach as I search out the killer." Campbell spread his hands to illustrate the vastness of the frontier that lay before him, so much in need of salvation. "On the one hand, I will bring an evil woman to justice; on the other, I will rescue poor, miserable souls from evil."

He was more excited than his wife had ever seen him. The word "possessed" would have described him well.

"For a while now, my dear, I have felt that my work here is mostly done, that another calling awaits me. How could I have known that the murder of my dear brother would light the way to a new and higher calling? Oh Lord, how mysterious are Thy ways, to bring us to the light of Thy salvation!"

"My dear husband, is it not up to God Himself to decide when my precious mother will go to her reward? As we know so well, she is not only a willful—a woman of spirit but strong and resilient, despite what Dr. Whitmire may say about her imminent demise. And your congregation?" Still beside him, Hannah shrank a little. How long would it be before she could once again enter the church with her two children and take up their places below the pulpit from which Campbell preached? How the women of the town admired her. How jealous they were of her, she was sure, the pretty wife of a tall, handsome preacher, an inspired man of God. So often she stole glances at the women, women of all ages, whose calculating eyes, shielded by their bonnets or hymnals held high, revealed their interest in the Reverend Campbell Harper.

He looked at her, his eyes glittering. "Only a few weeks ago, did not the Lord send us young Merriman, fresh from seminary and so keen to observe the homiletics of a master, if I may say so? He is a college man like myself, a true credit to my alma mater. He will take my place! How clear things become when one accepts a true call from the Lord." He took both of Hannah's hands and looked down sweetly at her worried face. "He will need your help, you know. Who better to acquaint him with the needs of the congregation so he should not err and undermine all of *our* good work? Can I count on you, dearest, to guide and protect young Merriman in my absence?"

The youthful and remarkably handsome Reverend Merriman was already the talk among the younger women, who seemed to sing like the prettiest songbirds when Merriman directed the choir. Hannah had mentioned to members of the choir that her own voice seemed to find itself more readily at such times. Some had urged her to join the choir herself.

"Glory be to God," Hannah said, gazing into her husband's eyes. "Above all, be safe. I could not endure your loss, dear husband."

* * * * *

Campbell knew little about firearms and other weapons of the law enforcement profession. He became uneasy when it occurred to him that, although the object of his search was a mere woman, that same woman had dispatched his brother with a hatchet. And a woman like that would surely fall in with the worst kinds of men. It would hardly do to ask Sheriff Rawlings or Deputy Armitage for advice. The town of Helena was full of veterans of the War Between the States; he would ask one of the many such men who attended his church.

He settled on a heavily bearded, bearish man known as "the Captain" for his rank in Dobbins's cavalry unit that had fought in the Battle of Big Creek, near the town. Although not a member of Campbell's church, he came highly recommended by two former soldiers in the congregation.

The man's full name was Calvin Mortimer. Campbell met with him in the dining room of the New Southern Hotel, where Mamie had worked for Wallace Washburn.

"So the boy you sent over told me you wanted advice on guns, and he thought maybe killin'," the Captain said. His long beard was streaked with tobacco juice. He leaned to his right and sent another stream into a small spittoon beside his chair. "Now I have to ask myself, why does a preacher want to know about such as that?"

Campbell had worried over what he would say. "First, I did not mention killing specifically. Yes, I am a man of God, and I do abhor the taking of another man's, of a human life. Yet the Lord preached justice, severe justice, Captain, and sadly it has now fallen to me to pursue that justice on behalf of my late brother, Rainey. I hasten to add that I shall not use my hand in violence if the party may be brought to justice without it."

"Justice. Hmm. I ain't all that sure you'd like the justice you might git over Rainey's killin'. I reckon Rainey was lucky to have lived as long as he did." The Captain sent another, smaller jet of juice toward the spittoon. "On the other hand, he was your brother. So there it is, justice or no. And the law ain't doin' nothin', I s'pose. I'm guessin' you ain't goin' out as a real deputy?"

"I have not asked for official status, nor would the sheriff grant it to me."

"One thing for sure, I wouldn't be usin' my real name if I was you, I mean with you bein' . . . unofficial. Might come in handy to use another name, in case things go amiss. Somethin' common is best. And here's another thing: In this case the people you're a-chasin' are gonna recognize you. You'll need to fatten up, I'd say, since slimmin' down don't seem to be an option. Grow a beard, try to look older. Might not be a bad idea to keep sayin' you're a reverend, though. Some folks think that means somethin'." The Captain spat again in the general direction of the spittoon. He smiled slyly, showing his discolored teeth.

Campbell barely managed to suppress his revulsion at the Captain's words and manner. "This has become my duty, Captain. That is how I see my mission. As a former soldier—a brave solider, I have heard—you will surely understand."

"It is true that I was a soldier who knew his duty. But what I really understand is killin'. Both the kind you need to do and the kind you don't. It's better if you need to, but it ain't necessary."

Campbell tried to sort out this statement for a moment or two but let it pass. "I am satisfied of the potential need either to do violence or, more likely, to protect myself. There are likely to be accomplices, ruffians who would do me harm, no doubt. What I lack is the means of protection. What do you recommend?"

After one more poorly aimed shot at the spittoon, the Captain pulled a filthy handkerchief from his coat pocket and wiped it across his mouth and the first two or three inches of his long beard. "First off, there's damn few crim'nals who'll come along voluntary. Somewhere along the way you will almost surely find the need of a weapon, 'specially if you aim to bring the culprit all the way back to Helena. So's the best I can say is you need a .36 Colt Navy revolver, holster, rimfire cartridges, and a good sharp knife for your belt. There's a newer Colt Army, a .45, but I don't care for it myself, and a lot of Colt Navy's are still around and cost less money. Oh, and you'll need a derringer for your inside pocket. I'd say a two-shot Remington .41 caliber would do. The Colt Navy is lightweight, but a fella like you prob'ly don't feel like carryin' around a six-gun all the time. Prob'ly need one small box of cartridges for the derringer. You'll need to practice with these weapons, understand. That derringer's got a real kick to it and sounds like a cannon goin' off. Now as for a rifle or a shotgun, that's a personal matter, dependin' on whether you'll be close or far from that wo—from your—"

"Murderess."

"Yep, that'd be her. A rifle or a shotgun does tend to git old when you're carryin' one around. If you find you need to act more in the quiet line, you might want a nice piece of rawhide about two foot long. You'll want to knot each end so's you can hold on if you find you must strangle the, uh, crim'nal."

The image of a garroted Catherine McCain struck Campbell like a blow to the solar plexus. In the next moments, the mission that had seemed so clear became clouded in his mind. Was that face, which had come to him unbidden more than once at night, the face of a person he could kill or actually bring to justice? Gathering himself, he knew there was only one way to find out.

CHAPTER 16

Dodge City, mid-April, 1879

One thing for sure was that there was no riverboat from St. Louis to Dodge City, Kansas. Frenchy—the alias Catherine had by now embraced—and Mamie had saved more than a hundred dollars apiece from their time at Bosse's, and after adding that to the small stash remaining from the trip to St. Louis, they felt almost rich. They discovered that the Atchison, Topeka, and Santa Fe train would take them all the way to Dodge City for only twelve dollars per ticket. That left them with enough money for room and board for several weeks if they were careful. Neither was in a rush to go to work after the stress and excitement of their job at the saloon.

They stopped over in Kansas City. Lacking the energy to search for a nicer place, they stayed the night in a cheap rooming house near the tracks. The remainder of the trip to Dodge was unpleasant. They both itched from bedbugs, and the soot coming into the coach kept Frenchy coughing and wiping her nose most of the way. All in all, they both decided that riverboats were much better, as long, of course, as they didn't blow up.

"I ain't stayin' in no more places that has them bugs," Mamie announced as she stood, scratching away at the station in Dodge City.

A porter who was passing by, pushing a trolley loaded with bulging suitcases and heavy trunks, overheard her. "Pardon me, ma'am, I couldn't help but overhear what you jes' said. There's only four hotels in Dodge. I cain't say which one is worse than the others. What I can say is that Miz Landsdowne will rent you a large room with two beds and feed you dinner every day for four dollars a week per head. Tell her Henry from the station sent you, and there'll be a little somethin' in it for me. It's the best place in Dodge, anyhow."

Mrs. Landsdowne's rooming house lived up to Henry's description, and they paid up front for a month. After a week of rest, frequent, long, and luxurious hot baths, and some of the best meals in town, Frenchy felt like doing some exploring. She and Mamie had retained their best dresses from St. Louis, after selling off some to earn travel money. Since it hadn't rained for several days, the streets weren't muddy, so they both wore nice lace-up boots. During their performances at the Bosse Saloon in St. Louis, Frenchy had taken to wearing her hair, re-dyed black, in a stylish pompadour as soon as it had grown long enough. Looking at herself in the mirror before they left the rooming house in Dodge, she had decided that it made her look more French, in accordance with her new name.

But Mamie hadn't worn her brown wig since they left Helena, despite Frenchy's repeated requests that she do so. "Even if I wanted to wear it here, I couldn't. I done throwed it away in St. Louis. That thing squeezed on my head so much, I had trouble keeping up with the cards on that boat."

"Your head is really important."

"Ain't it nice of you to say so."

"You know what I mean. We're going to work as a team. How's your head this evening, by the way?"

"Screwed on pretty good, but I ate too much beef."

"It's cheap here. Right outside of town there's probably twenty thousand beeves waiting to be shipped. Steak's not much more than eggs, less than pork I'm sure."

"Place stinks, though, don't it?"

"You think it's bad now, but I heard it was much worse a few years ago when the ground was stacked high with fresh buffalo hides."

They had been walking for only five or six minutes, but in that short time Frenchy counted four saloons and two dance halls. "Let's steer clear of the dance halls. After two months of having a bunch of men staring at me, I sure as hell don't want to do any dancing."

"Ain't that the truth."

"Can make good money that way, though, and it doesn't require any bed work; that is, necessarily."

They walked another minute or so. Mamie slowed, considering. "How's about that place yonder?"

The Lone Star Saloon was only a block away from the better-known Long Branch, but it was much larger. From time to time, the owner, Chalk Beeson, brought in more or less respectable singers and musicians to perform. Frenchy peeked inside when a drunk cowboy stumbled out. The place was maybe thirty feet wide but more than eighty feet deep. A fancy medium-sized bar ran along the right side of the front section, where the hard-core drinkers were standing and talking loudly and spitting tobacco juice in the general direction of the nearest spittoon. The rear section had more space, and Frenchy could see eight or ten tables and three faro layouts set up back there.

"Mostly men—cowboys, townspeople, probably a bunch from the railroad," she told Mamie, "but I saw a couple of women dealing faro, and some others talking to the bystanders and hitting them up for drinks. I like the feel of a larger space."

"So, the same as we did on the steamboat?"

"Yeah. I'll watch the dealer and check out the punters to see if any look to be working with the casekeeper. You watch the cards on the layout and let me know if the keeper cheats. While you're at it, let me know your picks for the last three cards."

"You ain't gonna be makin' any bets, are you?"

"Not now, but if our first plan doesn't work out, we might give it a try. It would be risky and we couldn't stay here long. I'd rather get the house to put me on as a faro dealer and pay you to watch out for cheating. Should be worth quite a bit in this place."

The next time the front doors opened, they walked inside and slowly made their way toward the back, receiving appreciative looks as they did so. Frenchy was watching the action. "It's like I thought. There's some men in here that make the sharps on the steamboat look damn near honest."

Mamie had been looking at the women. "Ain't you a little young for this place?"

"I'll be twenty next month. Besides, you never said I was too young to be taking my clothes off in front of a herd of wild men."

"I thought I was four years older'n you. Now I make it five. But I look young compared to these here gals. And as for you and taking your clothes off, them boys back in St. Louis had to be mighty quick to see much of those pointy little things of yours. Maybe when you get old as me, you'll have grown 'em some."

"Not unless I get fat. I'm not going to get fat. Not ever."

"You ain't sayin' mine are big because I'm a little on the plump side, are you?"

"No, I'm sure your breasts would be big if you were as skinny as I am in your other parts. On the other hand, you'd probably fall forward onto the street."

"That ain't nice. It just ain't."

"Now be quiet and remember, please remember, you're Molly again to anyone who asks. You know, things would be easier for us if you'd adopt Molly and forget about Mamie. I left Catherine in Helena, though I should've left her in Baton Rouge. How's your head—feeling sharp?"

"Since you ask, it's feelin' pretty good, but it's so heavy with this huge ol' brain of mine that I reckon I might fall over forwards any second now."

* * * * *

As they slowly made their way toward the back of the Lone Star, a young cowboy peeled away from the bar and offered to buy Mamie a beer. "I'm Harry," the cowboy said, adding himself to the long list of men whose eyes immediately fell to Mamie's chest.

"I'm *Molly*!" Mamie said the name so loudly that several other customers at the bar turned to look at her.

"Well, ain't that a beautiful name!" The cowboy barely shifted his gaze. No one offered to buy Frenchy a beer, likely because her eyes were focused intently on the first faro layout.

The bartender drew the beer, and the cowboy dragged his attention away from Mamie's bosom long enough to fetch the drink and hand it to her. "It's a Budweiser!" he said proudly. "Ain't it cold. Come all the way from St. Louis, and these people here bring in blocks of ice all the way from Colorado by train."

Mamie thanked him to be polite, but after a few minutes she stopped listening to the cowboy and joined Frenchy at the faro table. The young cowboy seemed to consider briefly whether it was worth his time to place a bet so he could stand beside Mamie but decided to rejoin his friends at the bar. By that time, Mamie was so absorbed in counting the cards and watching the casekeeper that she didn't notice. The ice-cold beer began to turn warm in her glass.

The casekeeper was a pale-skinned young man with a feathery straw-colored mustache and goldish wire spectacles. At first Mamie thought his occasional fumbling with the buttons in the faro box was because he felt scared or cowed by the punters. But soon she became suspicious. "I think he's only pretendin' to be nervous. Look at the way he slides the wrong button when a card is dealt and makes a show of changing it to the button that matches the card, pretendin' to be sorry and givin' the punters that little shit-eatin' grin."

She watched the keeper for another half hour. "So, here's what he's doin'. He's like the crooked keeper on the *Natchez*. When he thinks he can, he slides a button to show there's only one card left, but there's really two. See, now this time it's a seven. And there—he's scratching his nose, and his pinky is on the seven. That's him tellin' his punter to wait for the seven, 'cause there's one more seven card in the deck than the case shows. All them other changes he makes is playactin'."

Frenchy watched the punters who bet on a seven. Only one man bet on the seven successively, raising his bet each time. The seven came up on the second, higher bet, and he more than doubled his money. "It's that short fella standing up real straight to make himself look taller, the one with the striped suit and gray goatee. Looks like a banker or a lawyer, or maybe a big shot with the railroad. By now he's had a few whiskies." She nudged Mamie. "Look at him nodding and grinning at the keeper, now that his heavy bet paid off."

Mamie glanced down at her warm beer. "I reckon we earned us a cold drink."

Before they could take a step toward the bar, a stranger appeared beside them, holding two ice-cold foaming mugs of beer. He was about

Frenchy's height, maybe an inch or two taller, with wisps of sandy hair that stuck out on the top of his mostly bald head. Despite the baldness, he looked to be only in his late twenties, early thirties at most.

"On the house, ladies!" he said, holding out the beers. "Mick McGinnis, at your service. I manage this place for Mr. Chalk Beeson most evenings when he's away."

Frenchy was not impressed. McGinnis might once have been a nice-looking fellow, but considering the thin two-inch scar running from below his left eye toward his left ear and a smaller scar above his chin, he was at best odd to look at and at worst on the scary side. His scruffy beard had more red in it than the thinning hair on his head. The beard covered the shallow part of the longer scar, where it almost met his ear. Frenchy thought his blue eyes, a little bigger than beady, conveyed a bit of suspicion, despite his apparent hospitality.

"Hello," Frenchy gave him her gray-eyed stare. She took a small sip of beer.

He cocked his head, sizing her up. The sharp gleam in his eyes softened, giving way to what Frenchy thought might be respect.

There followed a smile from him, of the sort that transforms a face. In the war of smile wrinkles versus battle scars, the former prevailed. He extended his right and she shook it. He smiled again, this time at the firmness of Frenchy's grip, as strong as that of many men he had met. "How is it that you have such a keen interest in faro? Aye, very keen indeed?"

Mamie eased away from the man. "You talk kinda funny. I heard somethin' like it before—down where I used to live. I reckon you're a furriner."

"He's Irish, Mamie. He sounds a lot like my friend Sister Brigid at the convent school."

"Well, now. You see, I was born in County Donegal, but now I'm an American—as American as you." Some of Mick's smile remained, but it was joined by a firmness in his gaze.

"So you're what my mama always said was shanty Irish?" Mamie had yet to drink any of the beer he had brought.

"Now, ma'am, it is well that you are a lady."

Frenchy shot a look at Mamie. "Do you realize how much of an insult that is?"

"I seen some of them Irish, and they was in shanties."

"You're probably Scots Irish yourself."

Mamie stuck out her chin. "Meanin' what?"

"Meanin' your people are pretty much the same, but they're Protestants."

"Well, we sure ain't no Catholics!"

Mick had taken her measure. He crossed himself solemnly and looked into Mamie's eyes. "I'll pray for ye, miss."

"Stop it, both of you!" Frenchy said. "Let me answer the man's question." Almost comically, Mick and Mamie both took half a step back at exactly the same time and folded their arms across their chests. "We learned a lot about faro when we were going upriver to St. Louis. Mamie has a gift. Her mind sees and remembers every card dealt, in sequence. Even better, she can remember every ring the keeper moves—and see him when he cheats and moves them down and back."

"Jesus, Mary, and Joseph!" Mick was practically shouting at Mamie. "Why, bless ye, gal, for the Protestant genius you are!"

She frowned. "I don't know about no Protestant stuff, but what I can tell you, buster, is that the feller over yonder with the nice suit of clothes and a pointy beard is in cahoots with your straw-headed keeper."

Mick gave the man a glance and glared at the casekeeper. The young man seemed to suspect that the conversation he was observing might bode poorly for him. He took out a white handkerchief and used it to wipe the sudden spread of sweat from his face and put two fingers to his right earlobe. The man in the suit quickly departed. Mick took all of this in, but didn't seem concerned that the man had left.

Frenchy tapped Mick on the shoulder. "You should know, I'm almost as good as Mamie when it comes to watching the keeper, which gives her time to concentrate on memorizing the cards. I'm pretty sure we could split up and cover two layouts at the same time." Frenchy took a breath. "The fact is, what I really want to do is deal and run the bank."

Another look of mutual respect passed between them, but Mick shook his head, smiling. "No, sorry, my dealers have been with me now for two years. That keeper, aye, he will be gone, and gone with a bit of touchin' up, if you know what I mean. And that's just my way of sayin' farewell. Either the law or some acquaintances of mine will do a bit of chastisin' of the other fella, a Mister Jeanes, yeah. But as for ye ladies, I mean, *you* ladies—rest easy. Here is what I can do for you, if you are of a mind. Dress as you are now, if you're able. You'll act like some of the other girls—ah, ladies—here, meanin' if a cowboy wants to buy you the odd drink, you let him, yeah. But no side work, none, not that you would do any of that, as I can tell. If a lad buys you a dram or a good cold beer, make sure you're a-standin' near a layout and keep a sharp eye."

"And if one of them cowmen puts a dirty hand on my . . . self," said Mamie, "am I understandin' you right that you'd 'touch him up' and send him packin'?"

"Aye, and he'd never come back." Mick looked at Catherine. "Aye, I can promise you that."

It was disappointing that she wouldn't be dealing faro, but Frenchy thought the deal was good enough for now, depending on the money. "Now for the pay. We have our own clothes, and they're nice, better than most in here right now."

"How does a minimum of four dollars a night sound? More if it's really busy."

"So, two bucks each?" Mamie immediately calculated a total of four hundred and sixteen dollars a year apiece if they worked four nights a week, or only thirty-four dollars and sixty-six cents a month—far less than half of what they had made in St. Louis.

"Only if you say so," Mick said, laughing. "No, four dollars apiece."

After more quick figuring, Mamie smiled at the thought of making about three-fourths of her pay at the Bosse Saloon without baring her bosom. "Well, sir, I reckon I'll throw a good ol' Bible-type prayer your way when I git home tonight. I'm sure you can use it, and I know I'm feelin' plumb grateful right now."

Mick turned his gaze to Frenchy. "And what about you, Miss—I didn't catch yer name."

"I'm Frenchy. And I'm plumb grateful too. For now."

* * * * *

They earned enough to have separate rooms at the Dodge House Hotel. Mamie had fun buying dresses for every day of the week and outfits for carriage rides when the weather was nice for an outing along the Arkansas River. Mamie never stopped pronouncing it like the name of her home state. Frenchy thought she did it mostly to be ornery.

Three months went by before Mick let Frenchy handle a faro layout. He knew she could watch the keeper on her own and handle the fancy moves some of the punters would make. There was one young man, pretending to be a cowboy, who tied an almost invisible piece of silk thread to his copper, a personal betting chip, which he had placed on a nine card glued in the second row of the felt layout board. He pulled the thread quickly to withdraw the copper when a nine card wasn't dealt. Frenchy called him out: "Cover your bet! Cover it now or leave!" The layout nine card was on the side of the board away from her, but she had spotted the silk thread, green like the felt, immediately after she dealt the winning card, a king.

"Well how 'bout this, little lady? I say you're a goddamned good-for-nothing dance hall whore!" The pretend cowboy was leaning across the layout board, his head swaying, and his dirty, skinny neck stretched out as he snarled at her.

Calmly, Frenchy grabbed the purple bulb of the long hairpin near the crown of her pompadour and aimed the sharp end directly at the man's face. "And how about I stick this right in your fucking eye, you buzzard-necked son of a bitch?"

The drunken man tried to focus on the hairpin and didn't seem to clearly grasp the danger he was in. As he lunged toward Frenchy, Mick stepped in front of her and landed a full uppercut that caught the man right above his Adam's apple. Two of his friends dragged him off the board, scattering markers and money all over the place. From his back pocket, Mick pulled a straight razor, its white ivory handle framed with plated gold. "First man who touches that money will answer to me!" He placed the razor unopened on the board, only a few inches from his hands. The men walked away.

Mamie had been watching Frenchy's layout that evening and remembered exactly how much had been bet on each card and by whom. The punters were amazed when she calmly distributed the money and returned the markers to those who used them.

"Well done!" Mick gave Mamie a little salute.

In Dodge City there was a more or less settled line, known as "the deadline," that separated Front Street north of the railroad tracks from the rowdiest part of town south of the tracks. Frenchy learned that the term "deadline" came from the Civil War, meaning that if you were a prisoner and you wandered past a certain point, you were likely to be shot. In Dodge, if the drunkards began shooting up the town north of the deadline, they could surely be shot themselves because that's where the law mostly was. The wealthier people lived on the north side and wanted to sleep soundly at night.

Another rule more or less in effect held that cowboys and others coming into town had to leave their guns down at a place called the old brick house or at one of the liveries south of the tracks. This helped to keep much of the shooting south of the deadline. Since the Lone Star was a bit north of the line on Front Street, Mick never carried a pistol in the saloon himself, as most of the patrons were well aware of the extra risk of carrying arms in that part of town. He always carried the straight razor in his back pocket, but so far, thanks to his reputation as a ferocious fighter who used his thick heavy legs to leverage each punch, he had not had to use the razor and only had to show it two or three times. A straight razor was a scary thing to most men and to drunk cowboys, too, if they had checked their guns.

As the weeks passed, Mick and Frenchy made more time to talk. His people came from Ireland to New Orleans before ending up at a dairy farm near Kansas City. "Think of it," Mick said, "if they'd stayed in New Orleans, we might've run into each other on that big river."

"Not likely. I never left Baton Rouge except to go to my uncle's farm, and it was a long way from New Orleans."

"Anyway, I would have liked it, lass."

"Lass!"

"Would you be preferrin' 'mamsell'?"

"I go by Frenchy, but I'm half-Irish."

"Ah! I knew it! But you are full of secrets, I'm thinkin'. Aye, there's things behind the both of us—but behind us they are."

I hope you're right, Frenchy thought.

CHAPTER 17

Helena, July 1879

The reverend began to wonder if God and Matilda Winslow had conspired to delay his departure for four months as her condition and consciousness waxed and waned, at last leaving the reverend with thoughts so severe that he almost doubted his choice of vocation. When the end finally came in late July, he was so grateful that his eulogy probably seemed heartfelt, an impression he might not have been able to convey had she died according to his plans.

Believing that his mother-in-law's end was imminent back in March, he had begun his search for Catherine McCain then, at the steamboat station beside the dock in Helena. Recognized by the ticket agent, Mister Clune, Campbell briefly stated his mission: to find and bring to justice the woman who had killed his brother. Hardly had he begun to describe Catherine and Mamie when Mister Clune interrupted him.

"It's been a few months, but I do remember," said Mister Clune. "Yes, I sold two tickets and I recognized the woman you say helped the killer to ex-cape. She bought the tickets, you know. I thought it was odd that she was wearing a dark wig when she had such pretty blond hair. I could see some of her real hair stickin' out from under the wig. Not to mention that when she smiles, her front teeth ain't exactly how they should be. A man like me would see who she was at oncet."

"I am sure of it, good sir."

"She called me 'Mister Clune,' on account of she sold me my portion of liver pills every two months like clockwork down at the drugstore. I said, 'Miss Mamie, where are you headin' and I sure hope you ain't gone for long?' and she said, 'Mister Clune, I need two tickets on the *Natchez* up to St. Louis.'" Mister Clune poked gently around his upper abdomen, trying to determine whether he needed to get a new bottle of liver pills. Grimacing slightly, he went on, "And I started to ask her when she'd be back and to make sure they got the Carter's pills in on time, but I decided it wasn't none of my business so I handed over the tickets and tipped my cap goodbye."

Campbell studied the ticket agent for a moment. "Surely you heard later about the murder, and that this Mamie was an accomplice. Why didn't you go immediately to the sheriff's office with this information?"

Mister Clune had begun another probe of his abdomen but stopped and glared at the preacher. "Why? Because that big deputy come over here the next day, didn't he, and asked me about it hisself. And didn't I tell him the same damned thing, pardon me, *Reverend*, that I just told you?"

Campbell hastened to repair the damage. "I am sorry, Mister Clune. I did not know. And what did Deputy Armitage say after that?"

Mister Clune was not a man to pass off an offense easily. In fact, his doctor had told him that this tendency could be related to his unhealthy liver. "I s'pose you might ask him that yourself," he said sharply.

"Again, my apologies, Mr. Clune. By way of making amends and with the hope that your health might improve, please allow me to pay for your next bottle of pills." With this, the reverend took a silver dollar from his pocket and held it out to Mister Clune, who looked at it for less than a second before taking it and putting it into his pocket.

"Well, that's all right then."

"And Deputy Armitage said . . ."

"He didn't say a single word. He kinda gazed up the river, took a deep breath, and tipped his hat to me before he walked real slow back toward Cherry Street."

* * * * *

The reverend had never traveled farther up the river than Memphis, and that one trip had been on a packet boat that lacked the fine dining and social amenities of the *Natchez*, on which he had now booked a stateroom for one-way passage to St. Louis, for how could he know, he told himself, exactly how long his ambitious task might take? Thanks to the ample resources now firmly behind him, he had outfitted himself well for the trip: two new suits, a new pair of calfskin brogans, four fine shirts and as many cravats. He had two bowler hats, one soft gray and the other black. The suits were sober and professional, dark blue and brown. Putting himself forward as a clergyman might be helpful, so he could not dress in the latest style. On the other hand, he decided against the traditional black attire of many clergymen, as it might attract too much attention if his search required him to enter disreputable establishments.

In his initial zeal, Campbell had outfitted himself with some of the weapons that the surly Captain Mortimer had recommended. A dislike— no, a fear—of firearms kept him from purchasing a Winchester rifle, but he did buy a large clasp knife with a white pearl handle and a derringer, a .41 caliber Remington, but it held only a single cartridge. It was heavier than he had imagined. "It's a lot like the gun which kilt Lincoln," the gunsmith noted, approvingly. Campbell decided he also needed a Colt Navy revolver after he overheard two former soldiers in the gun shop talking about an incident during the war. A young Yankee lieutenant, riding alone, was able to capture both men because they had been unable to reload their Springfield rifles before the officer drew his Colt Navy revolver, with three unspent rounds remaining in the chamber. Campbell could not bear the thought of having to surrender to some brute who happened to be with Catherine McCain. Nevertheless, he now kept the revolver and derringer hidden deep within his big valise and had yet to fire either weapon.

Settled in his stateroom, he studied his face in the long gilded mirror across from the bed. "I need more years," he said aloud. He was thirty-one but wanted to look at least forty. He had allowed his dark hair to grow long, and now it reached well below his neck. He had not shaved; his mustache and beard had grown rapidly, something of a surprise. In a few weeks they would cover most of his face. Having associated the flowing mane with fervor or inspiration, he now thought he needed a different look. Recent photos of the Reverend Dwight Moody, a hero among evangelicals, showed the famous man with a full beard but hair much shorter than Campbell's. As for the extra years, it should be relatively easy to add a touch of gray to his beard and to his hair once it was trimmed.

There was a faux elegance to the stateroom, and of this he was vaguely aware. Something about it seemed appropriate for his new mission, like a dressing room for a star performer readying himself to go on stage. For more than a decade, he had been tied to church and family; now he was free of both. He felt a thrill as strong or stronger than what he felt at the height of a mesmerizing sermon.

When he stepped out of the stateroom into the long common area on which all the rooms on that deck opened, he walked past a mural of warriors dancing to the sun, beckoning from the west, where the wild free world awaited.

* * * * *

"Can you tell me when the barber will be in?" Campbell was disappointed at having to wait, since he had made a special effort to arrive at the exact time the boat's barber shop was supposed to open. He surveyed the room, his eyes going past but quickly returning to a small painting hung in the dark corner left of the door. There was a candle, as yet unlit, beneath the painting. The subject of the painting itself appeared to be—Campbell's eyes widened—a black Madonna with, yes, he concluded, a black infant in her arms.

"Good morning, sir. I am the boat's barber," said Gabriel Celiot, having seen Campbell staring at the painting. Gabe placed his broom in the corner behind the chair. He was smiling, as he was most of the time, and in fact was so used to being mistaken for a janitor that, in the interest of earning his fee, he let such things pass. Usually, he also found a way to increase the fee.

It took a moment for Campbell to accept that the Black man could be what he claimed he was. "And are you the only barber on the boat?"

"Yes, I am! And may I say, sir, that I am the finest barber on the entire Mississippi River, *le grand coiffeur . . . monsieur.*" Gabe had learned that throwing out a little French often worked to offset the negative first impression he regularly encountered. Even the most bigoted passengers were disinclined to challenge the preeminence of French taste in the fashion world. When he spoke his native language, whether or not his actual words were understood, the passengers could associate him with a sophistication they admired, requiring them to choose between their ingrained prejudice or the immediate demands of their vanity. Almost all chose the latter.

"Very well," Campbell said with a sniff. He waited for Gabe to gesture toward the barber chair and, after removing his coat and taking a last glance at the painting in the corner, took a seat. "I will thank you not to soil my shirt collar."

Gabe picked out his gaudiest apron, cast it with a flourish across Campbell's body, and tied it, a bit too tightly, at his neck. "There, sir, that should keep your collar nice and clean." Gabe was wearing a white shirt with broad short sleeves falling almost to his elbows. The shirt was unbuttoned at the top, and as Gabe bent to arrange the apron, Campbell saw a gold necklace from which a heart-shaped object dangled before his eyes. The center of the heart was square lattice, the perimeter with fine, elaborate scrollwork.

Campbell squirmed in the chair and tried to slip a finger inside his shirt collar to loosen it. His effort achieved little. Yet he would not allow himself to ask Gabe to adjust it. He settled into the chair and cleared his throat. "I do have some special requests. As you can see, I am growing a full beard and mustache. I believe both are coming along splendidly."

"Very much so, sir!" Gabe stepped back, as if only the perfect perspective could do justice to the scraggly outgrowths on Campbell's face.

"They need trimming, I am sure. My goal, however, is to have a full, thick beard."

Gabe moved closer to Campbell and framed his face with his hands, without actually touching him. He might have been sizing a fine portrait, estimating the space it would need on a drawing room wall. "Yes, yes, I see. Your face, it is not . . . broad, yet the thicker hair would add . . . *distinction*."

Campbell's face relaxed. He allowed a small smile to appear. "Now, uh, my young barber, it may be that few men such as myself request that their hair be dyed, but in my case, the request may appear even stranger."

"Many men ask that their hair be dyed, *monsieur*."

"Yes, but you see I am on a special, shall we say, assignment, and I would prefer to look somewhat older. Not old, mind you, but let us say forty years or thereabouts."

"How fascinat*ing*." Gabe stepped back again, clasping his hands together. "Of course, I can do as you say and provide you as well with the means to apply touches of silver-gray as you desire them. I will have to prepare a special formula, which I promise will stand for a full three weeks without washing, and therefore much longer for most men."

Doing his job on this boat was almost too easy for Gabe. Already he had found a sure way of charging this gentleman an extra three dollars. Most customers who wanted their hair dyed bought at least three bottles of brown or black. Since he did not keep a white formula on hand, he could charge a full dollar for each bottle of that new concoction. It would be simple enough. Already he had the pearl powder he required, made of bismuth, zinc oxide, and white chalk. Ladies often requested its application or purchased bottles for their own efforts to present what they hoped was a porcelain-like complexion. The addition of some joining paste, which he sold to the actors on the boat along with other make-up supplies, would complete the mix. The more he reflected on his new product, the higher the asking price became.

Gabe began by light trimming with a flashy pair of barber shears he kept on hand for customers like the present gentleman. Many of his customers could not be quiet in the chair, often distracting him but rarely enough to cause a mistake. But this fellow had said nothing beyond his initial requests. Absolute silence was itself a distraction for Gabe, so finally he said, "A special assignment, you say. How nice it must be to have a variety of things to do, true?"

"It is a departure from what I am used to." Campbell was enjoying the image of himself that was forming in his mind. "I have relied on eloquence in the past, but now I must become, I suppose, a kind of sleuth." He liked the word, the way it felt as he pronounced it. Being a policeman, sheriff, or marshal struck him as insufficiently subtle, not to mention completely inaccurate. He might have said "detective." And so he did: "I suppose the word 'detective' might be more familiar to you."

Gabe held the shears poised in the air above the customer's right ear. With a larger pair of shears, he could neatly remove that ear, into which a lesser person than himself might now want to shout a colorful expletive or two. He would have preferred a downright, freedman-hating, ex-cavalry private who had ridden with Bedford Forrest to this supercilious popinjay.

He began clipping again, very slowly so as not to tempt himself with bolder strokes. "*Oui, oui*, there are many detectives who use the *Natchez* to pursue their men. Some from the Pinkerton, yes, and many who work as I do for the steamboat line. It is their duty to watch out for thieves and to rid our boat of the cheating gamblers. We have many. It is true that they are very careful about their mustaches, though, and they are some of my best customers when they have won at the tables. And may I say that my Pinaud Brilliantine is absolutely the best product in the world for glossing the hair. And very reasonable it is too."

"Gamblers. A lower form of humanity, no doubt. I take it you also serve the ladies on the boat, as I see several pictures on your wall showing the many hairstyles that vain women now choose to call 'the fashion.'"

"Oh yes! So often, the men, they will let their hair and beards grow for weeks or sometimes months before—as they say—'suffering' themselves to be trimmed. But with the women, it is very different. Mm-hmm. They are so very careful of their appearance, it is true, yes, it is. I must admit it to you, sir, that sometimes I spend so much time with the ladies that I must sit and rest for ten minutes or so before I can accept a new customer. Oh, and they do love to talk! I must confess that I like to hear them talk, frequently one to the other rather than to me. They often come in pairs, and what one might like, the other sometimes does not. They are hard to please, yes, but they do like to be pretty, you know, and that is my job. I like it. I like them."

"Come in pairs," Campbell said to himself. He was quiet for a while. Gabe had stopped talking and, oddly enough, Campbell did not like the resulting silence. The trimming finished, Gabe began applying the silver-gray dye. The smell was somehow familiar to Campbell. Again he sniffed, in part to indicate his displeasure and in part to identify the odor more precisely. "Is that alcohol?"

Gabe backed away, holding the dye in one hand and a small brush in the other. "Ah, I knew you were a discerning man. Yes! A trace of bay rum—that is one of my unique ingredients. It is from the King's Tavern in

Natchez. Oh, but I cannot tell you more about the ingredients, *monsieur*!"

"It will go away? The smell?"

"Oh yes. Yes, it will be gone in, well, before the end of your journey, I am sure. Where are you going, sir? A short trip to Memphis, perhaps?"

"St. Louis. It is there where I hope to find my quarry." Quarry. Another word that was pleasant to speak.

"It is a big city. I have only begun to know it after a dozen visits."

"Yes, but one of the wom—one of the persons I am looking for is readily identifiable, and I have a description of her companion. As you may infer, I am looking for two females, one of whom murdered my dear brother. The law, if you can call it that, will do nothing, and so it falls to me to act. Thus, the need for my disguise. Both women know me at sight."

Gabe had been at the point of saying something more about St. Louis. At Campbell's words, he froze and closed his mouth. The dye was about to drip from the brush he was using; he hastily spread the dye across Campbell's hair. He turned away quickly, but not before he saw Campbell's dark eyes in the mirror behind the chair, studying his troubled face.

"I wonder," Campbell said, sounding more suspicious than not, "if you might have seen the pair yourself. Perhaps they—or one of them—sat in this very chair, entertaining you with her silly prattle."

Gabe kept a pitcher of water on the shelf of his walnut mirror cabinet. He poured himself a glass and gulped it down. Turning back to Campbell, he did his best to produce a natural smile. "You have no idea how many women have sat in that chair, *monsieur.* Next to the gamblers they are the, how would you say it, the foundation of my business on this boat. Not so frequent as men wanting shaves, but they pay much more and are so very interesting."

"Yet you do not ask me for their descriptions. I would think the very fact that you have so many women as customers would lead you to ask me about the appearances of these two."

"As I was about to do!" Gabe had recovered himself to some extent. "It is true that I have assisted many other detectives in this way. They appreciate my ability to study the human visage as few people can."

As I have been studying you, Campbell thought.

CHAPTER 18

It was no surprise to Campbell that the barber claimed he could not recall seeing the two women, even after hearing detailed descriptions. Yet after less than an hour in the steamboat's restaurant and saloon, where he managed a few sips from a glass of beer, Campbell found two people who did remember the women, one of them a barman who had decided they were up to no good because of the way they were watching the gambling tables. The barman was sure he remembered the women: One of them had such recognizable front teeth. And the other, while not beautiful, drew admiring glances from men in the room; but she was memorable to the barman for the plain, open, and direct way she spoke and for the straight-backed and confident strides she made after she turned abruptly, drink in hand, to leave the bar. "Like a man," the barman said. "Like a man who knew his business."

On the fourth day of the trip, less than twenty miles out from St. Louis, Campbell forced himself to engage in a conversation with a mere laborer, a short, thin Black man with remarkably large hands. His job was cleaning excrement and river filth from the paddle wheels with a long, heavy stick that had a stiff-bristled mop head on the end. He had set the long mop aside and was smoking a pipe in the shade of the wheelhouse, fully at ease as one of his boat's officers passed by and told him to take a rest before dinner.

Campbell managed a tone of levity, unusual for him, when he addressed the fellow. "My dear sister was a passenger on this same boat not long ago, and she spoke of a man, a Black man like yourself. She said he was kind enough to show her and her friend around the boat and explain the machinery, cabin names, decks and their functions, and much more. I would very much like to learn more about this vessel myself. Would you, sir, be that same man?" It surprised Campbell how natural and convincing he had sounded. How easy this mission might turn out to be!

"Nope," said the man, expressionless. The cob pipe clicked as he returned it to his mouth, foreclosing further discussion.

"Such incivility!" Campbell muttered as he turned away. But in any case, he was satisfied that the barber was surely protecting Catherine and her accomplice.

The next day, as Campbell stood in line on the gangplank waiting to disembark, he was watching an egret take flight and saw from the corner of his eye that the barber was watching him from the holiday deck above. Campbell pretended not to notice him and joined the group leaving the boat. He made a show of claiming his bags and noisily asked the porter for directions to a fine hotel. He hired a hansom cab, but after turning the first corner told the driver to wait. Campbell got out of the cab and stood next to a building at the corner, hiding himself as much as possible while still keeping the gangway of the *Natchez* in sight. Alarmed, he saw that the barber had already hurried from the boat and was heading down the same street where the cab was waiting. Campbell hurried back into the vehicle and drew the dark side curtain shut.

When Gabe was well past the cab, Campbell said to the driver, "Keep that young darky in sight, do you hear? The one with the gray bowler and striped coat. But do not get too close."

The strategy worked for about five minutes, during which time Gabe continued straight up Fourth Street, heading north; but when Gabe turned west onto Washington Avenue, heavier foot traffic forced Campbell to leave the cab. Swiftly, he gave the driver two five-dollar gold pieces to drop off his luggage at the Lindell Hotel, near at hand, along with Campbell's personal card and instructions to see the luggage brought to his room after checking in.

Campbell hurried through the crowd and slowed a bit when he was a safe distance behind Gabe. Never before had he found himself in such a place. He had been to Memphis half a dozen times, but now he was in a city ten times the size of Memphis with dozens of buildings on every street that would tower above the tallest in that town. Even New Orleans could not come close to the buzz and hum of St. Louis, which was half again larger than the South's biggest city. It was all he could do to keep from looking up and around, and to dodge laborers, businessmen, and shoppers in a hurry to be on their way. Two blocks later, the scene had begun to change. Here was a young woman in a tawdry red dress, slouched in the doorway of a dismal saloon. Only a little farther on, he heard shouting and swearing from a window above, followed by the howling of a young child.

At Tenth Street, Gabe turned right. Campbell paused at the corner and peeked around it in time to see Gabe banging on the door of a small rooming house. Directly, an old and disheveled man opened the door and shouted something at Gabe. All Campbell could hear were the words "None of your business, darky!" followed by the man slamming the door against Gabe's unsuccessful effort to wedge a boot against it.

"Lucky you weren't shot!" Campbell growled.

Gabe spat on the front step, turned, and began walking rapidly back toward the corner where Campbell was standing. Campbell dashed into a cheap dry goods store and waited, snatching glances out the front window to see if Gabe passed by. He did not. Campbell went to the door and looked out, first to the west. There, already fifty yards down Washington, he saw Gabe, still walking fast. Campbell slipped out of the store and followed.

Block after block went by. Gabe's pace was far swifter than the leisurely pace Campbell habitually adopted back in Helena, where he often stopped and chatted with prominent, well-heeled church members during his walks. Although the heat wasn't as bad as it was in Helena, he was sweating in his new suit when Gabe turned right at Garrison Street and stopped at the Bosse Saloon on the corner of Garrison and Franklin. As he watched the barber go inside, Campbell pulled out a small notebook and hastily scribbled the street names where he had made turns. Not daring to go in himself, he waited for what seemed like an hour but was actually half that time. Finally, Gabe came outside again and stood talking quietly with another man, also Black, on the front steps.

Campbell watched them for a little while but could glean nothing from their faces or movements. He took his chance to join a large group of railroad hands and shop clerks heading across the street to a loud restaurant and was safely out of sight when Gabe went back down Garrison Street the way he had come.

* * * * *

Hot and exhausted from the long walk, Campbell took a place at the lunch counter at the front of the restaurant. After a roast beef sandwich, he screwed up his courage and walked to the saloon. There was no one at the door, and inside, all was surprisingly cool, if dark at first. This in itself was a relief. Campbell tipped his bowler hat down so it sat more firmly on his head. Three steps later, he came to a hallway that ran to the left, and from a room off the hallway he heard the murmur of conversation, the clink of glasses, and the sound of a patron setting his beer glass down sharply on the bar.

Campbell walked into the room, stood near the end of the bar, and asked for a glass of "the best."

"Would that be beer or whiskey, sir?" the barman asked. "It happens that our bar has both."

Campbell managed to hide his distaste at the very thought of imbibing liquor. "Beer, please."

"A Budweiser for the gentleman!" shouted the barman to a younger man working the taps.

The younger man drew the beer and brought it over. Campbell allowed some foam at the top of the mug to touch his lips and pretended to enjoy it. "Young man, I wonder if you might help me find my sister? Although I would be surprised if she ever came this way, I fear it is possible. Please let me describe her to you."

The young man's name was Charlie. He had strict instructions to never, ever answer any questions about patrons or employees. The owner of the Bosse Saloon, who also performed on its stage in a solo singing act, had a prepared speech that he recited to all new hires: "This establishment is uninterested in the pasts or futures of anyone we serve and exists only for the purpose of shrouding the present with the haze of alcohol, the sound of laughter, and the indulgence of vicarious lust."

The owner had found it necessary to define the word "vicarious," but it was a word he liked, so he retained it in the script.

It was a joke among the barmen when they accidentally bumped into each other on busy nights that, but for the haze of alcohol, they could have avoided the collision. "Sorry, Charlie—couldn't see you for the haze." In fact, there was always a heavy cloud of smoke, not alcohol, in the Bosse from countless pipes and cigars. Only a few men rolled their own cigarettes. Occasionally, Charlie saw men light up prerolled cigarettes made in New York City or Richmond. Watching the beautiful Louise Pennette with more than casual interest, he noticed that she preferred Dubecs. Her friend, the pianist Baptiste, was seldom without a lit Bon Ton.

Charlie listened to the description of Mamie, the "sister," as well as one of Catherine, as Campbell remembered her. Scratching the fuzz of the beard he was trying to grow, he said, "Let me think for a moment, sir. Hmm. Sorry, no one comes to mind right now." He moved away and resumed pulling the taps, not bothering to come back to Campbell. Detesting the taste of the beer, Campbell decided that the order of another one would not be repaid with any useful information. He put a dime down on the bar and went in search of the Black man who had spoken with Gabe at the front door of the place.

The first notes from a piano reached his ears, from beyond some curtains closed off during this time of day. Seeing that no one at the bar was paying him any mind, Campbell pushed aside the curtains. Behind them was a much larger room, with a stage at the back and a piano set in a corner, down a few steps at stage left. And there was the Black man at the piano. Exhaling smoke, he carefully placed his cigarette in an ashtray. Campbell stood and listened, hardly believing what he heard. Abruptly, the music stopped. The Black man picked up his cigarette and pointed it at Campbell.

"Do you like music?" The man's voice was a deep, rumbling train of words.

"That was beautiful. I must say I am surprised to hear it, in this place." His tone made it clear what he thought of "this place."

The piano player shrugged. "I can play what I want this time of day. It is my time."

"Simple yet powerful, and, yes, so beautiful. 'Nearer, My God to Thee' has always been one of my favorites. In fact, I often ordered—that is to say, I often asked that it be included in the services of the church I used to attend."

"I learned how to play it from a boy."

The man's French accent made Campbell think he might have misspoken. "You learned it *as* a boy, I take it."

"I was the teacher of this boy. He is blind. I was his teacher at the school for blind children, here in St. Louis." His pronunciation of the city's name was French, with the words running together and sounding different enough to Campbell's ear that it took him a second or two to recognize them. "He is called Blind Boone. I played it for him one time. When he played it back to me, I felt I needed to learn it again from him, yes. He is now only fourteen years. Now when I play it, I think of him. It makes me play better. It makes me believe that music has power, that it is not only for—"

"Sinners." Campbell looked around the room, imagining the place full of drunken, lascivious, and howling men.

"—for entertainment. And for some of my people, this hymn that I have played is for hope."

"Hope? I might say that for my people, it is the ultimate reward, the fulfillment of a promise."

The Black man said nothing. He sat quietly, smoking his Bon Ton. The aquamarine ashtray atop the piano was overflowing with cigarette butts, most of them Bon Tons stuffed into the tray, shaped like a large conch shell. Yet others were Dubecs, more gently pressed down among the others. He stared at one close to the edge. The dark red lipstick remained on its tip, as on the other Dubecs he could see. Some time went by. He finished the cigarette and held it poised above the ashtray.

"I think it might not hold any more." Beside Campbell was a large trash can. Campbell saw a way that he might ingratiate himself with the Black man. "Here, I will empty it if you like." He took a step toward the piano.

"No!" The Black man's face turned fierce.

His response startled Campbell, but the preacher recovered swiftly. He might as well offer his story. "I am the Reverend Caleb Jackson, and

I am searching for my sister Mamie Jackson and her companion—"

The big man stood up and slammed the keyboard cover down so hard that the keys vibrated. Campbell gaped at him before collecting himself as best he could, and hurried out of the room.

Baptiste watched the white man scurry away. Around Baptiste's neck was a gold chain, and hanging upon it was a gold heart with square latticework on the inside and scrollwork on the perimeter. He touched the heart and closed his eyes, whispering, "By the power of the Mistress Erzulie, the white man, he must not."

At a much slower pace than the one Gabe had used to reach Bosse's, Campbell retraced his steps all the way back to the shabby rooming house on Tenth Street. He took care to knock politely. When the same old man who had quarreled with Gabe appeared, Campbell introduced himself as the Reverend Caleb Jackson and declared that he had heard from his sister Mamie that this particular boardinghouse had proved to be a fine place to stay, convenient to the riverfront and much of downtown. Might he have a room?

"I am all booked up at the moment," said the old man, throwing back his head with pride and tucking his thumbs under the frayed maroon galluses that held up his knee-worn pants. "Welcome to try back in a few days, young fellow. A reverend, you say. You'd be the first one of those to ever stay here."

"Ah! I was afraid you would have no rooms. Although my sister took care in her last letter to tell me of your fine establishment, she had to cut short her letter because her companion was in a great hurry to leave. Unfortunately, I do not know where they were going." Again, Campbell described the two women.

The old man's eyes narrowed. "It ain't likely that two men would be askin' about these same women all in the same day, now is it?"

"I'm afraid I don't know what you mean."

"There was a darky, all dressed up he was, here not more than two hours ago. I told him to git. Am I goin' to be tellin' a darky the whereabouts of two white women? No sirree. So one of them's your sister? Which one would that be? You said the one with the blond hair, the kinda plump gal? With the buck—now I seem to recall that she couldn't read nor write a lick. I heard that other lady tryin' to teach her a little.

Surprised your sister learned fast enough to send you a letter. That other lady, she was smart as a whip, I'll tell you that. Been a schoolteacher down south, she said, though she didn't say much. Heard her talkin' foreign one time, and I also heard her readin' out a newspaper story to the other lady, and I mean the words come so fast even I had a hard time keepin' up.

"Tell the truth, the both of 'em was a cut above most of the, uh, ladies who stay here. Dressed real nice too. They was stayin' on with me because, well, they liked me, don't you know, and they was all about savin' up their money. Worked over at one of them new type of stores—department stores, they call 'em now, on account of they have all kind of departments in that one store 'stead of havin' folks go to a bunch of stores to buy different things. I ain't been to one, but there's a bunch of 'em in this town now. I've had half a dozen women leave here once they got work in one of them stores. Don't make all that much money but they can get off the—they don't have to do hard outside work or do handwork all day in these factories we got around here. Now these here girls, they did a lot of night work. That schoolteacher, one of the few things she told me was that they hung up the women's clothes and laid out the perfumy things so's they'd be ready to sell next day. Never come back with a man, neither. Not once. They did smell good, I will say that. They would, I guess, bein' around all that perfume." The old man smiled and nodded with satisfaction at the thought of the two young women and the downright fetching fragrances they wore.

"Yes, sir, you are correct about my sister. Sad to say, she was raised by an uncle after our dear mother died and did not have the schooling that I was privileged to receive for the ministry. It was her friend, the schoolteacher in fact, who wrote the letter my sister sent me. Our uncle was a blacksmith, you see, and his notion of learning was limited. Did they happen to say where they were bound when they left here?"

The old man shrugged. "I wish I could tell you exactly where they went, young man. I heard 'em talk about buyin' railroad tickets, so's I guess that leaves out any more trips on the river. Lots of folks leavin' here on a train head over to Kansas City or maybe farther west. A few of the lower sort might go to Wichita or Dodge City or Abilene, places like that. But I don't see these gals doin' that, no siree. Cowtowns ain't much good for teachers. Ain't got no department stores neither, I 'spect."

CHAPTER 19

Tascosa, 1940

After a longer than usual absence, Tommy finally came by Frenchy's house, and as soon as she saw the proud look on his face, she knew what he had done. She was standing at the well, stooped from working the handle. Tommy came over and helped her to the front porch, despite her typical resistance.

"Well, say it." She held on to the front door.

"I went down to Amarillo and done it! Miss Frenchy, I am in the *cal*-vary." He had come down on one of the oldest horses that the boys could ride. There was no saddle on the animal, only a halter.

"That's *cav*-al-ree."

"Yes'm, that's right. You know what they told me? They said there wasn't but two calvary outfits in the whole damn army. That was them sayin' 'damn,' not me."

"I was about to say, what a damn silly thing for you to do, but come to think of it, if you're sittin' on top of a horse when this war blows up, you won't have any place to go fight. Horses can't fight against all these new-fangled weapons, Tommy. Maybe the worst you'll get is a chapped butt."

Only for a second did Tommy seem deflated by this news. "But that ain't so, Miss Frenchy. The sergeant done told us—Jimmy, he went with me—that the army still had horses out in some place in the Pacific Ocean where the army's been for years now. Me and Jimmy both know horses, that's for sure. The sergeant said there'd be plenty for us to do."

"There'll be much for you to do if those horses eat enough to shit all over the stables."

"Now wait, Miss Frenchy, that ain't fair. Me and Jimmy, we want to fight."

She opened the door and went inside. "I have some pound cake left. Want some?"

They sat at the kitchen table. Tommy ate two big pieces of the moist and heavy cake. Frenchy watched him enjoying himself. "So guess what, Tommy?"

"Whut?"

"You now owe me half a dozen eggs and a pound of butter."

Tommy grinned. "I will fight, Miss Frenchy. You'll see."

She looked across the table at Tommy, now almost six feet tall. He was already three inches taller than Mick had been, but today she saw a resemblance she had never noticed before. Tommy had gained weight, his face was fuller, and either his eyes had shrunk or they looked smaller now. All at once, she realized that the young man sitting across the table from her in this moment would leave soon and, as likely as not, would never come back again. Even if he lived. *I only know two or three other people now in the whole damn world. Have I been writing about my life for this kid at my table? No. I've been writing because our lives are the people who have made it, and we still owe them after they are gone. And then there are the things we owe them that we cannot truly repay.*

Frenchy hadn't cried in decades, not since maybe four or five years after Mick was dead and buried. One thing she knew: She wasn't going to cry now, either, not while this young man was sitting across from her and licking the crumbs of a rich pound cake from the corner of his mouth.

A week later she sat at the same table and took up her pencil. Looking back, she could see now how her time in Dodge City was so important in her life. There she mastered the trade of dealing faro, and not only the mechanical distribution of the cards but the ability to see the flurry of hands and fingers and bills and coins that came together and just as fast dispersed to make way for the next card dealt. Alone, she could catch most of the obvious cheating: the quick tug on the coppers that were meant to cancel a losing bet, the glances of the keepers and punters when they were in cahoots, the red-eyed glare in the cowboy's eyes that foretold an act of violence. The only thing stationary in the whole game of faro was the layout; the rest was change and chance.

> *I was learning a trade while I was learning about life. Faro was a means to an end. It worked a lot better for me than it did for Mamie. No keeper who knew about her skills would dare to fiddle with the abacus buttons when Mamie was watching, so she made good money simply by keeping an eye on the layouts. But I can see now how she was kind of left out. All eyes were on me, the layouts, the money, the cards, the fast action, and the flirty dance hall women. When men looked at Mamie, they saw one thing if they didn't see her teeth—no, two things—the same things they had gaped at in St. Louis. That was all they cared to see.*

* * * * *

Dodge City, August 1879
By now, Frenchy knew all of Dodge City's lawmen well. For her money, none of those men was entirely bad and none was entirely good. They were people. Lots of people out West left lots of bad behind. Most of them had guts, some were violent by nature, and many didn't give a shit about the finer points of the law. A few were middling faro dealers and honest. Wyatt Earp came to mind. But the arrangement in Dodge City was that most of the city's revenue went to pay the lawmen, and they could make real money running cowboys out of town or leaving their own cold beer or strong whiskey of the night and racing out into the street to shoot back at the drunk cowboys peppering the sky and some of the buildings north of Front Street with lead. In these more or less ritual-type affairs, one or more cowboys sometimes ended up dead. If folks really disliked the deceased, they might leave him in the street for a day or so. Other than that, Dodge was another bump on the prairie.

After only a short time in town, it was obvious to Frenchy that Mamie was less and less the Dodge City type and certainly not the Front Street after sundown type. Frenchy could hear Mamie rustling around on Sunday mornings after a long night at the saloon and finally figured out when she heard her friend's door slam shut one Sunday morning that Mamie had been going back to church. And meant for Frenchy to know it.

Mick had begun to stay overnight in her room at the hotel, and only a thin wall poorly papered over separated her room from Mamie's next door. Frenchy had not known what to make of love, but it was more true that she didn't know one thing about making love. It was a revelation. All that had happened to her in Baton Rouge and, worse, what had happened back in Helena, when they threatened to have a doctor examine her after Rainey Harper's assault, she quickly forgot once Mick caressed her body. Once they started going at each other, Frenchy found out about love and sex at the same time. It was all consuming. *Call me dirty, call me hungry, I really don't care. I'm almost twenty-one years old, and my body can feel desire about as fast as you can deal the winning card. That's how it is.* But now she realized Mamie could hear the bed knocking around on the wooden floor and against the wall or hear the bedsprings groaning like they would break. And then came the sound of Mamie's door closing on Sunday mornings.

She had come to love Mamie and cherish their differences, until now more a colorful stimulus to their friendship than a source of annoyance for them both. Mamie had saved her life and risked her own to make the trip to St. Louis, where in the end, poor Mamie was laughed at something cruel. Next was the long train ride to Dodge where Frenchy met Mick and, oh my, how life did change. Literally by chance, Frenchy thought, grateful that she was geared for change and strong enough to accept both the pain and exhilaration it brought. But she knew Mamie was not made that way. What Frenchy had brought to Mamie's life did not fit her naturally. *I should have admitted to myself that Mamie had been persuaded but not convinced.*

The truth was, the mostly unspoken tension between Mamie's strong faith and their joint escapades was tolerable so long as they were close— and also afforded them the means to survive. Frenchy didn't mean to hurt Mamie and surely didn't intend to ignore her. But some things take hold of a person, and one of those things was the different kind of love that came over her when she was with Mick, squinty-eyed, red-bearded, short-coupled, occasional son of a bitch that he was. It was love, and Frenchy loved it.

She wrote to Gabe and to Louise about the same time all this was happening in Dodge. She and Mamie had worried about Louise from the moment they had left her on the street in front of Faust's in St. Louis. Knowing her address was easy enough, and Gabe told them he picked up his mail at the St. Louis steamboat office. He lived on the *Natchez* unless he was on leave and staying with one of his many lady friends between New Orleans and Cairo. Frenchy didn't feel she could take off and go back to visit Louise, telling herself she needed to work but knowing down deep that she was loving her life and the man who was in it and didn't want to leave.

Weeks went by while she sent the first series of letters to Gabe and Louise. But since none of the letters came back to her by return mail, she eventually became more curious than worried. Sometimes she would wake with a start in the morning, and her first thought was that Louise was at the door waiting for her to go to dinner or supper or out for a shopping trip at the Market in St. Louis. Louise had never been inclined to write. Frenchy knew she had hated most subjects in school, grammar and math being at the top of the list. She used to cheat off Frenchy's work when they were girls at St. Mary's. Now, in her mind's eye, Frenchy saw Louise at her desk in Sister Francine's grammar class, capturing an answer from Frenchy's paper with a sideways glance, checking quickly to see if Sister had seen her, and then stifling a giggle once she knew her cribbing had gone undetected.

Louise–please answer; Mamie, please understand.

* * * * *

"And there you were last night, jabbin' me in the back and kickin' at me with those feet of yours, tellin' me to stop the goddamn snoring. But you know this, Frenchy *Pennette*, it's me now that can't get his sleep because of your blessed lovely legs runnin' like mad every night in bed. It's like yer chasin' or bein' chased by the Lord only knows what–and here I am tryin' to catch a wink before I have to pick up supplies for the saloon and kick the arses of the lazy sods who are to be helpin' me too."

Frenchy had finally managed to sleep a few hours, but only in the wake of nightmares about herself and Louise escaping from a series of menacing predicaments, after which they would try to smile and laugh reassuringly until the next grave threat appeared. Mick's snoring was almost incidental.

"I'm worried sick about Louise." Frenchy drew the covers around her shoulders. The August night had been hot, but the coolness of the morning that she would've normally welcomed now brought with it a chill. She lay there, the name "Pennette" echoing in her mind. She had recently, almost accidentally, adopted Louise's last name as her own.

Ten days ago, Mick's best barman, Old Pete Collins, had a stroke and died. There was a guest book at the funeral parlor. Frenchy followed Mick into the foyer, and before she knew it, she was standing at the table with the guest book, with Mick beside her and handing her a pen to sign her name. Louise was never far from Frenchy's mind, so she took the pen and wrote "Frenchy Pennette." She was reluctant to write or use her real last name publicly since anyone searching for her might think the name McCain, which was fairly uncommon, might be worth follow-ing up on. Frenchy soon admitted to herself that taking the name was also a way to feel closer to Louise—and a way to feel less guilty about leaving her alone in St. Louis.

Last week, Mamie overheard Mick calling out "Frenchy Pennette, get in here now!" They had all returned to the hotel only minutes earlier from an outing, and Mick was only pretending to scold her for dawdling in the hallway. Mamie and Frenchy were trying to decide where to go shopping after freshening up. Mamie was excited at the prospect, hap-pier than Frenchy had seen her in a long time. But at the sound of the name "Pennette," Mamie seemed almost to shrink, and from her face and eyes all of the cheerful anticipation vanished.

"You know, I ain't feelin' so good," Mamie said. "You go on without me."

Oh God, what have I done? Frenchy asked herself, as she watched Mamie walk away. The answer came quickly: The closer she became with Mick, and the more she tried to make up for leaving Louise, the less Mamie felt that she was loved. *I love them all but the sad truth is, I can only be with one of them.*

Finally, Frenchy threw the covers aside and sat up on the side of the bed. On most days, she was up and about early, and not only because the mattress was by now so bad that Mick complained to the hotel about it every day or two. Today was not most days.

"You should go and see Louise." Mick yawned and turned over to face her as she pulled her nightgown over her head, letting it drop to the floor. "But not right this minute."

"How do I know she's still there?" Frenchy ignored the leer on Mick's face.

"I think yer best bet is to get that little Black friend of yours to go and check on her, darlin'."

"Don't you call Gabe my 'little Black friend'! You of all people. It's not like you're a tower of a man yourself."

"From what you tell me about him, he and I do have things in common." Mick was not offended. For a man of only normal height, he was as unconcerned about his physical stature as any man could be. And with good reason. Almost all the men who had supposed that he could not toe the line had found out he could stand, and stand strong, for longer than they could ever do. "Gabe has made his way, and so have I. And from what you have said, he and I both have an eye for beautiful women." He had continued to watch her as she dressed. It was his favorite part of the morning. Lately, however, he had not been as successful as he would have liked when he attempted to coax her to return to bed.

"Sooner or later, he will pick up his mail in St. Louis. I have begged him to tell me about Louise. If I don't hear from either of them, I will try to write Baptiste at Bosse's. He might not be able to read himself, but there is some chance he might get my letter and ask someone to read it to him. If that doesn't work—well, I'm going to St. Louis." *We will never lose touch again.*

On that same day, in his stateroom on the *Natchez*, Gabe was sitting at a small table, pen in hand, staring at a blank piece of paper. To the side of the paper was the latest letter from Catherine. Again he read it, seeing in the well-formed letters and near-perfect handwriting something that, as much as the words, communicated the essence of his old friend from Baton Rouge. How much she cared; how earnestly she sought; how strong and hopeful she remained. Picking up the letter, he caught a faint scent that he associated with Catherine McCain. He dipped the pen in the inkwell and moved to create a word of his own on the blank white page. Then came a knock on his stateroom door; a boy whom he paid to bring him customers was waiting. A lady needed his attention. He got up and left.

CHAPTER 20

Mamie moved out of the Dodge House a week later, trying to make light of the situation as she packed her things and departed. Frenchy tried to do the same. But the parting words were sadly perfunctory, and Frenchy was left standing alone in the hotel hallway as she heard Mamie's footsteps grow fainter as she descended the stairs.

Mick and Frenchy took over her room, after the hotel put in a new door to connect it to theirs. In this second room they had a sofa, a small table, and two armchairs, as well as a vanity and mirror. The room was a little crowded; they called it their parlor.

The fact was, though, that Frenchy never enjoyed her time there now because she knew why Mamie had left. She had quit the Lone Star and gone back to her old trade, working in Herman Fringer's drugstore and greeting patients of Doc McLaren, whose office was in Fringer's building. She had moved to a small rooming house Doc owned on Spruce Street, well north of Front Street and away from the dance hall life. She and Frenchy kept in touch—lunch at the Dodge House, usually on Wednesdays. Sometimes they went shopping at Wright's or for short walks around town but never along Front Street unless they were at Wright's. Mamie was quiet and fidgety when they walked past the dance halls and saloons on Front Street, at a time of day when some of them weren't even open, and few were anywhere close to rowdy. Once, not long after she moved out, Frenchy asked to go with her to church, the Methodist Church up on Gospel Hill where all four of the town's churches sat, about a hundred feet closer to heaven than was the rest of the city. Unfortunately, Frenchy was jumpier in that church than Mamie was on Front Street, so she never went again.

It was a Saturday, and Frenchy was trying to get some rest in the so-called parlor. She heard a soft knock on the door, the mailman letting her know he was there. When she didn't get up, he slipped the mail through the space beneath door, wider than it should have been because the door was hung so poorly. Frenchy picked up a single letter off the floor. It had Gabe's return address on the outside. She tore it open, thinking that Gabe wrote such a beautiful hand. She would have expected that of him.

> *August 15, 1879*
> *Dearest Catherine,*
>   *I am now in St. Louis and found two letters from you as soon as I got off the boat. Oh, Catherine, I do not know how else to give you the news—elle est morte! This world is no longer home for our sweet Louise. When I was here not long ago Baptiste told me Louise had stopped coming to work at Bosse's. He expected the worst. Like all of us he loved our dear friend. I almost wrote you then but decided not to. It would have done no good.*
>   *Baptiste heard from the maid who works for that scoundrel Maurice that Louise passed away, here in this city. Baptiste went to the city morgue but he did not see our friend. She had been taken away. He did find the exact day of her death—August 5. He was in the morgue only five days later, on August 10. That is good.*

Here, Catherine had to pause and give in to the sobbing she had been trying to hold back. *I should have gone to her. I knew something was wrong. Why didn't I go to her? I was her best friend. I failed Louise, I failed her after all she had been through, oh my God!*

Catherine took three deep breaths and refocused on the letter. Lowering it moments later, she said, "But what the hell does he mean by saying 'it was good' to find Louise in the morgue?"

She choked down a fresh wave of sobs, wiped her eyes, and continued reading.

Baptiste was able to find a manbo that same day, August 10. A manbo is a spiritual woman, and within seven days of a death a manbo can help the soul to a resting place of dark water. It is now true that the soul of our dear friend is in that place from which it can be reclaimed in three hundred and sixty-six days. On that day, our dear friend will be free. This I believe. The day will be August 10, 1880, the day our friend's soul will be free. You must believe this, Catherine. You must.

You must also know that you could have done nothing for Louise. Baptiste begged her to leave that man but she could not. Not long after you left Louise found out that she was expecting a child, a child she was afraid to have. The man did not want the child of course. And he no longer wanted Louise. This she knew. Baptiste could see the sadness in her eyes, night after night. At first he thought it was because you and Mamie had left St. Louis. He could see changes in the way she looked and acted. She had no smiles, no energy. He saw she was sick almost every morning and finally she told him why. He knew about the man she was with, what kind of man he was. Baptiste told Louise he would take her away from this city to a place where they could live and raise the child.

But that night Louise did not appear as they had arranged. She was not in her rooms near Bosse's. No one knew where she was. Night after night the same, no Louise. At the morgue Baptiste could not find out how she died. Baptiste thinks the man had someone try to get rid of the child. His friend the maid thinks so too. She says the man has done it before. It is all I can do to keep Baptiste from finding this man and choking him to death. I tell Baptiste that the loa Erzulie will avenge or protect Louise—it is not his place to do so. He will get himself hanged. Yet he might not care if they hang him so long as he kills the man who caused our friend to die.

Baptiste does not know where Louise was buried. There is a pauper's cemetery. He says he will find out. He says it in such a way that I am hopeful but also afraid. Baptiste loves his music. He is a quiet man. But I know Baptiste very well. He is also a

dangerous man. The more he thinks of Louise, the more danger-
ous he may become.

Please know that I will write when I know more. I wish you
were here. I wish we—we three—were all here and walking side by
side, like we did only a few years ago in Baton Rouge. I can see
us now. I hear the laughter of our old friend, I see her turn your
way and then mine while she is walking and talking, shifting
her satchel from one shoulder to the other, smiling and teasing
me, hoping so much that you will be happy and stay with her
forever in Baton Rouge.

I am so terribly sorry to lose her. It is not for me to say, but
one must wonder how such a wonderful girl could end up the
way she did. It troubles my prayers to think of it. I cannot find
peace. I hope you can, my dearest friend.

Yours always, Gabriel Celiot

There was no need for Frenchy to reread any part of the letter. She let
it fall from her fingers, and stared at it on the small table in the room
once occupied by her friend Mamie. *I should have stayed in St. Louis.*

She slammed her fist down on the table. Then she did it again, and
again, until she gave in once more to her sadness, lowered her head,
and sobbed.

* * * * *

The following Monday she received another letter from Gabe. Opening
it quickly, she thought there might be more information about Louise's
gravesite, or maybe a report that Baptiste had found Louise's faithless
lover and given him the punishment he deserved. Before she read the
first lines, she was berating herself for wanting to endanger Baptiste by
making him the agent of revenge.

Catherine—

I had other news for you but did not want to include it in the letter about our friend.

You will not welcome this news either. A man is searching for you and Mamie, but I am certain that you are his true quarry. From what you have told me, I believe the man is the preacher whose brother you killed in Arkansas, but he did not identify himself as such. He wanted me to believe that he was some kind of detective.

He described you and Mamie and asked if I had seen you on the Natchez. Of course I lied, but the man has a kind of evil about him that I think gives him a special sight. He suspected me. He asked others on the boat about you too. I am sure he followed me when the boat docked in St. Louis because Baptiste told me the man showed up at Bosse's the same day I first asked about Louise. I know Baptiste told the preacher absolutely nothing, and he says the people at Bosse's are sworn to secrecy when anyone comes in asking about the customers.

The preacher might also have followed me to your former lodgings in St. Louis and talked to that horrible old man who runs the place. I hope you did not tell him where you and Mamie were going.

As a woman who knows her odds about many things in this life, you can guess the chances of this preacher finding you are not good. I believe that is true. The more one travels this big river, the more one finds that nothing in this world stays the same, and that from this city of St. Louis, a person could be heading for any place in the world at any time or vanish like foam on the river.

Again, I am sorry to bring more worry into your life. I feel so bad that I could not disguise myself and my feelings well enough to prevent that man from suspecting I knew you. Some feelings are too strong to hide, are they not?

Your affectionate friend, Gabriel Celiot

＊ ＊ ＊ ＊ ＊

"From what you tell me, I agree with what your Black friend says. How would a man be findin' you out here when all he knows is that you were in St. Louis last year?"

Frenchy had not let Mick read the letters from Gabe but had provided the briefest possible summary of their contents. She turned angrily toward Mick. "He is my friend. Black has nothing to do with it!" Frenchy could never know whether her going to visit Louise might have saved her. She did know that the main reason she hadn't gone was that she was preoccupied with the man beside her in the bed right now. At the present moment, however, it was all she could do to remain in their bed rather than move into the next room and sleep alone.

Since reading the letters, she had wondered: Did I tell the old landlord in St. Louis where Mamie and I were going? She was sure she had not, but what about Mamie? She was also sure she had not used either Frenchy or her real name around the old man.

She sensed that Mick wanted to ask her something but had decided against it. She felt his warm hand on her left shoulder. He kissed her gently and pretended to be smoothing some mussed hair back in place. *It isn't his fault. None of this is his fault. It's time I tell him what happened in Helena. The truth is, I've been afraid to tell him. He's been so happy— and how do I tell him the woman he loves has been on the run, that she's wanted for murder?*

When she had finished with the story, told quickly but honestly, Mick lay back in the bed and folded his arms across his chest. One minute passed, then two. "Do you remember what I told ya girl, back when we first met. I knew you were full of secrets and said so. And—"

"You said 'there's things behind the both of us, but behind us they are.'" *And I hoped it was so.*

"Yes. So it is now. Behind us they are."

"And here I was thinking that I wanted to be up and away from you. I'm sorry. The letter from Gabe—"

"I can see he is your friend, and a true friend at that." They lay as they were for the next half hour, Frenchy trying to face her deep sadness, and Mick thinking, considering, and at last letting his features relax as he made up his mind about something important, kept now to himself.

Frenchy waited two days, until her regular Wednesday lunch with Mamie, before telling Mamie about Louise. They were in the restaurant at the Dodge House. Frenchy had noticed that Mamie was less enthusiastic nowadays about eating there, although in the past it was her favorite place.

"I will pray for her, I will." Mamie sat very straight in her chair. She had lost more than ten pounds and never seemed to relish her food as she had before. The brightness that had always shone from her clear blue eyes was dimmed somehow, as if a translucent screen had been interposed between them and the objects they fell upon. "Oh, Catherine, I really am sorry. I know how close you was to her." With her right hand, slimmer than Frenchy had ever seen it, Mamie reached out and held Frenchy's own.

"Mamie, our old landlord in St. Louis, did you by any chance ever tell him where we were going?"

"Why, you told me to say nothin' so that's what I done!" She started to pull her hand away, but Frenchy held on to it. "I mean, I might've said somethin' about headin' out west, but that don't really tell him much since there's so much west to go to."

"I wasn't accusing you of anything. I only asked because Gabe wrote that Campbell Harper was in St. Louis recently, looking for us. I had assumed the law wouldn't bother with us all that much. I am surprised Campbell would take the time to do it on his own."

Mamie thought for a moment. "I don't know that I am. He was wrong about you, I know that, but he prob'ly talked himself into believin' what he does. He was always preachin' about how we all got to follow the Lord. I reckon he believes the Lord told him to find us."

Frenchy let this pass, although the idea that Mamie could see Campbell Harper as anything other than a lying zealot was shocking. But Catherine decided to make the best of it. "We did have some good times in St. Louis, didn't we, Mamie? The lunches and shopping trips and all the fancy clothes—how you loved the clothes. You and Louise. I didn't really give a damn, but I got a kick out of watching you two have such fun." For the first time since receiving Gabe's letters, Catherine smiled, and it was partly genuine. "And how beautiful she looked at Faust's the last time—" Frenchy's eyes began to tear up, and she couldn't finish the sentence.

"Yes." Mamie withdrew her hand. "She was wearin' that dark green dress. Got all gussied up to come over to Faust's and tell us she was stayin' in St. Louis. That's when she told us about that fella Maurice. I told her that no good would come of her bein' with a married man. Said I'd pray for her, and I did. Some. I guess not enough. I wish she'd listened to me. She'd still be alive."

"I don't think this is the time to be saying 'I told her so,' since we only now found out she's dead. And anyway, if what happened to Louise as a girl had happened to you, there's no way you could sit here and judge her for anything. And 'pray for her'? That's twice you've talked about praying for Louise. Well, goddammit, it's too fucking late to pray for Louise!"

"Oh no, dear me, I don't understand nothin' about bad times, since all that happened to me was I got pregnant and had a baby cut outta me and that baby died, and I cain't never have another one." Mamie managed to blink away some tears. "Me and Louise didn't always see eye to eye. But you know what? I did feel sorry for her, and I feel sorry for her now."

"You were always jealous of her. Of her and me."

"And now I s'pose you'll get around to tellin' me how jealous I am of you and that little Irishman you've taken up with, mm-hmm. Here's a fact: I don't want no little Irishman nor no other man right now 'cause I got all I can handle tryin' to get Mamie Jackson back to bein' right with the Lord. And let me tell you, that's a lot to do all right 'cause ever since I got you out of that jail in Helena, we've spent most of our wakin' time hangin' out with men and liquor and faro tables, and that ain't how no one gets right with the Lord. It wasn't me who wanted to deal them cards. No. It was Catherine McCain. And it wasn't me who wanted to get up on a stage in St. Louis, Missouri, in front of a bunch of drunken men and show parts of my God-given body just to make a few dollars. No, it wasn't me. It was you and that fancy friend of yours from when you was in that papist school down in Baton Rouge, neither one of you learnin' the Bible as it was wrote down. I reckon you always felt like y'all was sisters, and now you done taken her own last name!"

"You don't know!" The hum of conversations in the Dodge House restaurant ceased; the only sound came from utensils being put down as the patrons listened. Frenchy collected herself enough to continue in a low but furious voice. "Blame me all you want, Mamie Jackson, but do *not* blame Louise Pennette, who went to Mass every time they opened the fucking doors and could say the whole rosary in her sleep. It wasn't her that turned away from God, or the church, or the Lord. It was the church that turned away from her and ruined her life. As for loving her like a sister, you're damned right I did."

Mamie stood up. She bent and pointed her right index finger directly at Frenchy's face. "Listen here, girl. I ain't the smartest nor the purtiest nor the nicest female in this world. There's a lot I don't know, for sure. But this is what I do know. You are mad at yourself and full of guilt for what happened to Louise. And you takin' it out on me ain't gonna bring her back nor make you feel one bit better. Mm-hmm. Now that's it." Mamie gathered her scarf close around her bosom and left Frenchy alone in the restaurant, staring at the white linen tablecloth.

CHAPTER 21

St. Louis, late July, 1879

Campbell Harper soon discovered that the city of St. Louis had far too many of the new department stores for him to track down Mamie and Catherine, especially as he was all but certain that they were not using their real names. True, Mamie was more identifiable by description than Catherine was, the strong, confident demeanor of the latter accounting for much of the impression she would leave with anyone.

He allowed himself to luxuriate in his large, comfortable room at the Lindell Hotel for several days, taking hot baths and dining in the hotel restaurant or in his room whenever he chose. Along with his new suits and weaponry, he had almost three thousand dollars in cash, including two hundred in gold. It pleased him to think how much his parishioners loved him and to recall the zeal his dear wife had shown in turning over some of her inheritance from her mother.

He stood before a gilt-edged mirror and saw that his new brown suit fit him well. A pair of fine polished kid ankle boots clung to his feet so perfectly that they might have been made for him personally, and by hand. Such was in fact the case: The hotel made all the arrangements, and all he had to do was open the door to his room and spend half an hour with a busy little man bearing a variety of measuring devices that he put to good use. The boots, only three days in the making, were the result.

All of this was very well, but he was not making any progress in finding his quarry. At such times, he thought, one must let God lead the way. A path would appear. A clue would jump out at the most improbable moment. In the meantime, what he needed was a good walk, some fresh air, and, most appealing of all, some lively and wholesome entertainment. He had overheard a party of guests on the mezzanine level recounting their wonderful evening at the Grand Opera House where a minstrel show was playing. "Never have I laughed so hard in my life," one of them said.

Campbell had never seen a minstrel show, but he had longed to do so since the former mayor of Helena went on an extended trip through the South and saw a performance in Atlanta. Already thinking of himself as a man of the big city, Campbell immediately had the concierge look for a ticket to the show for the evening. The ticket was expensive: ten dollars. The concierge had confided that the locals, that is, those of substance, knew the place by the name of DeBar's Grand Opera House, the late Mr. Ben DeBar having been the owner. He was famous for his portrayals of Falstaff. Mr. DeBar, the concierge added in a low voice, had adopted the niece of none other than John Wilkes Booth. "Mr. DeBar favored productions of a pro-Southern type," the concierge said, having sized up Campbell early in the conversation. "Unfortunately, he was harassed by federal investigators immediately after the war. But the minstrel shows are the thing now!" Campbell swelled with this newfound inside knowledge, feeling more like a real St. Louisan. But for his mission, he might have considered a move to this fine bustling city.

Campbell paid for his ticket with a flourish and considered tipping the concierge a full silver dollar but, finding only one in his pocket, decided against it. He was furious when the man later sent up a note along with the ten dollars saying that the show was sold out, except for "a few much cheaper seats in the balcony." Campbell took this as a personal affront. If a concierge could find transportation, restaurants, theater tickets, and, he had heard, entertainments of a questionable nature for certain gentlemen, then why could he not accommodate an upright man such as Campbell himself? If the fellow expected more money from Campbell now, he was a scoundrel and a fool. Cheap seats!

Deprived of his entertainment and finding no consolation in his dinner at the hotel, Campbell woke early the next morning after a troubled sleep. After lying in bed for ten minutes, it hit him that it was Sunday. "Why, man, are you lying abed when it is the Sabbath?" he said aloud. He got up and pondered his suits, deciding not to wear the brown suit of yesterday. The blue one, with a cravat of a darker blue, was much better.

Having passed by the Union Methodist Church the previous evening, he resolved to go there for his Sunday worship. He had not managed to attend church regularly since his departure from Helena. The thought of attending excited him, especially as it would permit an opportunity to evaluate the message and manner of the minister. Campbell's brand of Methodism had more in common with many Baptist churches than it did with Methodist churches in big cities. While Campbell did detect a Northern intonation in the pastor's words, the sermon itself was most satisfactory, anchored in Philippeans 2:12. Campbell made a mental note to strive for the same exact emphasis the next time he himself cited these verses, for the pastor spoke the words "with fear and trembling" in such a way that a scruffy boy of eleven or twelve who had been dozing in the next row jerked awake and remained so until the service came to an end.

Campbell left the church, congratulating the pastor on the way out and, of course, mentioning his own similar role, "though in a somewhat smaller parish." Walking down the front steps, he noticed a large group, mostly women, standing in a half circle around another woman, who was being questioned by two men Campbell took to be newspaper reporters.

Campbell heard the woman say to the reporters, both young men, "Yes, mark my words, the both of you: There is no innocence in alcohol, only evil. Taking *only* one drink is the same as taking *only* one bite of a poisoned apple. Nothing leads a man more surely to ruin than alcohol in all its insidious forms. You may say, 'Well, I am a man and can handle my liquor. A real man can always do so and enjoy his hard-earned freedom from domestic cares in the full companionship of his fellows. There is no harm in a bit of whiskey or a pot of beer. We are all hail fellows, well met and well parted.' But I say that not only will you and your cheerful companions trod the path to perdition—but ladies—they will leave their wives and children bereft, having squandered their earnings on nothing more than the devil's own elixir."

At this, the women applauded, and seeing the speaker walking past the reporters, followed her, chanting, "The lips that touch liquor / Shall never touch mine! / The lips that touch liquor / Shall never touch mine!" Campbell himself had preached on the evils of drink, so he followed the group as it headed north up Fifth Street. The group grew into a crowd. The crowd walked on and on, but not so fast that Campbell was unable to keep up.

To his surprise, the crowd stopped outside the Lindell Hotel, whose excellent environs he had left only three hours before. He went around the throng in order to place himself near the main entrance to the hotel foyer. There, with luck, he hoped to meet the fine, spirited woman who was causing all the hubbub. The woman had looked familiar to him, and now he realized that she was Miss Frances Willard, recently chosen as the new national president of the Woman's Christian Temperance Union. He had seen her picture more than once in the St. Louis papers.

He felt some trepidation at the prospect of meeting a national figure. "Yet she is only a woman," he told himself, bucking up his confidence. "I should say, she is a fine Christian lady. How can we not be of the same mind?"

As the lady turned to enter the hotel, the crowd took up a new chant, "On to Kansas! On to Kansas! Keep Kansas pure!" Campbell had never heard a single soul speak of Kansas as being pure. He recalled that, on the eve of the war and throughout its terrible duration, there was wide-spread use of a very different term: "Bloody Kansas!"

* * * * *

Frances Willard had a handshake like a man, as Campbell immediately discovered upon meeting the small but forthright woman in the lobby of the Lindell.

He had had time to consider which name he would use before he actually met Miss Willard. There was something freeing about using another name, similar to the way he felt when he thought of himself as a detective. On occasion, he had thought of his dear wife and children. Certainly he would write to them, as soon as he could find time to do so. Yet already he found it difficult to keep them in the forefront of his mind while he was conducting his search and adjusting his identities. By the time Miss Willard entered the lobby, he had made his decision. He had already pretended to be the brother of Mamie Jackson, and he might need to do so again. Holding out his hand, he said, "Miss Willard, may I introduce myself? I am the Reverend Caleb Jackson, a Methodist minister from Arkansas, and like you, a worshipper at Union Methodist this morning."

Her eyebrows rose. "Arkansas! We could use your help down there. Mostly moonshine, I hear."

"The saloons, I believe, serve beer and bottled whiskey, although I wouldn't be surprised to learn it was only moonshine or worse out in the country. I have preached against the evils of alcohol repeatedly; I fear that in some cases, my words have made little difference."

"So what brings you to St. Louis? I am here because yesterday I made a long-winded speech over at the Temple Building, not far from Union Methodist." By apprising him of her own reasons for being here, she seemed to be encouraging him to be forthcoming. While not large in stature, she was remarkably imposing. Her pale eyes were not unkind but steady in their gaze while her small but well-formed mouth never quite reached a full smile, conveying more intelligence and curiosity than civility or good humor.

After a brief hesitation, Campbell recalled that he was on a special mission. "I felt an urgent call, Miss Willard, a call to preach to the people most in need. In my judgment, most of those are to be found in the big cities or in the newer towns on the frontier, often battling the twin evils of drunkenness and licentious behavior." He watched her carefully as she took this in and felt he needed to say more. "So often they go together, don't they, Miss Willard? And of course there are the horrors that drunkards visit upon their own loved ones. They become the ruination of their own homes."

Campbell could see his remarks were well received. He was acutely aware that impressing this woman had become very important to him. Why, he did not yet know. So used to the deference and adulation of his wife and the women of his church, he felt unsure of exactly how to proceed. A woman Miss Willard surely was—but deferential she certainly was not. She was obviously admired, and expected to be admired. But that was what Campbell expected, too, especially from a woman, and especially in matters of religion. What was it that gave her prominence and made him almost a supplicant when he was near her? Ah. It was fame. The woman was famous throughout the land, famous and powerful. Righteous in her cause, and righteousness could not be ignored. Fame, power, righteousness—he could make this woman his instrument to gain the very same ends.

"You are in the right of it, Reverend. You may call me Frances. I actually prefer to be called Frank, but, oh my, how it confounds so many people when I tell them that."

Campbell merely nodded, finding himself to be one of those confounded.

"What you said a moment ago caught my attention," she went on. "You used the word 'urgent.' It has come to me that where I am going next—Kansas—could do with a lot more urgency. The state, you may know, has already prohibited the manufacture and consumption of alcohol, a leader among states in that regard, yet the devil has had his way with the law. Saloons and dance halls abound and so does heavy drinking, not to mention the debasement of young women, many of whom have been deserted or abused by so-called fathers or husbands in the grip of alcohol. So, yes—urgency. You know, my family were all Congregationalists. Intelligent, well-intentioned people they were. I became a Methodist. Do you know why?" She gave him no time to respond. "Our denomination, Reverend, knows how to inspire a sudden, commanding desire for commitment, not only to Jesus and Christian salvation but to change the world, to fight its evils to the death."

Campbell could certainly see that Frances was capable of practicing what she preached.

"I'll tell you what it is," she said, again allowing no time for him to speak. "For many of the people in the West, newly arrived, struggling, threatened, what they need, and need now, is *salvation*. When we speak of temperance and the terrible evils of alcohol, what we are really talking about is *salvation*. What we need, Reverend, are men and women who can conjoin Christian salvation with total abstinence from demon rum. And I mean to tell you, sir, that they must feel, must know, in the very marrow of their bones, that their salvation, their abstinence, must happen not in the next month, nor in the next week, nor tomorrow, nor before the sun goes down. It must happen *now*!"

"Yes, yes, I see!" Campbell couldn't help asking himself if his parishioners ever felt the same fervor after listening to him that he felt now.

Well, of course they did.

"And how do we do that, Reverend?"

Campbell sensed that she knew what his answer should be. After reflecting for only a moment, so did he. "Hell. We must show them hell, make them believe in the way you have described, that 'demon rum' is the Devil and that we stand on the knife edge of hell—"

"The edge?"

"—that liquor is that very hell pouring down our throats, scorching our souls, incinerating our hearts, and laying waste to those we love."

"Yes, scorching our souls. There is no time. There is only now."

* * * * *

And so it happened that Campbell was enlisted in the cause of temperance and scheduled to depart for Topeka, Kansas, the following Wednesday on the same train as the famous Frances Willard. Campbell was exhilarated, so full of energy that he bounded through the humming city as if his legs had belonged to Leonidas himself. His face lost some of its natural pallor. His head was filled with Scripture and rhetorical flourishes, one feeding off the other. The sky was blue; the weather fine. The smells of St. Louis—toasting hops, tobacco smoke, horses and their waste, roasting coffee beans, sauerkraut, the perfume of the ladies, the sweat of the laborers in the street, and, yes, the stale beer smell of the taverns as he passed—neither attracted nor repelled him because all were one and part of the city, and the city seemed to be his.

In this state of euphoria only one unhappy thought intruded: That man Baptiste at Bosse's Saloon, he was surely lying, in league with that young barber. Into Campbell's mind came the image of the barber, gold necklace hanging down to the curly black hairs on his chest. And the picture in the corner of the barber shop: a *black* Madonna and child. "Ah, yes," Campbell said to himself. "They are papists, after all, and foreign colored into the bargain." The little barber, the piano player Baptiste, and, of course, Catherine McCain, the woman who had killed Rainey Harper—she was black in thought and deed if not in color. He imagined them all huddled in that small dark corner on the *Natchez*, the candle lit beneath the black Madonna, all of them whispering and conspiring, papists all. "The true word of God means nothing to them," he whispered. "It is only their schemes and images they embrace. Hocus-pocus, as Rainey used to say. And far worse."

Then it occurred to Campbell that the barber, as part of the crew of the *Natchez*, would of necessity come and go through St. Louis on the big steamboat. The boat's arrival and departure times would be readily available at the wharf. Campbell still had time at his disposal before his own departure to Topeka, Kansas. "I wonder how readily I might return to my role of sleuth?" he asked himself.

The answer was not long in coming. The next morning Campbell ate a big breakfast—oh, how his appetite had improved!—and hurried south to the wharf. The *Natchez* was scheduled to arrive from Memphis by 4:00 p.m. "But don't be surprised if she ain't here till long afterward," the station agent said. "Hard to predict exact times—she ain't no goddamn stinkin' train."

As Campbell waited, gazing at the sky, he imagined an encounter with the barber. Emboldened by his recollection of him as being a small man, Campbell saw himself glowering down at the barber and intimidating him by his presence, a well-dressed white man, a man with a mission, a man guided by the word of God and not under the sway of crude graven images.

Emboldened or not, he grew restless with the waiting. Not wanting to move far from the wharf, he looked out at the new Eads Bridge, more than a mile in total length, spanning the Mississippi from east to west. As a boy, Campbell liked to draw. The bridge was worthy of a fine drawing, he thought, admiring the three giant arches beneath the main bridge and watching more than a score of boats—riverboats, packet boats with cotton baled high, and a dozen barges loaded with all manner of freight. Smaller craft and sailboats dodged their way back and forth under the bridge. He would have liked to go down to the bridge itself, perhaps to wait near the abutment at the west end, finding welcome shade beneath one of the five smaller arches there. But the closer to the river he walked, the more he was unable to bear the smell—of fetid water, dead fish, floating vegetation, and Mississippi mud gathered hundreds of miles upriver and deposited at this busy port.

So Campbell stood at a distance looking at the twin American flags flying high in the breeze, each flanking the top of the bridge abutment.
He sniffed in his peremptory way and turned his back on the flags.
Whether he looked to the north or the south, the scene was one of constant activity. Amid the disembarking passengers and shouting bosses
on the boats and wharf, he saw what had to be more than a hundred
Black laborers, some rolling casks from the boats to the wharf, others carrying chicken coops—so many chickens, more than Campbell
thought possible in any one place, cackling and filling their coops
with droppings.

Everywhere he looked, he saw sturdy hand trucks, about as tall as a
tall man. And seeing a Black man pushing one near him, loaded with
a giant cotton bale, Campbell had to give the coloreds credit, they did
have great strength. From talking to farmers in Helena, Campbell had
learned that each bale could weigh as much as three or four hundred
pounds. The bales on the wharf, as at home, had all burst through their
burlap wrapping in places, showing white tufts of cotton and leaving
others strewn about the wharf. Only half a dozen metal bands kept the
bales from coming apart. Not far away, a wagon arrived, the pair of horses harnessed to it sweating and panting in the September sun. A crew of
Black men began loading cask after cask of something, he did not know
what, into the wagon. Hundreds of casks remained to be loaded, all
up and down the wharf. Other wagons reached the wharf, their teams
crowding one another for space, whinnying and struggling against their
harnesses as they tried to bite or kick.

Campbell heard the men singing, had heard them intermittently
since he arrived at the wharf. What they were singing, he could not tell.
Watching and listening to them for another minute or so, he sensed that
the movements of the men, measured and steady, fell in with the songs.
Campbell understood but few of the words; some of the singing struck
him as sad, some as more spirited.

There—two men dropped a cask and it burst open at the top, where it
was not bound by metal bands. A dark liquid poured out of it. Singing

and not paying attention, you were, Campbell thought. Now, the smell of whiskey came to him, reminding him of his visit to Bosse's Saloon in search of Catherine McCain. He imagined he could hear the sizzle of the liquid on the hot wood block pavement. *All those casks, all that evil congregated right here before my eyes.* "Dear Lord," he said aloud, "please know I have set myself against this evil."

Somehow it made Campbell feel better to see the magnitude of the Devil's work, placed directly in his path on the very eve of his mission to Kansas. It was surely a sign. A sign to help him see clearly, to reinforce his zeal. And then he heard a familiar voice.

"Look at that!" said Gabe Celiot. "Forty gallons of whiskey, Henry! Watch now, watch those rascals. See! They are looking for the boss man; they do not see him around. Now, now, *see*, they will take their cups from the water bucket and scoop up whiskey as soon as they turn the cask upright. And why not, it cannot be sold now?"

Henry frowned. "I do not have a cup."

"It would do you no good, my friend. You did not spill the whiskey, so you cannot drink it." Gabe amused himself by watching Henry ponder this statement. Henry had only recently joined the *Natchez* crew in Memphis. Clearly, it made no sense to him that those who spilled the whiskey should be rewarded. But Gabe had heard that the men would have their pay docked for breaking a cask, and their few drinks would not offset their loss. Telling Henry about this would likely satisfy his sense of justice. But Gabe loved to tease Henry and said nothing more.

Campbell turned and saw the riverboat barber coming his way. Their eyes met. Gabe whispered something to the much taller Henry who quickly turned toward the white man standing on the wharf. Campbell had stretched to his maximum height, head held high, defiant.

Henry fixed Campbell with a stare that would have caused him to shiver if the sun hadn't been so hot on his back. When Gabe and Henry were well past, Campbell raised his fist and shouted, "Liar! You will pay! I will find her! I would have you thrashed back in Arkansas. Whipped to your knees!"

An older man leaning on a nearby wagon was sipping the last of his share of whiskey from a cup. He licked his lips and, smiling at Campbell, said, "I reckon Arkansas where you belong."

CHAPTER 22

Dodge City, late August, 1879

Leaving Dodge City happened so quickly—and that was the best thing for Frenchy.

"I'll be needin' to put up a house before winter, so it's now that we'll be goin'." Mick had finished his breakfast with Frenchy at the Dodge House. She didn't seem to hear him. "Now listen to me darlin', ya need to pack yer things, and now would not be too soon."

"I need to do what?" Frenchy looked up from a plate of eggs and bacon, growing cold.

"I've been puttin' back some money. It's time we did somethin' more for ourselves. We've been hearin' about that new cowtown down in Texas, in a place they like to call the Panhandle. To my mind it should be easier to make money off of drunk Texas cowboys if you go where they are all year round."

"How much money do you have?"

"As much as you have, girl. Five hundred, give or take."

"How the hell do you know how much money I have?"

"I counted it. Do you think I'm stupid? You're a-lookin' into that little brown case of yours every other night. When you close it up you give it a little pat. That's the only time I ever see you happy now."

"Which cowtown?" She was not happy now.

"They call it Tascosa, I believe that's the right of it."

"So here we are in a nice pair of rooms with decent food and a town big enough to stretch our legs and you want to pick up and move to a godforsaken place in the middle of nowhere that nobody but Comanche Indians have wanted till now. I hear the Comanches like fair-haired scalps. God be with you. But maybe they'll give you a pass since you're almost bald."

Mick ignored the comment. "You will no doubt be thrilled to know I've bought us a stagecoach, the open-air kind you see, and ever so slightly used. We'll have a lovely ride down there, I am sure of it. Well, there may be the odd renegade Kiowa or Comanche or maybe a would-be robber, but nothin' we can't handle. I'm wantin' to open a livery stable once we get there, and I can use the old stagecoach as a wagon, you know, for haulin' hay and the like. Bein' born on a wee plot in Ireland and workin' on the family dairy near Kansas City, I kinda miss the outdoor work—but not the actual milkin' mind ya. I know I can pick up some bartendin' on the side, I've heard of a saloon that might take me. We'll build a place of our own, start afresh. There'll be an end to livin' in a damned hotel and hearin' the neighbors belchin' and fartin' through the night. What do ya think, girl?" He reached out his hand. "You need to get movin', my darlin'."

Frenchy spiked a piece of egg with her fork and ate it. She didn't look up for a while. When she did, Mick could see that her eyes were moist. She reached across the table and took his hand. "You're a sneaky little Irish rascal, but thank you, Mick. Thank you."

"You'll find her one day soon, girl. The pair of you—you've been through too much. It cannot stay this way. Before I came along, Mamie was all you had."

"Doc McLaren says she told him she was going to find someplace quiet to settle down and then up and left town. I'll have to tell him where we're going. Sooner or later, she'll get back in touch with him. He's been so good to her, he and the druggist both. She's bound to run out of money, with no friends, nothing but a couple of bags and a Bible, Doc says."

"Dodge is almost a closed town. We're doin' all right, but it's not gettin' us anywhere. I can't see startin' a business here a'tall. Have Mamie come join us when she can. Hell, she can start a church or somethin'. Maybe find a right fella. Might be one or two down there, I reckon. We'll put up an adobe house—that's what they have down there, you know. A house made out of the land it sits on. An approach well known in Ireland. Very little timber in that part of Texas. But who knows, maybe we'll stay down there for more'n a year or two. People do stay in the same place, I have heard."

"All the work, it will be good. It will take my mind off Mamie, and I still think about Louise every day. You're forgetting she was my friend before Mamie—Louise, and Gabe too. But Gabe is a survivor. He will make it, no matter what, and make it look easy even when it isn't. Yes, Gabe is fine. But I didn't know till Louise died and Mamie took off that I was the missing kind, that I would miss them and worry about them and blame myself." She paused. She knew Mick would try to console her about her guilt, and she didn't want to hear it. After a while she said, "I guess there was nobody to miss before them."

"Ah, but now you've got me, girl."

She smiled; it felt good. "It's getting rid of you that'll be hard," she said.

* * * * *

Mick's "stagecoach" was a twelve-foot box wagon with a weather-worn canvas top. Still, he was proud of the shelter the canvas could provide. When open, it rested flat across some wrought iron framing, forming a sort of roof over their heads. If the weather turned ugly, he could pull the canvas sides straight down, hook them to the frame, and enclose most of the wagon. The front seat, on risers, was big enough for two people. Another seat of the same size sat behind it, and together they took up the front third of the wagon. In the back they packed two faro layouts, a bridle and saddle, blankets, their clothes, water, coffee, pans and utensils, and enough staples to last for two weeks on the trail to Tascosa. For ready access was a large canvas tarp. At night they would make a lean-to with it, using the wagon for support. Mick had a double-barreled twelve-gauge shotgun and a hinged Smith & Wesson .44 caliber revolver, easy to reload. Frenchy had her own weapon, a two-shot derringer of small caliber.

The first day out was a long one, eleven hours. They made more than forty miles, all the way to Hoodoo Brown's sod house store at the wells on Crooked Creek, near Meade. Sweaty and exhausted, Frenchy only wanted a drink of cool water and some Double-A whiskey, along with as many johnnycakes as Mick could buy from Hoodoo's wife.

"Are you goin' to be helpin' me with the horses girl, or not?" Frenchy was licking her lips from that first drink, a big one. She walked back to the team, a pair of matching bay swing horses Mick had bought along with the wagon. "I've taken care of the reins. Now you take the bridle off the near beast, my dear, and soon these poor creatures may be watered and fed."

"I'll help you, all right," Frenchy muttered. She walked to the horse nearest her and began to fumble with the bridle.

"No, no, not that one! The *near* horse. The horse on the *left*!"

"Well, goddammit, why don't you just say the goddamn fucking horse on the left?"

"Ah. A silver spoon you had as a babe. No hard work on the farm, I see. Hmm. Yet you do not sound so much like a lady now, darlin'."

"I worked on a farm—but not for long. Milked cows, shoveled shit. And yes, dammit, I rode the horses at Uncle Connor's farm, but the only thing I got out of that was a—" The thought of what happened on that horse was inseparable from thoughts of Arkansas, so she paused and reached for the whiskey bottle. Wiping her mouth after a swig, she said, "All I got was a sore butt."

"So, little good it will do me to ask you to unhitch the martingale and pull off the hame, I'm guessin'." He grinned at her slyly.

"Ask me later. Tomorrow. Maybe. We'll see." She sat down on a barrel and ate another cake. "Hame, my ass," she muttered.

Three days later they crossed into Texas and ended another long day, most of it rainy, at Cator's Zulu Stockade, which was actually an enormous dugout fronted with pointed cottonwood stakes.

"You'd be soaked to the bone but for my canvas top!" Mick hurriedly dismounted from the front seat. "Aye, and I'll be expectin' a kiss of thanks!" Frenchy had moved to the back seat, letting Mick, in his slicker, take whatever rain blew in.

James Cator came out of the dugout, dressed in an old swallowtail coat that was still far too nice for the surroundings. From a horned pipe clenched between his teeth came wisps of smoke. Frenchy, out of the wagon by now, saw the pipe bowl redden as the tall man drew on the pipe again.

"Ah, 'tis not often I hear the sound of a true paddy in these parts," said Cator, after taking the pipe from his mouth.

Mick stowed the harness, slowly. He had already removed the slicker. Turning to Frenchy, he smiled. He walked toward Cator. "Have ya ever seen a man smoke a pipe when it's stuck up their bum? Mind ya, I mean the stem part, not that glowin' bit in front of yer nose."

"Aw, shit," Frenchy said.

Cator took another puff, reddening the bowl again. He was a tall man, lean and hard from years of hunting buffalo on these plains. Mick had heard that Cator had killed more than fifteen thousand of the beasts in only three years, before the great herds were wiped out. Self-made entirely, though he came from a good family, the word on the trail was that he could shift from being hospitable to lethal in less than a second.

"I prefer the traditional way." Cator blew out a little smoke.

"And I am an Irishman, not a 'paddy.'"

"I can see that. A touchy race."

"Oh, he'll touch you up all right," Frenchy was wet, tired, and hungry. There was no time for these stupid men to be having a pissing contest out here on this prairie. Worse, it was raining again.

"Yes, I can see that he might do so." Cator had noticed the scar on the left side of Mick's face. "Well, sir, although I am a proud Englishman, born of two English parents, it happens that you and I have something in common besides our language. On second thought, maybe we have only one thing in common." He smiled at Mick, who by now had his right fist clenched behind his hip, ready to let fly. "For you see, lad, I was born in County Donegal, where my father was on naval duty for Her Majesty."

"County Donegal, by God! Me too!" Mick extended his hand and Cator took it. Now both men were smiling and slapping each other on the back as they walked toward the dugout.

"Don't mind me!" Frenchy grabbed up the bottle of Double-A, hiding it inside her shawl.

Inside the dugout, after she had eaten her fill of stew, she got around to asking Cator about the name of his place.

"Ah, yes, the Zulu name always comes up. It happened this way: My father was a military man, and he had many friends who had served the world over, for Britain, as you know, ruled the world." This with a sly grin was directed at Mick. "But to the point, dear lady, when my father looked upon a desolate place, he would always say, 'James, that is Zulu land, it is for a fact.' You see, there is a Zulu tribe in South Africa. It was his opinion, but not of the first impression, that nothing could be more desolate than the land the Zulus occupied. As you may have observed, it is not a stretch of the imagination to apply the term to my own modest holdings here."

"No, it isn't," Frenchy said. "Thanks for the stew."

Two hard days passed, one rainy and one cold to the bone for early October, but in better weather, the Dodge City to Tascosa Trail ended not fifty feet from the front door of the Exchange Hotel. Asleep, sitting up on the seat behind Mick, Frenchy jerked awake when the seemingly endless motion of the wagon ceased. It was dusk, and the fast-approaching darkness softened the harsh, mostly treeless landscape. For days now Frenchy might have been on another planet compared with what she knew in Baton Rouge, what she saw on the Mississippi River, and what she experienced in Dodge City, Kansas, where one could often see tall grass, green hills in the spring, and a respectable array of trees.

"God bless America, that sign says 'Hotel,'" she muttered. Studying the unimposing adobe building, she looked skeptical, however. *I suppose you could call that two stories high, so long as you were dealing with folks no taller than Mick.* Light streamed through one of two windows on the ground level. Down the block, some familiar sounds came her way, and she imagined she could smell the saloons. What she didn't have to imagine was the occasional stink of marsh or, worse, something dead or dying to the southeast of her. She felt the wind shift about that time, bringing slightly cooler air and also freshening the tiny piece of the planet that she, Mick, and the old stagecoach occupied at that moment.

For that first night it mattered little that the bed was springy and the mattress malodorous, or that the noises down below and off somewhere in the darkness included the occasional scream and a loud pistol shot. The next morning was mostly quiet, depending on how one defined morning. At 9 a.m., Frenchy and Mick were still sound asleep, he in his clothes and she mostly undressed but covered by a sheet.

She woke first. Shaking off the night, she sat up on the side of the bed. "That goddamn house of yours better not be long in coming."

Mick wasted no time. He found a job bartending at the Jenkins and Dunn Saloon, the place some freighters in Dodge had told him about. It wasn't too far from the Exchange Hotel—but in that relatively short distance, less than half a mile a little south of east, one was at the fringe of a part of Tascosa known as Hogtown. Closer to the Canadian River, and only a few hundred yards from the bayou that ran to the northeast off the Canadian, the section might have gained its name from any one of several sources. The bayou could be rank smelling, was often muddy, and could have accommodated any number of hogs.

In the shacks near the bayou and close by the saloons in Hogtown lived many of the women who had come to Tascosa from other cow-towns and mining towns on the western frontier. In not much time at all, Mick and Frenchy came to know Frog Lip Sadie, Gizzard Lip Annie, Rowdy Kate, and Rocking Chair Emma, among many others. It was said that during the day, some of these enterprising women were available to help out the town's more conventional citizens with chores, who returned the favor on many occasions. Thus did Frenchy find and appreciate a surprising level of tolerance and civility between the inhabitants of Hogtown and those who lived to the north and west of them in Tascosa.

It did not take Frenchy long to share Mick's vision of making a home in the town. She liked the fact that hypocrisy did not hover over most of Tascosa's human relations. People saw what they saw, knew it for what it was, accepted it, and went on with their business. A circuit-riding preacher or a severe Bible-toting proselytizer from the Woman's Christian Temperance Union would find few converts in Tascosa, Texas. On the other hand, after a man named Russell was shot dead one day, Mick persuaded the townsfolk that Tascosa was in need of a civic improvement he had observed in Dodge City, a small section of real estate destined to grow: Boot Hill.

CHAPTER 23

St. Louis, mid-August, 1879

When the time came for him to board the train to Topeka, Campbell was still replaying in his mind the encounter on the wharf with the barber and the other man. "If I had been in possession of a cane, I would have whipped them both," he told himself. Campbell had cut it close in getting to the station on time. Now it seemed to him that the Black porters were slow in getting his bags on board. He snapped at one, an older man who was still wearing his dark blue jacket in the noontime heat. "Hurry along with that, boy. This train is about to leave and I am bound to be on it."

The porter had already seen to Campbell's heavier bags. Now he threw Campbell's valise into the aisle of the second-class passenger car. Campbell was seething now. "I'll have your job for that!" The train began to move. Smiling, the porter waved goodbye.

For a few seconds Campbell was so upset that he couldn't figure out where to sit. And the motion of the train almost caused him to lose his footing. Half the people in the car were staring at him. Two young boys, dressed in their finest clothes for the trip, were pointing their chubby fingers at him and giggling.

He was supposed to be preparing a speech, really a sermon, on the evils of alcohol and the dreadful consequences of its use. Frances Willard herself had given him, under his alias of the Reverend Caleb Jackson, a place on the program for the big tent meeting at Bismarck Grove, outside of Topeka, in two days' time. Yet for half of the ten-hour trip, Campbell did no constructive work at all. In his entire adult life, from Little Rock to college in Clinton, Mississippi, and finally on to

Helena, Campbell had never seen Black people forget their place the way they had in the last few days in St. Louis. Why, it was one shameful display after another! Lies from the darkies, those were expected. But as soon as Campbell had salved his fury over one incident, another would return to his mind. Now it was that laborer on the wharf. Swilling whiskey, idling against the wagon he was meant to fill with casks, smiling at Campbell and saying, straight to his face, not more than ten feet away, "I reckon Arkansas where you belong."

It was this recollection that provoked Campbell to action. Taking a notepad from his valise and choosing a recently sharpened pencil from the lapel pocket of his coat, he readied himself to write. The recollection of the wharf clashed with his growing perception that he was now on a mission much larger than the one he had embraced at his church in Helena and the task of sleuthing he had accepted when he left that city. Now, his mission was the defeat of evil in its clearest form. Its *distilled* form, in fact. He was amused and self-congratulatory for having conceived the term "distilled evil." He should mention it to Miss Willard.

Later, settled in at the Windsor Hotel in Topeka only a few blocks west of the train station, Campbell found his quarters suitable but not on par with those at the Lindell in St. Louis. As for what he had seen of Topeka on his short walk to the hotel, he was unimpressed. He might as well have been in Helena. Few buildings of any distinction did he see, now considering himself capable of judging them after his stay in St. Louis. Even the state capitol building looked half-finished at best, and the Windsor itself was more imposing.

To his initial dismay, he realized that he had gained weight, perhaps more than ten pounds. But on reflection he thought it was a positive development. His face was fuller, his beard and sideburns were well out of fledgling territory, and the gray dye had aged him ten years. He would never be obese, he thought, and the pounds he had gained so far had brought him up to a solid, proportional figure of a man whom most would take to be about forty years old. It would not be long, he mused, until his appearance might deceive Catherine McCain if he came upon her without warning. Briefly, he considered that his own dear wife might not recognize him in a photograph or from afar. *Afar, indeed.*

Before leaving St. Louis, he had decided that, as the Reverend Jackson, he needed a traditional black suit. So he had purchased one before boarding the train to Topeka. In fact, that was what caused him to be late.

The next morning, he went to the hotel restaurant for breakfast. There he saw that Frances Willard was seated across the dining room at a table near a large window. With her was a companion, sitting across from Frances and leaning forward in her chair. To all appearances, she was imploring Miss Willard to agree with her on some point.

Brimming with confidence in himself and in his distinguished appearance, Campbell waved aside the young man who sought to guide him to a table and walked straight across the dining room to Frances Willard. He was conscious, or thought he was, of some admiring glances coming his way as he proceeded toward the table.

Frances saw him right away, and her face indicated she was relieved to be distracted from the talkative woman with whom she sat. "Oh, do join us, Reverend Jackson. Anna, this is the Reverend Caleb Jackson. He will be speaking at Bismarck Grove."

"Anna Gordon," the other woman said crisply, annoyed at having been interrupted. Reluctantly and without looking at him directly, she held out her hand. Like Frances, Anna had a very firm grip. By now, Campbell had learned to prepare himself for such handshakes, however odd he thought them to be.

He sat so that Frances was on his right and Anna was on his left. "I am sorry to break in on what must be an important conversation. Please do continue."

Frances had requested a fresh cup of coffee, the first having grown cold. She eagerly held the new cup to her lips but put it down without tasting it. "My dear reverend, all my conversations are important. With so many horrors in this world, I have no time for anything other than caring and doing. You see, one without the other is meaningless. Anna and I differ only as to emphasis. My own view is that the violence done to the young women of this country is as important as battling the evils of drink, and, of course, the two are often linked. Did you know, Reverend, that the age of consent for a girl to lie with a man in this country is only *ten years old*? Many thousands of very young girls are alleged to have consented when the brutal act of rape has befallen them. To prove they did not consent, they must show that they were beaten senseless, with limbs broken and blood oozing from their wounds, or that they were held down with the force of Hercules. Few go to court when such high thresholds of evidence are required; almost none prevail. All are shamed. Many cannot be saved. The current law, sir, is nothing less than a license to rape young girls. But hear me, Reverend, someday we will abolish such laws. Moreover, we women will have the vote one day, and you watch what happens after that, sir."

"I—I did not know. So young . . ." *Women, vote? Surely not!*

"The rape laws themselves will take much longer to change. But at least the young girls—we might save them." Frances picked up the cup again, taking a deep breath before sipping from it. "Anna here is so very passionate about forming a national temperance legion, as she calls it, for children six to twelve. She would go at the problem that way, as I would change the laws. Anna, please tell the reverend all about it."

"I know this," Anna said firmly. "The salvation of this nation requires an end to the sale of alcohol, which means the shuttering of all saloons. We have to get at the children to do that and then to their parents. The churches cannot or will not do it for us. The Bible rarely condemns drinking in itself, but only drunkenness, as I am sure the Reverend Jackson knows. We, however, know that drinking is the root cause and must be stamped out."

Campbell was not comfortable in this conversation. He picked up his own cup, pretending that Anna's reference to him was not a summons for him to speak.

"Well, is that so, Reverend?" Frances leaned toward Campbell, her eyes issuing a challenge.

Campbell had bought himself a little time to think. "'For the kingdom of God is not a matter of eating and drinking, but of righteousness.' I believe I have it right. It is from Romans."

"See! The Bible does not condemn drinking outright." Anna looked triumphant.

Frances looked doubtful. "The thing we must remember is righteousness is the one true goal."

* * * * *

Frances had chosen to stay in Topeka, partly because the accommodations were better than in Lawrence, which was much closer to Bismarck Grove. But her main reason was to confer with Governor St. John, one of the most prominent men in the national temperance movement. Bismarck Grove was hallowed ground for the movement. Only last year, big crowds had descended on the beautiful elm-covered grounds, giving the cause of temperance more national prominence. Frances hoped to persuade Governor St. John to run for president as the champion of prohibition. He had led the successful fight in his state, despite the scofflaws in many towns who ignored it. She was confident that she would do a better job, but she was a woman and could not vote, much less run for president of the whole United States of America. But men had their uses, and she had ideas about how to use them.

Campbell was now fully alert to the sound of "the Reverend Caleb Jackson" when he heard it. He was satisfied with his plan thus far but had come to second-guess his decision to use an assumed name. After all, he was now on a train to the famous Bismarck Grove meeting grounds, the same train and destination as Frances Willard and Governor St. John of Kansas. Although his place on the program was in one of the smaller venues, an open tent in fact, only a hundred yards distant his two famous companions would be addressing thousands in the enormous tabernacle erected on the grounds. It was not difficult for him to see himself there someday. Who knew, maybe during this gathering he would receive a summons, based on what was sure to be his brilliant sermon under the tent.

Sure he was of success, but how disappointing it would be to receive accolades from the large press contingent at the meeting and, later, read that it was "the Reverend Caleb Jackson" who had been so brilliant. Soon he chastised himself; all that mattered was that he was following God's will. What was it to God if "Campbell Harper" received worldly praise or not?

Ah, but it came to Campbell that he, as the Reverend Caleb Jackson, could now spend the rest of his life as a crusader and never again be confined to the restrictive precincts of Helena, Arkansas. The Lord would provide for his dear wife and children; surely, he thought, the young and handsome Reverend Merriman might be inclined in that direction already. He was mentioned frequently in his wife's letters from home.

About thirty miles east of Topeka, the train circled to the north of Lawrence and headed into Bismarck Grove. The train moved slowly past large exhibition halls, used in local and regional fairs to display carriages, buggies, work wagons, and the latest in farming machinery. Beyond those halls was a large racecourse, in the center of which was an imposing tower. Between that tower and the grandstands were two smaller towers, one on each side of the track. These marked the starting and finishing lines for the races. He assumed there would be no such entertainments during the meeting.

The Union Pacific pulled up alongside a depot the company had built especially for the grounds. Campbell remarked that it was larger than the depot in Helena. Waiting for Frances, Anna, and Governor St. John were two shiny carriages with gilt furnishings and burgundy leather seats. Each had a coachman decked out in striking livery: dark green coats and black top hats. Campbell finally guessed that the green coats were a tribute to the leafy elms that formed a welcome canopy over most of the grounds. Less than fifty yards from the depot was a graceful arched sign that read "Bismarck Grove," as if the grounds were a small town.

After waiting sometime for his own luggage to be loaded onto a much less imposing flatbed wagon, Campbell took his place on the seat beside the plainly dressed waggoneer and looked up at the sign as he was transported along the graceful curving lane to his own lodgings. On the way he saw many fancy carriages and smaller buggies, their passengers in a festive mood. Handsome horses and their well-dressed riders, both men and women (the latter riding sidesaddle), weaved in and out of the vehicles on the lane.

He was grateful to find that he was to be housed in what reminded him of the officer's quarters he had seen at the Little Rock Barracks a few years back, when he participated in a religious program for the soldiers. Simple, but in his case, private. Thank God, I am not in one of those tents, he thought. The tents were located much farther away from the Dicker and Morton dining halls and from the tabernacle, which had a prime location near the agricultural exhibit hall. He settled in for the night, relishing the fresh sheets if not the loosely bound straw mattress beneath them. Through the half-open window came the sound of hymns, too many for him to make out a lot of the words individually, but all conveying to him a sense of righteous destiny.

Campbell chose Morton Hall for breakfast the next morning, a fine sunny day. He emerged to see half a dozen women gathered around another who seemed inconsolable. There were groups of women, and of men, too, in lesser numbers, scattered all over the grounds, some lying on blankets and others standing and loudly debating strategies for the temperance movement. From the group nearest him, he could not help but hear the words, "Why would God take my little Billy? Will he go to Hell?" The young woman at the center of the group began to sob.

"We cannot know, my dear Judith," an older woman said, probably the younger woman's mother. Her voice, while patient, was heavy with sadness. "If only Billy's father had been there, but no, he had drunk himself to death in that filthy tavern."

"But Billy wasn't baptized! He wasn't baptized!"

On his way to Topeka, and again on his way to Bismarck Grove, Campbell had worked on his message, to be delivered the next day under a large outdoor tent not far from the racecourse. Confident of success he was, yet his work thus far was missing something. He had hoped to convey an urgency to be saved along with a demand to abstain from the evil of alcohol. In doing so, he had not thought enough about children. Now the anguish of the young woman—Judith—had shown him the way. Did not Anna Gordon emphasize the importance of saving them from the horror of drunken fathers? And did not the great Dwight Moody himself begin his own work with children, when others would not hear him?

The following morning, the day of the great event, Campbell did not rise for the 5:30 a.m. service in the tabernacle. He had stayed up late to finish his sermon and had planned to hear only parts of Frances Willard's and Governor St. John's speeches at the tabernacle before making his way to the tent where he would speak, beneath a big stand of shady elms. As he headed to the tabernacle after a late breakfast, this time at Dicker's, he found himself in a kind of reverie, listening again to the strands of hymns, to the confident hum of people gathering in righteousness, to the soft murmur of leaves in the elms above. Their branches swayed easily in the gentle breeze, allowing the sunlight to fall in shifting patterns across the grounds. Campbell found a bench and rested.

It was going to be hot later on. All to the good, Campbell thought. The tabernacle was said to be stifling already, with a thousand souls stuffed inside. By 2:00 p.m., when Campbell would speak, people would want some shade and a place to sit. Seeing the tent, Campbell knew they would have to sit on twenty-foot planks with no back support; still, that was better than standing or even sitting in the hot and crowded indoor venues.

* * * * *

"And so it was," Reverend Jackson intoned, "that Little Billy's father had left his wife destitute, spending every cent, *every cent* of his meager wages on cheap rye whiskey. Now we might hope that all turned out well; we might pray that Our Lord intervened; we might rejoice at this very moment in this sacred grove to see Little Billy walk past your benches and, smiling and straight-backed with confidence and pride, come to me and say, 'I am here, and I belong to Jesus.'"

The reverend paused, gazed beyond the last row of benches, most of them still full now as the sermon was drawing to a close. Most in the crowd turned around to follow his gaze.

"What do I see? Is that Little Billy, grown up enough to know, love, and accept the Lord?" The reverend lowered his head, shaded his eyes, and squinted. "Or . . . is it his dear mother, bereft and longing for the peace of the Lord's blessing, coming to us now, her suffering unbearable at the loss of her only child?"

And now as the gathering looked on, there came a woman, shuffling along, wiping tears from her eyes as she made her way to the crowd and moved, as in a trance, up the tent's center path.

"Come along, dear woman," the reverend said softly, causing the on-lookers to lean forward to hear his words.

"Little Billy is dead." The woman's voice was barely loud enough to be heard by those closest to her. "I thought I heard him cry. A soft crying sound. A pitiful sound that slipped away. It just . . . slipped away. That was all we had of Billy."

"What did she say?" yelled an old white-bearded man seated only ten or so feet away.

"We can't hear!" was the cry from many others, not angry but desperate to hear the woman's words.

"He did not know the Lord." Not waiting for the crowd to ask again for her to speak up, Judith turned to them and screamed, "He did not know the Lord!" Then, again in a lower tone, "I could not pay to bury him. We had no money. The church paid for the service. All I want is peace. Peace for Billy."

The reverend held out his hands. Judith came closer but remained beyond his reach. The reverend whispered to Judith, "How can you be sure he did not know the Lord?"

She leaned closer. "Well, he was not baptized, so he was not saved."

A murmur went through the crowd.

"He was not baptized! He was not saved!" the reverend told the crowd. Some in the audience groaned in despair.

"Yet how could he not be saved?" the reverend said. "In Luke, Jesus says, 'Suffer little children to come unto me, and forbid them not: for of such is the kingdom of God. Verily I say unto you, Whosoever shall not receive the kingdom of God as a little child shall in no wise enter therein.'"

Another murmur. The reverend held out his hands, palms upraised, and the crowd quieted. "You may say Billy could not *receive* the Lord because he did not know of Him; you may say that, therefore, he cannot know Him now. But I ask you, who gave Little Billy to this world? A drunken father, a righteous young mother yearning for a child to love? No. It was our Lord who gave Billy to this world. Would He give him to us and deny him in the same moment? I challenge anyone to show me clear proof in scripture that such would be the case for a child taken from us, whether stillborn or granted breath on this earth.

"And ask yourselves, what is the true meaning of Jesus's words? We are not to *forbid* the children who would come to the Lord, is that not the truth of it? And what is the essence of receiving the Lord? Is it not acceptance, acquiescence, of Him, to Him, and Him alone, yes, above the greatest good in the world, the gift of a mother's love?"

The reverend looked into Judith's eyes. "Might it not be that the plaintive sound heard by this dear sweet woman was the *grateful* cry of one who was losing the greatest gift of this world but who had *received* the greatest gift of all: everlasting life with our Lord Jesus Christ? What a blessing it is now to know that Little Billy was not hindered, no, he was in fact rushed to the fore, finding salvation in one pure breath. So now as I stand here, amid the lengthening shadows still dappled by the light, whom do I see?" The reverend stood quietly for several seconds, looking into Judith's eyes.

"It is Little Billy," Judith said, placing her hand on her chest. "He is here, and he belongs to Jesus."

* * * * *

About the time Judith appeared, Campbell was aware that Frances and Anna Gordon had quietly made their way to a place to his left, only a few yards away. Although he could not see them clearly, he felt, without a doubt, that they had watched much of his sermon and thought it was worthy. When at last he turned away from a grateful Judith, they were waiting, Frances with that almost smile that could communicate at so many levels. Now, he believed, it conferred admiration.

Before she and Frances left their place, Anna leaned down and whispered, "He will do, don't you think? For now."

Frances smiled, this time actually parting her lips. "A wonderful sermon, Reverend Jackson." She took both of his hands and pressed them firmly.

"Wonderful, yes," said Anna, only nodding at Campbell while keeping her eyes on Judith, who was now more the center of attention than the reverend. Campbell observed Anna without concern. The fact was, he had only invited Judith to attend, merely whispering that his sermon might be of special interest to her after the sad loss of her son. He had given her no instructions, although she might have inferred that she would receive some attention herself. The result was that he was more impressed with the impact of the sermon than anyone in the sizable audience. His true mission—how strongly it had been confirmed. Feeling that the power and grace of God had come to him, and to such great effect, was the closest he had ever come to an authentic religious experience. Like many others in their youth, he had proclaimed his faith and walked forth in a white cotton gown to be baptized, in his case, in the runoff waters of the Mississippi River. He had shown emotion at the time but was conscious of a lack of it internally. How sublime to experience the real thing now!

After Judith drifted away, he looked about him and saw in the faces of those who had lingered a kind of awe as they gazed upon him. He waited to shake their hands and bid them farewell, and to bless them and their own children in the eyes of Lord, until all but one had gone. On the last row of the rough-hewn pews there remained one woman still. He caught her eye as she stood up. She smiled shyly, despite the tears rolling down her face. He took one step toward her, and her mouth opened to a full smile—and there, unmistakably, was the irregular contour of protruding front teeth that he recognized immediately as belonging to one Mamie Jackson, the very same woman who had helped Catherine McCain escape from Helena.

CHAPTER 24

The reverend's first thought upon seeing Mamie was to turn on his heel and seek out Frances Willard in order to bask in her compliments on his "Little Billy" sermon. Then something told him that the woman before him, one of those for whom he had been searching so long, would not have remained, alone at the back of the pews where she was sure to be seen, if she had recognized him for who he was: a man who wanted to bring her to justice.

He walked toward her slowly, his arms out so that she might touch him if she so desired. She gripped his hands, desperate for hope and salvation.

"Oh, oh," she said in a quaking voice. "You don't know, you can't know. I lost my own baby boy. He was cut out of me. He was dead. He was blue-white dead. For so long all I seen was him dead like that. Now I see him. He's on the other side. He's growed up. He's smiling down at me. I been scared of what God done to him ever since that time. My husband, he made me leave home after our baby died, didn't want nothin' to do with me 'cause I was ruint from the childbirth. Now God done sent me to you, and when I heard you this evenin' I believed you was speakin' to the pain in my heart. It was somethin' strange and powerful." Mamie glanced up at the sky. The breeze parted some thin clouds.

Through her tears she now looked straight into his eyes. He saw no sign of recognition in her, a great relief. In the six or eight paces he had taken to reach her, more than a few thoughts had gone through his brain. His first steps were those of a man who felt no ground beneath him. Then it struck him, almost literally, that her being here might force him to choose which of his missions had the greatest claim on him, on his life, on his very identity. Sleuth, detective, righteous avenger; preacher to the masses, an instrument of the Lord, redeemer to so many enslaved by alcohol; or, simply, the Reverend Campbell Harper, minister to a small flock in a small town, husband, father, a humble and ordinary servant?

Now, in the grip of Mamie's strong hands, he could see that he would not be constrained by her awareness of who he really was, or had been. He remembered her clearly from her attendance at his church in Helena, a woman with a decent voice; but his efforts to disguise himself had certainly deceived her.

In his sermon, he had striven to project a serious, somber tone, and he was aware that his voice had found a deeper register, more in keeping with his new appearance. Lowering his head, he gave thanks to the Lord for keeping his way open, if not altogether clear. And now he began to see that he might be able to reconcile his missions, or still combine them as he had hoped to do in the beginning. Did not God demand justice as well as the spreading of His word?

"There, there, dear woman." He dared to move closer, allowing Mamie to rest her tearful face on his shoulder. She wrapped her arms around him, pulling him close, too close. His first thought was to pull away. He glanced around, seeing no one near at hand, no one paying them any attention. The persistent press of the woman's remarkable bosom against his chest caused a stirring within him, which he sought to extinguish. Still she held on, and he was aware of another, more startling manifestation of his desire, one that caused Mamie to look downward and blush.

* * * * *

The next morning, after the five-thirty prayer meeting in the tabernacle, Frances Willard made her way through the crowd to find the reverend, with Anna not far behind. Seeing Frances coming their way, the small group of admiring women who surrounded Campbell parted, as they might have done if a four-horse carriage had been approaching. Frances grabbed his left arm and led him to a quieter place near a side window.

"I must say, Anna was quite taken with your 'Little Billy' sermon yesterday. You know how determined she is to reach the children of the nation, to protect them, of course, but also to bring into their homes a sense that prohibition is the way for the whole family to thrive."

"Thank you, Miss Willard."

There followed an awkward silence. For half a minute Frances studied Campbell. She and Anna exchanged glances, with Anna nodding somewhat reluctantly. Frances displayed yet again her enigmatic smile. "When Anna and I leave here, Reverend, we will return to Illinois, to my home in Evanston. Thanks to good rail service, we are able to schedule meetings throughout the winter months with leaders from Iowa, Indiana, Wisconsin, Michigan, and Ohio—"

"—and New York and Pennsylvania," Anna interjected.

"But you, Reverend Jackson, will remain in Topeka." It was in no way a request from Frances but a direct statement of fact. "Someone has to keep us apprised of Governor St. John's actions. It is our hope that he will achieve passage of a state prohibition amendment in the near future. Beyond that, well, I'll say that our nation *must* have a prohibition president someday, and someday soon."

"I see," was all Campbell could think of to say in response.

"You will of course be compensated," Anna said, unable to hide a tone of regret.

"Yes, certainly. Moreover, Anna and I are persuaded that 'Little Billy' is a sermon that will do well in our Kansas tent meetings when we return in the spring. As it benefits from the presence of the boy's mother—Judith, that was her name, I believe—I wonder if you might locate that dear lady and ask her if she can accompany us in the spring, with an appropriate companion of her choice. Her own mother, perhaps. I believe I saw a woman who could be her mother there, under your tent."

The reverend felt uneasy. He had not seen Judith since the end of the sermon. She had left quickly. He had thought to look for her at the early service, but he did not see her or anyone in her group. "Please let me try to find her. I will make that my sole purpose of this day."

And, in fact, the reverend did search that day and the next and the final day, when he stood watching as hundreds of people boarded the last Union Pacific train out of Bismarck Grove. Waiting so long that he almost missed the train himself, he finally decided that Judith and her group had probably arrived and departed by wagon. Given the fact that she had achieved a kind of celebrity at his sermon in the grove, he was surprised that no one he had talked to could provide any information as to her whereabouts, or even her last name. He did notice that, after the sermon, the woman thought to be Judith's mother had stood by her and received, with the appropriate mix of gratitude and solemnity, the money offered to help Judith through her ordeal.

The reverend spent most of the journey back to Topeka searching the cars for Judith and her mother but with little hope that they would be found. In the car next to his own, however, also riding in second class, was Mamie Jackson in one of the seats immediately in front of the un-fired stove in the aisle. The reverend's first impulse was to retreat from the half-open door, but it was too late. Upon seeing him, she smiled and offered a quick wave of her hand, without raising it from her lap; the two of them might have been sharing a wonderful secret that they needed to hold close.

The reverend was repelled, but suspected that he and Mamie Jackson were actually sharing a secret. When he turned away from her after their embrace at the grove, he had been shocked to see a bulge in his trousers. He had thought about sitting down, or walking off at an angle that would make it less obvious. Thanking God that no one else was present to notice, he had retreated when he could. Yet surely, he thought, Mamie herself had noticed, had felt the bulge against her own body. So, was that their one secret? If she had recognized him but hidden her knowledge of who he was, which he doubted, that would be another secret. One thing was certain: She was not frightened or wary of him now, not with that confiding little wave and sweet, if unbecoming, smile.

And what of his original mission? With Catherine McCain's accomplice barely ten feet away, how could he not pursue Catherine herself? At the thought of her, he did not feel a rush of vengeance or righteousness; he felt an almost irresistible urge to *see* her. It was not the first time he had felt there was something compelling about Catherine McCain, something that had little or nothing to do with justice. The reverend did not like feeling unsure about himself. He relished a sense of destiny, the pure connection between the exalted calling he imagined for himself and the affirmation of that calling by God. Forward in this same train was a pair of famous and formidable women who had marked him to share their prominent mission. Was that not something to heed? And, once more, he saw that the Lord had shown him the way. His instruments were so different but so intertwined: Frances Willard on the one hand, and Mamie Jackson on the other. With his position secure in Kansas until the spring, Campbell could assist Frances while ingratiating himself with Governor St. John; and he could keep an eye on Mamie, with the goal of learning more about the whereabouts of Catherine McCain.

Managing a smile of his own, he entered the car and moved down the aisle toward Mamie. He found himself unable to look at her during those few steps but instead kept his eyes fixed on the stove. Therefore, when he came to a halt beside her and looked down at her still-smiling face, the effort to summon a natural and friendly smile was especially difficult. He ignored her teeth and concentrated on her eyes, bright, blue, and shimmering with happiness. At that moment, he decided that she did not recognize him but was responding to their shared experience at the grove.

"May I join you?" he said, bowing slightly.

"Yes, *you can*. I was hopin' to see you again before I went back to Topeka."

Yes, Campbell thought. It was surely possible that Catherine McCain might herself be in Topeka, the very town that God had sent him to on his mission with Frances Willard. Now he had six months to find out. He smiled.

"You shore seem happy today," Mamie said.

"'This is the day which the Lord hath made; we will rejoice and be glad.'"

"I know that one. It's from the Psalms, ain't it?"

"Why, yes, yes it is. Psalms 118, verse 24. You know your Bible well, I see."

"It's what we have in this world. The Good Book and the ones who can preach it right." The look she gave him, so pure in its conviction that he was certainly among those who could do so, came close to touching his heart. "I wish you had been around when I lost my own baby. I only saw him when he was dead. I hadn't been able to git that picture of him out of my mind till I heard you speak. He had a name, and all it was good for was to put on the wooden cross at his grave. Then my husband, he made me leave on account of I couldn't give him no more children. I been supportin' myself, you know. Workin' for druggists—why, I can name every patent medicine you can think of." She paused and lowered her eyes. "I done some other things too, no, not the worst, but bad enough I need the Lord to take ahold of me, and right now."

"How terrible that must have been for you, losing your child. Yet, as we know absolutely as people of faith, the Lord must have had a higher purpose when He took little . . ."

"Willie. Willie Jackson."

". . .Willie from you. There is always a reason, always a path the Lord gives us to emerge from the suffering we all must endure."

* * * * *

The reverend waved to Mamie as she left the train with a lively and confident stride. She had mentioned that she was staying in a boarding-house across the street from the Windsor Hotel until her new job began in a week. "I got on at the drugstore near the hotel," she had told him. "They was real happy to see I knew all them medicines already."

Good, Campbell thought, now I know where to find her. He would plan what would seem to be a chance encounter and at that time give her the news that he would be staying on for a time in Topeka himself. He must remain in contact with Mamie, but at the same time not get too close.

The reverend hurried back to the ladies' first-class car near the end of the special train. He made it just as Frances and Anna stepped onto the platform, where they were met by two porters carrying their bags.

"Did you find little Billy's mother?" Frances didn't bother to offer any greeting. "Anna and I were working on the schedule for the spring meetings and want to arrange a good location for 'little Billy.'" Anna took a moment to smile at the reverend, for his preaching at the grove had shown the importance of her emphasis on saving children.

The reverend knew how he would respond. "Even better, a woman who lives right here in Topeka heard me preach—and she, too, lost a child at birth. All she could see since that terrible day was a vision of that poor thing lying dead, but now she sees him, little Willie, as safe and blessed in the arms of our Lord."

"'Little *Willie*,' you say?" Frances turned to Anna, whose smile was fading.

"But you see, it's almost exactly the same story. The only difference is that this woman was in the audience, seated at the back. It is true that Judith's appearance was wonderfully dramatic, but I'm sure that this woman—Mamie is her name—would be willing to appear in much the same way. She is a devoted Christian, though not refined."

"And what does 'not refined' mean, Reverend?" Anna stared at him skeptically.

"Her speech is that of the frontier, the speech of the common person, one might say. Her husband abandoned her after a would-be physician's efforts to deliver the child left her barren."

Frances squinted at the reverend. "And what role did alcohol play in the death of the child or in the abandonment of this—this Mamie?"

At first, Campbell was unable to respond. Mamie had said nothing of the evils of drink. In fact, she had said little about her husband at all. "The same, the very same. The man was a drunkard, abusive, profligate in his spending, and gave her nothing while demanding that she leave." The reverend blinked when he said this but recovered almost immediately. Surely, the husband of such a common woman, a man who would send her away under such circumstances, must be a drunkard as well.

Frances and Anna headed for some shade near the station office. The reverend, along with the porters, followed along behind. "On the one hand," Frances said, "we have a woman who was not only cruelly cast away by her husband but physically damaged by the terrible experience. On the other hand, the woman herself might not be outwardly impressive, possesing nothing of the almost ethereal quality that poor Judith had. What do you say, Anna?"

"What do we really know of this Mamie's background, Reverend? It would hardly do for us to involve a woman whose own virtue and character are open to question."

"Why, as to that I can say she has been supporting herself by working for druggists as a shop clerk, one who has become something of an expert on the best medicines available to the populace. If you would like, I am sure I could obtain references."

Frances let out a long, deep sigh. "Anna, I am tired. My back aches so badly from all the standing we did at the grove that I would welcome a recommendation from the woman right now if she were here." She paused to stretch toward one side, grimacing. "I am of a mind that your new woman will do. She will do for the spring camp meetings. You will see to it, Reverend."

"Yes, you shall," said Anna.

The reverend was left standing alone at the station as the two ladies and their porters walked slowly to a waiting carriage. *Dear Lord, let it be that the two strands of my destiny may be joined by your hand.*

CHAPTER 25

Topeka, Kansas, April 1880

Campbell put down the latest letter from his wife and sipped some tepid tea. With each letter, there were more mentions of the young Reverend Merriman. His sermons were now "approaching the heights of your own, Dear Husband," and "my own voice is now prominent in the choir." The congregation "misses you, of course, but the church membership has held steady." Campbell had told her that he was preaching in the small town of Tecumseh, whose inhabitants, he found, shared his pro-Southern views. As for Governor St. John's plans for prohibition, Campbell, as the Reverend Jackson, of course, was able to report to Frances Willard that the state's voters were certain to ratify the amendment by year's end. Campbell had to admit to himself that he did not miss his wife, and thoughts of his children entered his mind only glancingly. *Ah, but all that matters is that they are happy and safe.*

Not long after the departure of Frances and Anna, he had appeared at the drugstore where Mamie worked, his confidence in his plan surging as he saw how pleased and impressed she was to see him. He had already decided he didn't want to be around her too much, especially at the local Methodist church that he was sure she was attending, so he told her of his ministry in Tecumseh. "But I will drop by from time to time," he said.

Mamie was pleased when the reverend asked her to recommend a medicine for low back pain. "Now is this for you, Reverend, or for . . . a lady?"

"It is for Frances Willard. I want to have something on hand to give her when she comes back here in the spring."

"Well, for a lady I'll say Piso's Tablets. If it was you, I'd say Balm of America." She smiled, and he made himself concentrate on her blue eyes.

He dropped in at the drugstore at least once a month after that. But two days ago, he made a special trip to tell her that Frances Willard wanted her to appear at the next tent meeting in May.

"Me! I ain't no preacher. I cain't talk right half the time. If you have a number problem or you're needin' some medicines, I'm your gal. But preachin'? No, sir."

Fifteen minutes later, Campbell had succeeded in gaining her cooperation. For the next two evenings he explained what she should do and assured her that she would have to say very little. "It's about your little Willie. We must do it for him."

A week later, on a Saturday afternoon, with the shade of twilight enveloping the quiet but attentive crowd a few miles east of Topeka, the reverend came to the end of his sermon. "And so Little Willie's father, seeing that the infant was dead, turned away from his poor wife, discarding her like a broken wheelbarrow or a rusty plow. She was no longer of use to him now that the doctor had told him she could not have any more children. There she was, praying in her pain for the soul of her dead infant, now carried away from her to be buried. Little Willie would never be baptized. He would go straight into the cold ground. Leaving his wife destitute and alone, the father spent every cent, every cent of his meager wages on cheap rye whiskey. Now we might hope that all turned out well, we might pray that our Lord intervened, we might rejoice at this very moment to see Little Willie walk among us and, smiling with confidence and pride, come to me and say, 'I am here, and *I belong to Jesus.*'"

The reverend paused and gazed beyond the last row of benches. The words "belong to Jesus," spoken loudly, were Mamie's cue to walk slowly toward him from her place behind a tall elm thirty feet away. He could see part of her mostly hidden face peering at him. Finally, he nodded, more emphatically than he would have liked. At last Mamie came forward, slowly, as planned.

"What is that I see? Could that be Little Willie, now grown up enough to know, love, and accept the Lord?" The reverend lowered his head and shaded his eyes. "Or, or is it his dear mother, longing for the peace of the Lord's blessing, coming to us now, her suffering unbearable at the loss of her only child?"

But Mamie stopped when she reached the tent, seemingly frozen. They had gone over her small part five or six times. But she could not remember what to do. It was a part without pictures, without numbers, and her mind could not recall it. Honest Mamie, she always was, so she said, "What do I do now, Reverend?"

The immediate derisive snickering of the audience caused the reverend's face to turn scarlet. Spreading across his chest and down to his gut was a flood of shame, an unbearable sensation that filled the vast, dark space between who he imagined himself to be and who he actually was. Daring a glance toward the bench behind him, he caught a glimpse of Frances Willard and Anna Gordon hurrying away from the tent. Seeing them leave, the crowd began to disperse as well, at first only a few people at a time, followed by larger groups, laughing and gesturing toward the reverend as they departed. A sudden rage consumed the deep shame he felt. He was able to glare at those nearest at hand, silencing anyone whose eyes stayed on him long enough for him to notice.

He knew, of course, that he would never see Frances Willard or Anna Gordon again, unless he was skulking at the back of a crowd. Nor did he want to see them. Failure was something he could not admit to himself. Seeing them face to face would put him under their contemptuous gaze, a definitive judgment that he could not bear.

"Well," he uttered, after taking a long, deep breath. He stood to his full height and thrust out his chin. He gazed skyward, seeing Venus peek through the clouds. "So this is how the Lord chastens a worthy man who has lost sight of his one true destiny?" Then, only a minute later, "I see it now, Lord." What Campbell saw was that his gifts of the spirit had been corrupted by his infatuation with power and adulation. The Lord had now brought him low so that he could be raised high once again. His way forward now, at last, was clear—to be the arm of God's justice by tracking down Catherine McCain. "Ah, yes," he said softly, his eyes falling on Mamie, still standing at the edge of the tent. Her head down, she was sobbing. Many in the audience had pointed at her and laughed as they walked past.

"Miss Jackson, please follow me." She did so, her head still down, knowing she had failed him but afraid to call any attention to herself by speaking. Suddenly, the reverend stopped and turned, smiling down at Mamie. "I have a carriage waiting. May I offer you a ride back to your lodgings?"

This gentlemanly offer was so at odds with what Mamie was expecting that she could only blush and mumble "Uh-huh." And a second or so later, "Thank you so much, Reverend." He gathered her in his arms and held her with some conviction, for after all, it was Mamie who would lead him to Catherine, and as he knew very well, using Mamie would be no challenge to him at all.

Mamie had yet to find permanent lodgings in Topeka. It turned out that they were both staying at the same hotel, Mamie only for two days thanks to a small contribution from Frances Willard, who had wrongly anticipated that Mamie would continue to be a part of their Kansas tour. The reverend accompanied Mamie to her room, standing close behind her as she unlocked the door. She entered, turned, and smiled at him. Overcoming his disgust at the sight of her front teeth, the reverend made a slight bow and wished her a good night.

The next evening he sent his card, the card of the Reverend Caleb Jackson, to her room along with a note inviting her to supper in the hotel restaurant. Mamie could not read the invitation, but she entreated a hotel bellboy to read it to her, tipping him half a dollar. "Please tell the, the gentleman that I would be honored to eat—to have supper with him, I would."

The supper was one of the most splendid events of Mamie's life. A handsome man sat across from her, fixed his eyes on hers, ordered the best steak in the house and, for good measure, a bottle of chilled champagne, served only at the hotel and at a premium charge the reverend readily paid, his biblical admonitions against imbibing no longer useful to his purpose. Mamie did not need the champagne rushing to her head to feel a deep surge of happiness. Reaching across the table, she grasped the reverend's hand and said, "Oh, thank you, Reverend. Thank you so much. I ain't never had a supper like this before. No, never. I—I'm truly, no, deeply obliged."

Seeing the tears welling up in her eyes, the reverend struggled for a moment to find a reassuring smile. Quickly, he summoned the waiter and paid the bill, adding a generous tip.

He gestured for Mamie to walk ahead of him up the stairs and on down the hallway to her room. On the way he tried to concentrate on the shifting motion of her hips. At the door to her room, he was pleased to see that with a quick movement she had shifted her light shawl enough to reveal a generous glimpse of her large breasts. Willing himself at first to be sexually aroused, his interest soon became pronounced, so much so that she noticed and moved close against his body. She opened the door and took his hand, leading him inside. Releasing his grip, he went straight to her bed, sat on the edge, and removed his coat and fancy dress shirt. Sitting there in his undershirt, he motioned for Mamie to turn away from him. "Will you kindly undress?" His voice was quiet, but firm.

Mamie fumbled with the buttons and hooks on the elaborate garments she wore, but in less than a minute she had unlaced her corset and was standing naked, except for a garter belt and stockings. She began to turn toward the reverend, but his left hand was strong on her shoulder, forcing her to keep her back toward him. A minute, two, and it was over. When Mamie turned to him, moving closer for an embrace, he was already reaching for his pants. He quickly moved to a nearby chair where he had placed his shirt and coat. He yawned. "Mamie, you can put your clothes on now."

"My goodness, that was quick. I reckon it's been a while for you. Well, for me too, not since I was married to Dale. Anyhow, it'll get better with practice, you know." Mamie laughed, proud of her witticism. "I'm gonna put on my robe and go tidy up a bit. Now you stay right there." She gestured toward the chair and stepped behind a three-panel room divider, its red paint long since faded. It stood next to a maple vanity with a wash basin, a pitcher of water, and two small towels. Two water glasses were on a shelf above the basin.

When Mamie was occupied and humming some cheery tune, the reverend went to a bedside table and jerked open the drawer. Inside were hairpins, rouge—and two other items that caused his dark eyes to gleam, a small envelope and a larger, letter-sized envelope, both unopened.

Taking out his clasp knife, he opened the small envelope first, as the postmark date was earlier. In it was a plain two-sided card. *Sorry & missing you*, it read, on the back. *Gabe writes Campbell Harper searching. Unlikely to find us but be careful. Love, Frenchy.*

Frenchy? It had to be Catherine! It was all he could do to keep from ripping the larger envelope open, but he carefully used the knife. The letter inside was in fact signed "Catherine" and revealed that she was in a place called Tascosa with a man named Mick. *They have a house, he has a livery stable, she is dealing faro. Misses you so. Sorry for everything.*

He was so absorbed with the letter that he was slow to realize Mamie now stood across from him in her robe. Somewhat clumsily, he tried to put the note and letter back in the nightstand drawer. "I—I was merely curious, that is to say, I was wondering if these had been sent by a former beau—"

Mamie shook her head and giggled. "Naw, there ain't no former lovers if that's what you mean. It was only Dale, and he done left me." She was flattered that he could be jealous. "Anyhow, what do they say? I ain't had time to get Doc McLaren's friend here to read 'em to me."

"I do apologize. They're from someone named Frenchy . . ." He knew he didn't have to reveal more.

"Yeah, I knew it was from her. I can tell her handwritin'. Anyhow, I figured out during supper who you really was when you started to talk more like you did back in Arkansas. I don't care. It don't matter. All that stuff in Helena, it's over. You and me, we'll make a life. It don't have nothin' to do with Catherine. Not really. I need to tell you—she was innocent. Sorry for your brother, but innocent she was. You knowin' that, I'm sure, will put all that behind us. I cain't have no kids, but I'm guessin' you have enough as it is. I hate it that you and your wife must of split up, but you and me, we was meant to be." She smiled at him, her big front teeth squarely in his face. She had idolized the reverend since the first camp meeting and considered his attention, such as it was, to be not only a high compliment but the will of the Lord, whose servant she thought the reverend to be. She felt wanted, despite his treatment of her during sex. It wasn't all that much different from the way Dale had treated her, after all. "And how nice that I won't have to change my last name now that you've changed yours, all in line with your new life, I'm thinkin'! See, we was meant to be."

"Meant to be!" He jumped up from the bed. The thought of having her as his wife and the sting of knowing that his subterfuge had failed, and with such a naïve woman, triggered the outburst. "Me—with you? A half-witted country bumpkin with teeth like a jackrabbit?" He stared at her loose bathrobe, which barely covered her large breasts. "You think *those* are enough for a man like me?

Ashamed, crushed by the sudden change in him and the awful words coming from his mouth, Mamie pulled the robe tightly around her. He was almost fully dressed. She watched him put on his tie and vest, watched him arrange his hair and toy with his beard and mustache until they suited him. Standing back from the big mirror, he put on his coat and again made slight adjustments until he fancied that what he saw in the glass was what he saw as himself. Watching him now, she finally saw *him*, knew he was worse than any cowboy or cold-eyed gambler she had seen in the last three years, knew he was worse, by far, than her ex-husband, Dale.

Mamie was no longer in tears. "A man like you, you ain't no man a'tall. If you ain't the devil, you're his close kin. I wonder what your woman back in Helena will think when she finds out what a fine man she married? What about all them people down there thinkin' you're a man of God when you're more evil than the evil you preach about? You're less than nothin', is what you are."

The reverend's face, having just been composed to his standards, contorted yet again in rage. "You would tell my wife! You would ruin me!" He raised a fist and smashed Mamie in the jaw. She staggered back and fell against the bedroom wall. Dissatisfied with the damage he had done, the reverend looked frantically about the room until he spied the pitcher on the vanity. He grabbed it and turned back to Mamie, who was shoving aside the mattress in order to reach for the derringer she kept beneath it.

He threw the pitcher at her head. As she ducked, he lunged toward the derringer that was now in her right hand, wresting it away from her. He lost his balance and fell to one knee. She came for him, her fingers formed like claws, her blue eyes blazing with absolute fury. He pulled the trigger. Blood rushed from her head, inches above her right eye, as she crumpled between the bed and nightstand. *"God help me!"* he cried out, and ran out of the room.

He was inside his own room nearby, with the door locked, when he heard someone in the hallway say, "Was that a gunshot?" Had he remembered in his panic to close the door to Mamie's room? Yes, yes—he had pulled it shut just before he ran down the hallway but, of course, it was still unlocked. Still, it should take the people some time to figure out where the shot had come from. He must make his escape before then.

He swiftly packed as much as he could into a large valise, waited for the hallway to clear, and took the back stairs to the narrow alley behind the hotel. No one was there. Trying to look as nonchalant as possible, he made his way to the raised wooden walkway above the mud and waste in the street alongside the hotel. The nearest livery stable was four blocks south. Although he wasn't much of a rider and hated horses in general, he bought the gentlest gelding in the place, telling the stable manager he only needed it to get to Lawrence before dawn. In fact, he rode west instead of east, hoping to catch a train to Dodge, either in Junction City or Salina. He had to wait until the next day for the train out of Junction City, but he camped out near the station and, slapping the gelding on the rump, set it free to go where it pleased.

Once he reached Dodge City, he removed the gray from his hair, shaved off his beard, and bought some work clothes and boots. In his hotel room, he scrutinized himself in the mirror and felt his fear of being apprehended fade away. He looked eight or ten years younger—and, he thought with satisfaction, almost like one of the nesters he had seen on the train: plain, hardworking, law-abiding, and quiet.

He soon discovered there was no train to Tascosa, only freight wagons and stagecoaches, including an express stage that would get him down there in about three days. But before he could book passage, he fell ill, attributing the sickness to the strain and lack of sleep from the past two days. In his hotel room, he sent for a doctor, who told him his fever, red rash, and whitish spots in his mouth could mean but one thing—measles.

"How can it be that I am brought down by a disease for children?" he whispered hoarsely, with malice in his tone.

"Hmm." The doctor, a red-faced, jolly-looking fellow whose bedside manner was generally conducive to recovery, stepped back from the puffy-eyed, petulant, and sneering face of his patient and considered. "One might hypothesize," he said, pausing to foreclose on a grin, "that given the reactions of the patient in this instance, the persistence of certain personality characteristics from childhood might, in fact, have made this adult patient equally susceptible as he has aged."

CHAPTER 26

Tascosa, April 1880

Mick McGinnis met Casimero Romero through the priest who lived in Vega. Once a month, Casimero paid for the priest, Father Miguel, to make the thirty-mile trip from Vega up to the Romero rancho east of Tascosa. Mick and Frenchy built their adobe house in the same block where a courtly gentleman named Ysedero Sierna lived with his wife and children. Ysedero was well acquainted with both the priest and Casimero Romero. He took a liking to Mick, one of the few Anglo Catholics in Tascosa. Soon Mick was riding along beside Ysedero and his family when they made the short trip each month to hear Mass at the rancho. Frenchy never went along, preferring to spend the day resting.

Whether because they were neighbors or because they shared the faith or both, Mick and the two much older men quickly became close friends. Mick and Frenchy had not been in Tascosa six months before Mick came up with an ideal plan for a livery stable, the business he'd dreamed of starting when he and Frenchy left Dodge City. In the meantime, he'd been working for Jess Jenkins at the Jenkins and Dunn Saloon, not far north of the shacks and cribs of Hogtown at the southeast end of town, close by the Canadian River.

One Sunday, while lounging in the shade of Casimero's long patio with Ysedero and Casimero himself, Mick pulled out three cigars, one of a dozen Henry Clay *habanas* he had bought off a gambler down on his luck in the saloon. Offering them to his friends, he was satisfied with the delight in their eyes, for the Henry Clays were among the best cigars to be had in the entire nation. Mick took a cigar cutter out of his vest pocket. It had a wooden handle, and on the end a piece of metal with a circular hole cut in it. Above the circle was a spring-loaded blade. Mick inserted the rounded end of the cigar into the hole and depressed the blade, neatly cutting off about a sixteenth of an inch. He often bit the tips off the smaller end of his cigars, but with such a fine cigar as the Henry Clay, he preferred a perfect cut. Casimero and Ysedero carried fancier cutters, Casimero's made of silver and Ysedero's having a handle of carved oak. Each man fired up a match and held it flickering beneath their cigars' larger ends, letting the small flame slowly ignite the prime tobacco.

The men smoked silently for several moments, savoring the first drafts. Finally, Casimero held his cigar out and admired it, as one would regard a finely crafted blade or a piece of art. "Ah, I would say this: If God smoked a cigar, this would be it, señor."

From frequent conversations with Ysedero, Mick learned that his neighbor held Casimero in the highest regard. Casimero had left his land in New Mexico in 1876 and set out for the open range to the east, traveling in a procession like a prince, bringing his large family, twelve wagons, and more than one hundred *peónes* to work the land. With them were four thousand sheep tended closely by Basque sheepherders, most of whom had gravitated to New Mexico from California. Only an inch or so taller than Mick, Casimero was more heavily built, with a broad chest and shoulders, a flowing black mustache, and a dark and commanding look about him. As callous as some of the white ranchers could be toward the vaqueros who helped work their cattle, not one ever thought about looking down on Casimero, or Ysedero for that matter. If the cattlemen didn't like Casimero's sheep, they seemed to accept them, probably a tribute to the man himself.

"And what is the occasion?" Casimero was smiling at Mick. Casimero and Ysedero looked at each other, already guessing what Mick had in mind.

"Well, gentlemen, this is the way of it. Tascosa needs a new livery stable, and I am the man to build it. I know livestock as well as any man—well, almost as well as any man on these plains. I can have the necessary lumber delivered from Dodge City in ten days' time. I will build behind the Jenkins and Dunn Saloon. It will be the only livery on the south side of Main Street, the most convenient spot for the cowboys riding across the Canadian River to hit the town."

"And all you need, my friend, is money, *verdad*?" Casimero smiled again, and took another draw on his cigar. He now stood nodding at it slowly, as if to say, "What a magnificent creation that cigar is, a thing that is the best of its kind."

Mick's blue eyes were on Casimero. "Well, in fact, money is not the most important thing. What you have done with your irrigation system is a wonder to us all. You have water all year. You have alfalfa, oats, and, of course, tall prairie hay, all in abundance. If you front me the feed I need, after three months I will give you back the cost of the feed plus twenty percent more into the bargain."

"Twenty percent? And that would be one hundred and twenty percent of the feed cost, and not twenty percent of your net profits?"

Mick paused. It wasn't a surprise that Casimero might want more than twenty percent over and above the value of the feed, since he could use it all himself for his own livestock and because Mick might fail. But a share of the net profits? Mick didn't have time to do any calculations. "You're right. The twenty percent is over and above the cost of the feed."

Casimero gently tapped half an inch of ashes from the end of his cigar. "Well, my friend, I have more confidence in you than you do yourself. So here is what I will do. I will provide your feed if you pay me only fifteen percent of your net profits. But this arrangement must last one full year. It is good, no?"

Ysedero was nodding repeatedly, though very slightly, a mannerism he often used to signal strong agreement. It was possible that Casimero would gain by the counteroffer, but Mick had not calculated what the difference might be. One thing was certain: He had to have feed for his livestock, and what little money he possessed had to go toward building the stable. "Agreed," he said, extending his hand.

Casimero took it. "Now we will drink to our new business." He addressed one of the house servants, a pretty young woman standing near the door to the large hacienda, about ten feet away. "Mariana, *tres tequilas, por favor*."

Mick turned to look at her. At first, she did not seem to hear Casimero's order. Her eyes were elsewhere, fixed on something or someone just inside the door. Then, she quickly said, *"Sí, sí, Jefe."* Looking flustered, she hurried inside, muttering something as she disappeared from view. A few seconds later, the voice of Father Miguel came from the house. Mick looked at Ysedero and Casimero. Both were studying the smoke from their cigars as it floated upward and drifted away in the gentle breeze.

* * * * *

The livery stable was a great success, receiving a quiet endorsement from the Tascosa sheriff, Cape Cunningham. The sheriff had implemented a form of gun control, requiring the cowboys to leave their rifles and pistols in the livery stables before they hit the saloons in Hogtown or on Main Street. Mick now welcomed the sound of hooves pounding up the road from the Canadian River more than he had before, since his livery was closest to the river yet convenient to all the saloons. Jess Jenkins wanted a piece of the business, offering to pay wages for a hand in the stable in exchange for eight percent of the profits. This allowed him to keep Mick at the saloon much of the time. Mick quickly agreed to the deal. He could keep an eye on Frenchy who was now dealing faro. Her encounter with the cheating cowboy who had tried to attack her in Dodge City was fresh in his memory.

Jenkins was surely aware that Mick's concern for Frenchy was a way to keep Mick working at the saloon. The rough, tough, and sometimes rowdy cowboys knew of Mick's reputation as a fighter. None of them wanted to be whipped by a man who was, as often as not, smaller than his opponents. On him, they could not use their pistols, stowed safely in Mick's own livery stable and supposedly watched over carefully by the new stable hand, Slats Tomlinson.

Frenchy had never seen Mick so excited, nor had she thought they could be so successful, living in their own house, and accepted by Tascosa residents both north and south of Main Street. Since 1877, Frenchy had been constantly on the move, escaping from Baton Rouge and Helena, leaving the big city of St. Louis, and finally making the wagon trip from Dodge City to Tascosa. Often, she had dreamed of lighting out for California, heading north to Colorado, or going south, far south, to

Old Mexico or South America. After less than a year in Tascosa, those dreams melted away.

When she thought about Helena and the news from Gabe that Campbell Harper was trying to track her down, she took to heart Gabe's words that it was most unlikely that Harper would find her. In fact, she could not imagine the man in any sort of detective role, his undoubted gift for deceit not being matched, she was sure, by the toughness and perseverance that real detective work required. And after living so long in rooming houses and hotels, she had come to love their modest adobe dwelling, snug during the hard Panhandle winter. Cooking for her drunken mother, however, had soured her on doing any kind of domestic chores. Now she rarely had to cook their meals or clean the place, a luxury that freed her from memories of the demanding Marie Fleurot McCain, sodden with cognac and wrapped in bitterness. Casimero Romero recommended a young Tejano woman to them, Fatima, and God bless her, she did the cooking and cleaning around the house. Often, Frenchy slept in, dozing blissfully and finding it a comfort to hear the soft sounds Fatima made as she went about her tasks, taking care not to wake "*la señora.*"

But a "señora" Frenchy, in fact, was not. She had known for months that Mick wanted to get married, but she didn't give a damn for a piece of paper or a priest's pronouncement that she and Mick were "man and wife," as the saying went. She also suspected that if she agreed to marry him, Mick would feel the union was somehow incomplete if it had not been sanctified by a priest. He had talked a lot about his early years in County Donegal, where he had been, she was astonished to hear, an altar boy. His mother thought the parish priest was a man of God; his father thought the priest was close to senile but generally lenient and understanding. The fellow went about the village blessing things seen only by himself. Mick's father joked that the priest was the only man in Donegal who had actually seen the little people and could call them all by name. Frenchy could tell that Mick's view was closer to that of his mother's: The priest might have been daft but that did not alter the fact that he was a man of God.

The last time Mick returned home after Mass at Casimero's rancho, he spoke of how important the day had been for him, how much he appreciated Casimero's friendship, and how the priest had a special quality about him, a profound humility, a kind of absence, so that in the space before them, the worshipers beheld only the presence and no mere ritual. Frenchy then felt that Mick was on a journey that she could not share. A distance began to develop between them, growing out of things left unsaid, but not actually unknown.

Frenchy did not fear much, but the thought of losing the life she and Mick had created because of her disdain for the Catholic Church was so unsettling that she again began to have trouble sleeping.

One Sunday evening, Mick returned from Casimero's ranch, still feeling the effects of agave tequila. In the house for only a minute or so, he grew somber, literally not at home in some way.

"Go on and say it," Frenchy said.

"Marry me?" Mick said.

She had been expecting him to go on about the day at the rancho, the warm family atmosphere, the excellent food, the fine wine and tequila—all blessings in his mind, all owing to the family's faith and the influence of the priest. Either that, or he would say a few meaningless words in passing, before he went off to bed.

"It's all I want," he said.

She was quiet for a few moments, relishing a deep sense of relief.

"I suppose we can't have children," she said, raising her eyebrows and smiling.

He laughed. "Sure it isn't from lack of tryin'. Anyhow, I don't care."

"So you'd marry me even if we stood up before our crackpot justice of the peace and that priest friend of yours wasn't in sight?"

"Yes."

"But you'd be disappointed?"

"That's like askin' me if I'd be disappointed if a man gave me a thousand dollars in silver 'stead of gold."

"You're a clever rascal, you know."

"A rascal I am not, Miss."

"And I know how much you like gold."

Two nights later, they were walking home from the Jenkins Saloon, arm in arm, Mick with his eyes on the shadows as they turned left on

Main. They always departed before midnight, leaving the worst of the drunks in the care of a bartender and bouncer, who together weighed four hundred and fifty pounds. At night, before going home, Mick went next door to the livery and picked up his Smith & Wesson revolver and stuck it in his belt. So far, he had never needed it. They knew people up and down Main, many of them residents, business owners, and cowboys from nearby ranches who were still up and about. They walked along the south side of Main to avoid the crowd at the Exchange Saloon across the street. When they turned right on Water Street to head to their house, Frenchy pulled her arm away from his. They stopped. He looked at her but said nothing. But in his eyes she saw the question.

"I'll need to have a long talk with that priest of yours before I can turn into gold."

CHAPTER 27

The next Sunday, Frenchy was up and dressed and sitting at the kitchen table eating a piece of the berry cobbler that Señora Sierna had left for her after returning from Mass at the rancho. The señora was generous with her gifts to Frenchy, but she and most of the other Tejanos who were devout Catholics were disappointed that the colorful pair continued to live together without benefit of marriage.

Frenchy knew that the priest was going to pay her a visit on this particular Sunday. Mick was taking his ease out at the Romero rancho, having armed himself with half of the remaining Henry Clay cigars. She finished her piece of cobbler and eyed another large hunk that remained in the señora's baking pan. She should save a piece and offer it to the priest; after all, there was little else in the house to offer him, although the coffeepot was still hot and more than half full. On the other hand, Frenchy knew that the priest would have had every woman at the rancho trying to stuff him with charbroiled lamb chops, beef flank steaks, puddings, pies, cobblers, and dulces that Frenchy couldn't begin to pronounce. So she pulled the baking dish in front of her and began eating all the cobbler that remained.

She was almost done when she heard the sounds of a snorting horse, clomping hooves, and the faint jingling of the traces as a buggy came to a stop outside. She got up and stuck the empty baking dish into the stove oven that only her cook ever used. She was waiting for the priest as he walked past the well in the front yard and stood, black hat in hand, on the front porch.

"I am Father Miguel." The priest's voice was soft and had only a trace of the lisp that was common among priests who had been trained in Spain. Frenchy already knew he spoke English. The Masses at Romero's rancho were in Latin, as they were elsewhere, but Mick had once mentioned that the priest heard confessions in both languages. The priest did not offer his hand. Frenchy offered hers anyway, finding to her annoyance that his grip was reluctant, flaccid, and quickly withdrawn. She gestured for him to come inside; hesitantly, he did so.

"Coffee?" She picked up the hot metal pot from the stove.

"No, thank you, Sen—"

It was clear to Frenchy that the poor man didn't know whether to call her señora or señorita. "Please call me Frenchy."

"Frenchy?" He stood uneasily, fumbling with his black hat.

Frenchy poured herself a cup of coffee and sat down, motioning for him to do the same. She took a sip and put the cup down on the table. "I am done with your church, and that's the way it is."

For someone who had seemed so diffident up to this point, the priest's response came quickly. "I know. I understand. Completely."

Frenchy looked into his large, dark, and sensitive eyes. She believed him. "You can accept that?"

"I must. Yes. I must."

"How can that be? Isn't it your job—your mission—to show people how to believe, or scare them so they will?"

"No, I cannot do that. Especially not with the belief. Some would say 'faith.'"

This is the saddest man I have ever seen in my life, Frenchy thought. She became aware of how humble and honored she felt that this priest had confided in her what he could not disclose to any other soul in the world.

"Why do you tell me these things?"

"Ah, that is simple. I know you do not believe. And you will not believe. You are honest and strong, and in this matter you will not change. But I also know, I have heard, that you are a good woman, still very young but wise for your years. People trust you. How else could they bet their money before your eyes, time after time, night after night?"

"They are foolish, and much of the time drunk."

"Yes, but I hear what they say about you. You are a person of trust. So is your . . . so is Señor McGinnis."

"So tell me, Father, why do you require nothing, not even belief, as you have said?"

He was quiet for a good while. She thought he was drifting off, or shutting down.

"I cannot ask of others what I cannot do myself."

Frenchy leaned forward in her chair. "But in years past, when you were young, surely you believed . . . had faith?"

Another spell of silence. When he spoke again, very quietly, it was as if he had recalled an obscure event from long ago. "Yes, as I understood belief at the time. But in this land—it is much like a desert in many ways—I found something else. Something stronger than belief." Another hesitation, but brief. "I found that I needed love. Human love. I wanted life. It was denied me because I am a priest."

"So don't be a priest."

He looked into her eyes. "For you, yes, remaking your life has been your life. I have heard something of your story. It is, I think, a story no one truly knows but yourself. But I know enough, all the more as I look at you now. The truth is, leaving the priesthood would not help me. It is not for the Church that I stay; it is for what I have of love. You see, I do have love, and it is love for a woman. But for her, it is more important that I remain a priest than for us to be together. She loves the Church more than she loves me. I love her more than I love the Church. So, you see, I do not have her and I do not have the Church. In the Church, she believes she finds salvation. I find a prison, but one from which I appear to offer salvation."

Frenchy was for once at a loss. She finished her coffee, got up from the table, and placed the empty cup in the washbasin. "Water?" He nodded. She dipped up enough for two tin cups. He drank thirstily.

"Too much talk," he said, wiping his mouth. "I mean, at the rancho."

Frenchy sat down, moving her chair a bit closer to the priest. "Here you can say anything."

For a moment, she thought he would smile. At one time he must have displayed a dimple, to the left of his mouth and a little above, when he smiled. Now she saw the slightest movement there, nascent lines in his face converging, but not enough to fully change his expression. "I am making a confession, not to another priest, but to an unbeliever, a very young woman, who works in a saloon. It could be humorous, you know. But it is not."

"You wouldn't be the first. Well, you are the first priest, Father."

"You know, I am almost a real father. I have a daughter, you see. She is of my blood, I can see my blood in her. But she does not know I am her father."

"Would you like for me to call you Father or Padre?"

"Please to call me Miguel. But only between us. Otherwise, Father is fine."

"You say you do not have the Church . . . Miguel. You have lost belief, or should I say faith?" Frenchy felt uneasy; she would have to keep this conversation from Mick. He would, in the end, be angrier with her for telling him about the priest than he would be with the priest himself. Mick, too, saw salvation in the man.

"If God sees me, He knows that being cut off from the woman I love and our daughter is penance enough. I do not feel sinful. No. But the fact is, I only remain in the Church because it is her desire, and there is nothing else. It is a destiny to which I must yield. In the Mass, I raise the chalice because it is what is given me to raise. Yet, I see meaning in the eyes of those who come to Mass. So maybe God wants me to be nothing other than a, what is the word, a *vehicle* for the Eucharist? To be like the freighter who brings supplies from Dodge City to the dry goods store in Tascosa. It is only a job. Like a freighter, I grow tired of my constant rounds, in my case tired of mouthing the words of consecration; but it is my job to do so. Sometimes I believe my limited role, man's role, is a sign that no man, no woman, and in fact no *institución* really matters. That only the mystery, only the constant presence of suffering and a longing for peace are important. At those times I feel that the chalice is held higher in the air than I am myself holding it. And in that bit of air, perhaps there is not emptiness. But I do not see redemption. It is simply a space where suffering and peace come together. If I have faith, sometimes, it is in that space. At its best, my life is lived just there." Miguel closed his eyes. He sighed, breathed deeply, and got up from the table. "I must go."

* * * * *

And so on a fine April day in 1880, Frenchy became Frenchy McGinnis, saying only the minimal words that she and Miguel had agreed could be used in the brief ceremony. Before it began, Frenchy could see that Mariana was the woman Miguel loved and that her little girl, Luciana, with a quick smile and a dimple on her left cheek, was certainly his daughter. Of the large crowd assembled at the Romero rancho, no more than four or five people knew the full story of Miguel, but surely others thought they did.

For her part, Frenchy wished Miguel had not been asked, required actually, to conduct the marriage ceremony. He had confided that Casimero had ordered Mariana to take Luciana to Amarillo for baptism four years past, not wanting Miguel to perform it. Now, Miguel's voice was shaky, and he struggled to keep his eyes away from Mariana. His final blessing was rushed. Frenchy gave Mick a quick kiss and practically pulled him away from Miguel. While the others were loud and cheerful in their congratulations and eager to enjoy the fine array of food and drink, Miguel remained standing for a minute or more before making a half-hearted effort to circulate among the crowd.

"You go on," Frenchy told Mick, releasing her grip so he could join Casimero, Jess Jenkins, and Ysedero on the patio. He was down to his last four Henry Clay cigars, having saved them for this occasion. She had never seen him happier. Frenchy was happy for him, and for herself, almost in equal measure to his own joy, but underlying her feelings was the concern she felt for Miguel. With everyone outside now, he seemed abandoned, a small dark man with a sad face and large, pain-absorbing eyes. She went to him, placing a hand on his shoulder. He did not look up to see her face.

CHAPTER 28

Tascosa, early May, 1880

"Nobody but a damned fool like Tom Harris would start mouthing off against the new cattle syndicate," said Jess Jenkins, principal owner of the Jenkins and Dunn Saloon.

Mick was drinking a glass of beer at the bar. "A strong man he is. A strong man who speaks his mind." Mick rarely drank on the job, but his livery stable was doing so well that a little celebrating was called for. He might even have a tot or two of whiskey later on. After all, he of all men had persuaded Frenchy to turn herself into gold, an accomplishment that seemed to him but little short of a miracle. He took a big, satisfying drink from the mug, smiling like a man whose life was all it should be.

He put the empty mug down on the walnut bar. "Strong—and proud. Tom will not put up with bein' treated poorly. Can't really blame a man for that now, can ya?"

Jenkins gave him a sly look. "Now you're wantin' to have it both ways, tricky Irishman that you are. And I don't think you know for sure what the syndicate is up to with this new, what do they call it?"

"The Panhandle Stock Association," Mick said in a loud and formal voice, sounding like a big shot making an important official announcement. He picked up the mug and drained it, licking a bit of foam from his lips. "Otherwise known as a bunch of rich cattle barons, some not even livin' in the state of Texas."

"They claim they only want to stop all this cattle rustlin' and keep the damn tick-ridden South Texas cows out of here so their own herds can stay healthy. And here's you makin' money off the gunmen the syndicate has brought in to deal with the rustlers and run the sick herds away from the Canadian. Half the horses in your stables belong to the 'special' cowhands hired by the LS Ranch and the other big spreads, and you cain't deny it."

"Well, here it is, Jenkins. Back in Ireland, my pap never owned an acre, nor half of one, not ever. Here, some of the real and actual cowboys have got their own tiny pieces of land. You say the ranch owners want to stop the rustlers—but the question is, who will they say are the rustlers? Right now, as things stand, the cowhands like Tom Harris can round up a few stray cows and calves and raise them up on their little plots. But you watch, the syndicate'll put a stop to that, and guess who'll be called rustlers then—the hands themselves. And you can bet the syndicates won't pay more to make up for the hands' losin' their few beeves. So what's left to 'em, eh? Low wages, hard work, bad food, and worse whiskey. Aye, especially here. No stake for themselves, no, and no chance of one neither, not with the way things are gonna be. So. Well here it is. Yes, I board the syndicate horses because they own most of 'em within three hundred miles of here. But I give a few of the cowboys a little bit off when they come to town. It is my way of sayin' I think they'll be in the right of it when all this comes to a head."

Jenkins downed a shot of whiskey. It was the good stuff, Double-A, from a bottle he kept hidden under the bar. "You're more full of shit than Tom Harris. But you are an Irishman, so I guess it's your due." Jenkins belatedly made a little smile after he said this. More than once he had witnessed Mick's temper in action. "I say you're walkin' a fine line, and you had better watch yourself. The syndicate ain't done any harm so far, and here you been pourin' the odd free one to the cowboys and don't think I ain't seen you. And if I've seen you, others have seen you too. You're borrowin' trouble, Mick McGinnis, and so is Tom Harris and his bunch if they keep carryin' on about somethin' that ain't happened yet."

Mick went behind the bar and drew himself another beer. "And here's what I see. You are havin' it both ways, too, bein' my partner at the livery and caterin' to both sides here."

By now Jenkins had refilled his whiskey glass. "Yes, but I am a silent partner at the stables, as you well know. If it wasn't for me and Casimero, you'd be boardin' Mexican donkeys in them stables. Here's the thing,

Mick, I'm a shrewd businessman and you're an honest one—exceptin', of course, the free drinks you slip to your favorite hands. I'd consider takin' it out of your pay, except I know this won't last. Already the syndicate ranches have more hands than they can use comin' in here from other parts of Texas, and from north and west of here too. If Tom Harris and his kind want to quit, there ain't no syndicate ranch goin' to give a shit. Not to mention they've hired some of hardest men in New Mexico, fresh from all those squabbles out there. Already been a few killins around here."

"I hope I live long enough to see you die," said Mick, with a reluctant smile, "because maybe I can get old Bloomfield the undertaker to tell me what you have in that chest of yours in place of a good honest heart."

"Heart my ass," Jenkins said. "I'm a businessman, Mick, and it's my head that I look to for answers."

"Aye, and a Protestant into the bargain."

"All I know is I ain't had a killin' in my saloon for two months and more, and I want to keep it that way. You're the man to keep 'em under control. But the fact is, that one wasn't a real killin'."

"If you mean Jess Leigh I think you'll find his grave out on Boot Hill with little more than a few sticks of wood to mark it. If he wasn't killed, what was it that made him dead, aye, and dead right inside those doors over there?" Mick gestured to the double doors at the front of the saloon.

"None of that went on in here!" Jenkins stabbed the bar with a thick and disfigured index finger, broken cruelly years before when a freight wagon bolted while his hand was caught up in the reins.

"Well, I was here and it went like this. Jess Leigh came in one afternoon and had five or six whiskies, not countin' the ones his friends bought and slipped to him when I cut him off. He goes outside and bumps into the cleanin' woman from the roomin' house, who happens to have her arms filled with a stack of towels and doesn't see that one of those damned ducks from the bayou is in her way. She steps on the duck, the duck makes a ruckus, a true ruckus it was, and flutters back into Leigh's horse, which he's holdin'. The horse gets spooked by the duck, rears up, and throws its front hooves toward Leigh's face. He pulls out his Colt, which he had not stowed in the stable, and shoots the feckin' duck. Well, the cleanin' woman took to hollerin', and Louis Homan called Leigh a crazy bastard for shootin' the duck. Next thing you know, Leigh is pointin' that Colt at Homan and swears he'll see him deader than the duck ever was unless he crawfishes real hard and says he's sorry. Now comes Sheriff Cape Cunningham, him with his double-barreled shotgun. So he says to Leigh that he shouldn'ta shot the feckin' duck in the first place, but however that may be, he damn sure had best drop his pistol uncocked to the ground and get the hell out of town if he knew what was good for him. But Leigh, bein' in fact and in the eyes of Jesus himself a true and actual son of a bitch, went and pointed that Colt at Cape. Cocked it was. And the next thing, that scattergun went off and blew Jess Leigh right off his horse like he'd been struck by a North Sea gale, and I'll be damned if he didn't land all the way over there, right across the threshold of this establishment. So there it is, and it's a fact you had a killin' here and that's the end of it."

Mick waited for Jenkins to say something, but Jenkins was silent, his eyes on the spot where Leigh had fallen, his upper body full of double-ought buckshot. The cleaning lady had taken care of the mess for free.

Less than five minutes later, Tom Harris came in and stood at the bar in front of Mick. He gave Jenkins a cursory nod and ordered a whiskey. Then another, and another. "I been demoted from wagon boss, on account of I told the boss straight out I don't like what's comin' with that new group they done formed," he told Mick, after drinking half of his third drink. "I reckon I cain't find no work with another outfit, neither. Hell, anybody with any sense can see where all this is headin'. If what they want is to get rid of real rustlers, let 'em go git that damn little fart Billy the fuckin' Kid who was in here drinkin' up all your whiskey not so long ago." Tom was staring straight at Jess Jenkins.

"That young man was a good solid customer." Jenkins nodded, devoted as he was to all such customers.

"He is a cold solid killer, is what he is. And he's gonna be a cold, dead man 'fore long."

One of the big front doors slapped against the wall, and two syndicate men came strutting in. They sometimes made it their business to hang out in the vicinity of the saloons and, for sport or for money, liked to harass the hands who had begun to speak against the new association. It wasn't the first time Tom Harris had attracted a syndicate man.

One of the men remained near the door while the other came to the bar, standing no more than two feet away from Harris. With a nod at Jenkins, Mick moved out from behind the bar and Jenkins took his place. Mick's right hand made a quick pass at his back pocket to make sure the straight razor was in place.

"I'll take four of your finest," said the syndicate man at the bar, known to all as Lon King, late of New Mexico, where he had done duty for the big ranch owners out there. "That'll be one for my friend at the door, one for the little Irishman over yonder, one for me—and one for our friend Tom Harris here. You'll be needin' a handout every now and again, Tom, what with you no longer bein' a wagon boss. I figure that's fifty dollars a month that you just pissed away."

Tom turned slowly to face King. "Take that drink and pour it in one of your ears so I can watch it come out of the other, you empty-headed son of a bitch."

It was early in the day, and neither man had checked in his guns at the livery stable, the usual requirement later on, when things became more tense in the saloons near Hogtown. Quickly, Mick stepped between the two men, both taller than he was. The syndicate man standing at the saloon door moved his right hand toward the pistol on his left hip. "Get outside and settle this with yer fists!" Mick pushed the two men farther apart.

King spat toward Tom's boots. "No man calls me a son of a bitch."

Tom reached across his body to the bar, and downed his third whiskey. He set the small glass down carefully when he was finished. His right hand was now closer to the holster on his left hip. "Not really any need for it. It's wrote all over your face."

The man at the door pulled his pistol. Mick moved a foot or so toward him and put out his hand, trying to get the man to back off. Tom Harris and Lon King drew their own weapons, Tom turning slightly toward the man at the door. King kept his eyes on Tom.

Jess Jenkins came out from behind the bar. "Goddamn your eyes, I'll send for Sheriff Cunningham!" He started toward the three men closest to him. He thought later on that the man at the front door fired first, but it was impossible to know exactly what happened because all three men fired more or less at once. When it was over, the man at the door was writhing and cursing on the floor, a bullet wound in his thigh. Mick lay crumpled and motionless, a trickle of blood coming from his mouth and a bullet wound on the right side of his chest. King ran out of the saloon, leaving his companion behind. Tom Harris pulled off his long bandana and held it against Mick's wound.

Later, when Frenchy saw Mick laid out on a table in Doc Shelton's house, she thought he was dead. He was naked from the waist up and unconscious. She could see where the bullet had entered his chest, an inch or two right of his breastbone. The hole was almost purple, and around it were dozens of small spots almost the same color. Frenchy looked up at Doc Shelton, her eyes asking what she could not bring herself to speak.

"The bullet went almost all the way through," he said. "Those little spots are from the gunpowder, he was shot at very close range. He hasn't lost a dangerous amount of blood yet, so he has a chance. I'll know more tomorrow. Now you've got to get on out of here so I can get that slug out and bandage him up."

Ten days later, Mick was able to come home. Doc Shelton said it would be another month or more before he could think about going back to work. Frenchy found that she was a poor nurse, losing patience with Mick's impatience to get up and move around. "Yer a right vicious woman, you are!" he yelled at her one morning. "Who are you to tell me when I can get out of bed, when I can eat, when I can have a dram or two to pick me up?"

Frenchy had not slept well. It was seven in the morning, long before her body was ready to deal with the simplest demands, much less the temper of a wounded Irishman. "Ysedero knows a woman who'll come by and take care of your ornery self. You've scared Fatima half to death. I told him the only requirement I have is that the new woman also doesn't know any English. You can complain all you want to when she's around, and she won't know the difference. I've got half a mind to take a room at the Exchange till you get over yourself. For God's sake, Mick, use some common sense. You have to rest! That goddamn syndicate man nearly killed you. You had no business being in the middle of that fight in the first place."

"I'll not have you tellin' me what I shoulda done or ought to do now! You know that part of my job at the saloon is keepin' good order—well, tryin' to, anyhow. What would you have me do, hunker down behind the bar and wait for them boys to kill themselves?" He tried to get up from the bed but fell back, his mouth contorted in pain. What he said then she could not say—some words from Donegal, in the old language, spit out like bitter arrows aimed at her and the world at large.

CHAPTER 29

Dodge City, early May, 1880

One sunny morning, Campbell Harper awoke in his room at the Dodge House Hotel and felt well enough to summon the hotel housekeeper with something approaching civility. A short, rail-thin woman of about twenty-five, she had knocked ever so softly on the door, and now slowly opened it, at first showing only her head, for she knew that the same miserable, condescending brute who had occupied the room the past week and more would still in there, his head buried in his pillow, his twisted mouth ready to spew out the harshest criticism of her timing, her appearance, or the food she brought up from the hotel kitchen. But the brute was sitting up now. His face bore something that resembled a smile. He quickly devoured the poached egg and toast before him on the tray. "I will have more," he said, a dark yellow bit of yoke tucked into the corner of his mouth. "And I must have a shave. Send for the barber now."

When the barber had come and gone, Campbell remained in his chair, looking warily at his image in the mirror behind the wash basin. He had only glanced at it while the barber was at work. He had lost weight during his illness. The gray dye was long since gone. "I look like myself," he said, a note of surprise in his voice. It had been months now since he had closely resembled the preacher who had left Helena, Arkansas.

An urgent thought came to his mind: *I will be myself!* He could not go back to being the Reverend Caleb Jackson, a name known to people in Topeka, including some who had seen him with Mamie. His sudden departure from the hotel in Topeka was tantamount to an admission of guilt. But no one in Kansas knew him as himself, and now no one between Dodge City and Tascosa, Texas, would know him either. Not until he reached that town; not until he was face to face with Catherine McCain—or Frenchy, as she was now. Shocked she would be when she saw him standing before her, thus giving him the upper hand. He imagined her gray eyes as they must now be: bold, fearless, sure of what they saw. He narrowed his dark eyes and cast a fierce look at the mirror, seeing in its reflection the expression of a man in charge, dominant, forbidding, and unstoppable.

He spent another few days in Dodge City to restore himself to full strength and decide how he would make the long trip to Tascosa. He already knew that there were no trains to the place. Freight wagons were too slow and far too uncomfortable for a gentleman's passage. Riding on horseback would leave him exposed to the elements—and God only knew to what else. I wonder, he thought, are the savages subdued down that way?

When he asked around, he could not tell whether the answers were meant to frighten him without grounds or to falsely reassure him, depending on who was doing the talking. The Comanche had been subdued; the Kiowa were on reservations. But there were reports of renegade bands. Others said that cattle rustlers and former Indian traders might bring harm, and probably murder, to nesters or single travelers caught out on the prairie.

He soon learned that the stagecoaches had an armed man perched next to the driver. The coaches were small and dirty, with unraveling purple or maroon seat cushions and frayed curtains on the windows. They were not suitable, but nothing was suitable out here in this godforsaken land. His strength restored, he decided to take a regular stage, not the express, so he could spend the nights in well-known way stations where one might hope the brigands of the prairie were not welcome.

* * * * *

The trip was worse than Campbell had imagined. The stage reached the Exchange Hotel in Tascosa just as darkness fell. He had seen the lights on Main Street from miles away, peeking at him intermittently through the dust churned up by the stage. Slowly they grew brighter, larger, and by the time the stage was only a few miles north of town, he had begun to feel their glow as a welcoming embrace, beckoning him toward a warm meal, a clean bed, and a peaceful night under a safe and solid roof.

But as he stepped stiffly out of the coach, he had to dodge three swaying and singing cowboys making their way down to the Hogtown saloons from the livery stable north of Main. It was a Saturday night, and inside the Exchange, the dining room was full and half a dozen people stood ahead of Campbell in the line to sign the hotel register. The hotel clerk was maddeningly slow, taking far too much time to count the coins and notes made in payment and to return any change that was due. Campbell urgently needed to relieve himself. He had seen no privy when he got off the stage, although one of the cowboys he had barely avoided simply stood in the shadows toward the back of the hotel and, singing all the while, splattered the adobe wall with urine.

When Campbell had at last registered and paid for his room, he hurried upstairs and made use of a smelly chamber pot. The hotel was somewhat quieter when he went down to the restaurant. The only things on the menu were beefsteak and beef stew. He chose the latter. The clientele surprised him: Here was a man dressed in a decent suit and wearing a cravat; at the table next to him sat two women who might have wandered in from a nearby dance hall, each heavily painted with lipstick and rouge. A tall man wearing a white shirt, tie, vest, and bowler hat approached the well-dressed man at the table. Campbell watched and listened as the two men talked. The newcomer carried a pistol in a right-handed holster, though slung on his left side.

"Well, Doc, what's the latest on Mick?" the newcomer said. "We ain't seen him or Frenchy for several days now."

Campbell was holding a big spoon poised over his bowl of stew. He set it down on an adjacent plate that held three slices of bread and a square chunk of butter.

"Frenchy thought it was best to take him over to Vega. I reckon she's there now, but for how long, I don't know." The doctor chuckled. "From what I hear, that adobe house of theirs up and shrunk when they were both cooped up in there all day."

The man with the pistol laughed. He turned toward Campbell and coughed, covering his mouth with his hand and then wiping it on his pants. He had a star pinned to his vest.

"You know, Doc, I haven't been able to find one person who can tell me where Lon King might be," said Cape Cunningham. "Most likely New Mexico."

Doc nodded. "I hear the Kid's back there, too, somewhere around Fort Sumner. Folks were kind of surprised he behaved himself when he was here last fall."

"Showed some sense," the sheriff said.

Doc studied the sheriff for a moment. "Smartest thing he ever did."

"He won't last much longer. He's been running between too many fires for too long."

Doc tapped the cloth napkin against the edges of his mouth. "I'll let you know when Frenchy and Mick come back from Vega. I take most of my meals here, and Frenchy'll be in as soon as they're back in town. That woman won't cook for anything or anybody."

"Good. I'd like to visit with 'em. Both of 'em. I mean, they are in fact good friends of mine. Mick, well, he needs to let somebody else take care of the rowdies over at Jenkins's place."

* * * * *

Campbell slept well that night. He awoke with something like a plan. He would take his meals in the hotel, too, but try to sit so he could see everyone who was coming in. He wanted to see Catherine—but only when and where he chose. It would not do for her to come in, see him first, and be forewarned. He ordinarily removed his hat when he was dining, but now he kept it on, tilted toward the entrance to the restaurant. If she came in, he would need only to lower his head to avoid being recognized.

Already he had learned where she lived, had walked by the simple adobe house, amazed at how plain it was, how rudimentary, wondering that such a woman could ever be content in a place like that. He longed to go inside; it was all he could do not to return after dark and break in. He imagined what he might find in the place. There would be her clothes, no doubt—*all* of her clothes. He saw himself opening her chifforobe, running his hands across the silk, cotton, linen—all the surfaces that touched her skin. Her shoes and boots, unlaced, waiting for her to choose among them. There might be a dresser, a vanity; her brushes, powders, combs, and rouge. The strands of her auburn hair in the brushes and combs. Her smell—he did not know it but would know it at once, and once known he would never forget it. The small things, so close to her, so intimate, in a chest perhaps or in the drawers of the vanity. The pillow where she laid her head each night; the smell of the pillow; the smell of her hair, scents, flesh, lipstick. He would—but now he sought to stop himself, to ward off such thoughts.

Four nights passed, then five. Campbell was tired of the hotel food and increasingly irritable that his long mission, so close to ending in triumph, continued to drag on. It was not that he was eager to return to Helena; in fact, the more he thought about Helena, his wife, and his children, the more he was able to persuade himself that by now they must be settled into a life without him. Almost certainly, his return would be disruptive. He did not need to worry about their material comfort. What he had taken of his wife's inheritance to finance his mission was less than half of what she had received from her mother's estate. And, happily, most of the share he had taken for himself yet remained.

He thought back to the letters he had written home, two from St. Louis and three more from Topeka. In the last, he had written that his religious life suited him well. And the regular preaching life was one he could always go back to. Before he left St. Louis, his wife had encouraged him to continue his work. His mission, she said, was "ordained by the Lord," and who was she to stand in the way?

Mamie. The foolish woman had given him no choice. Throwing herself at him, baring her bosom shamelessly and rubbing her body against his—yes, his will had let him down, he had succumbed, he had sinned. But how could a common woman like that imagine he would want to stay with her, be her constant lover, *be seen with her*, day in and day out, to have people pointing and smirking, making rabbit faces, withdrawing at the first sight of those awful teeth. He couldn't bear to think he had been so close to her face; a lesser man might have kissed her. The thought made his stomach turn.

Yet he could not in good conscience say she deserved to die. A terrible accident, that's what it was. If only she had kept quiet, remembered her place, not been led astray by her preposterous delusions. Yes, she would be alive today. But, if so, wouldn't she have warned Catherine? Soon he had satisfied himself that Mamie had to die in order for him to find Catherine. Finding her, might he not save her, redeeming the death of poor Mamie and the life and soul of Catherine herself?

Campbell wearily and slowly made his way through yet another bowl of stew. He saw the town doctor come in and take his usual seat at a table in the center of the dining room. As Campbell was settling his bill, he saw Sheriff Cunningham enter and noticed that the doctor stood up and waved excitedly for the sheriff to join him. Campbell left too large an amount in the waiter's hand, but he was eager for the man to be away. Leaning toward the doctor, Campbell listened closely.

"They'll be back in the morning," the doctor said. "Mick is still weak, but he can stand and mostly take care of himself. I figure Frenchy'll be glad to be home so she can go back to dealing at the saloon. You know, Cape, that's a pair to draw to, speaking of cards. Love each other, they surely do, but when they're forced to be together, my oh my, the sparks do fly." The doctor paused for a moment, savoring his simple rhyme. "Here's hoping Mick will get back to work in a week or so."

The sheriff was about to risk a bowl of chili when a tall barman from his favorite saloon came in, out of breath and flushed with anger. "Sheriff Cunningham, it's the boys from the LS and some other outfits, and there's gonna be trouble!"

"Not in my saloon, by God!"

*****

The next evening, Campbell again waited in vain. Against his better judgment, he walked slowly around the block and approached the bridge over Tascosa Creek. From there he could see the house where Mick and Frenchy lived. Yes, there was light coming from one of the windows on the east end of the house, flickering, a dull yellow in the dark. Campbell knew he should not go any closer. There would be little he could see through either of the windows. Soon his ears caught the sound of a harsh, passionate argument. "Ah, they are at it again," he said. "It is clear that she must leave such a depraved man." They probably aren't really married, he thought. "Calm down, man. All you need to do is wait. You are where you are meant to be, and all will happen as it is meant to happen."

Somehow, he was sure she would come to the hotel the next evening. He had taken special care with his attire, paid for a shave in his room, and applied drops of an expensive cologne he had purchased in St. Louis. At first, he felt so confident of himself and his appearance that he thought he would sit, bareheaded, at his customary table and let her be overwhelmed when she saw him sitting there. But he was aware that any sort of public recognition would not do, no, not at all, because he must be prepared to take her away at a moment's notice, with little or no commotion. Accordingly, he had made arrangements with the livery stable on the west side of town. Until further notice they must keep two horses available for Campbell. He was also prepared to buy a wagon and team if he had to but hoped the horses would do. For fifty dollars the livery manager said he would be happy to help Campbell in any way he could. Campbell made up a story that Mick McGinnis was well known in Dodge City for his unsavory business dealings. The livery manager eagerly absorbed the news. He would make sure two of his best horses were available when Campbell needed them.

Campbell knew he would have to get Catherine out of Tascosa in a hurry; she and Mick were friends of the sheriff. Whatever claims Campbell might make to him would likely be dismissed. So Campbell's plan was to take Catherine and ride north to the Little Blue stage stand and wait there for the next express headed back to Dodge City. From Dodge City—well, he wasn't sure what to do after that. The unfortunate business with Mamie in Topeka had left Campbell with no desire to remain in Kansas for any length of time. He still carried the WANTED poster he had torn off the wall of the sheriff's office in Helena. He could use that as leverage against Catherine. He could force her to stay with him for a little while—long enough. Surely she would fall under his spell. He would save her. She would never know what happened to Mamie.

He was sitting at his usual table with his hat on, his body aligned so he could hide his face with only a slight movement. The doctor was having his nightly supper, sitting alone and mostly unbothered. A few minutes later, Campbell heard the rough scraping of a chair being pulled back from a table and the doctor's excited voice. "Frenchy! It's so good to see you! I trust Mick is much better."

"Strong enough to be more ornery than before. He's still having trouble breathing, but the pain's mostly gone."

"I'll pay him a visit first thing in the morning."

"How early is first thing in the morning?"

The doctor chuckled. Everyone in Tascosa knew Frenchy McGinnis liked to lie in bed till noon, or later. "After lunch," he said, taking his seat.

"Well. See you then." Frenchy picked up a bag of food that the new maid had ordered earlier in the day and turned to go.

The manager of the hotel restaurant fancied himself to be a man of style. He always wore a vest and a cravat and sat behind the counter on a high leather-backed chair. His name was inelegant: Hank. He smiled and nodded as Frenchy made her way out and let his eyes linger for a moment on her departing figure. When he looked up, he was surprised to see another pair of eyes, dark and intense, doing exactly the same thing.

CHAPTER 30

Campbell Harper had begun carrying the Colt Navy revolver tucked inside his belt, where it was hidden by his coat. On the way down to Tascosa, he had persuaded the grizzled shotgun guard on the stage to give him a lesson when they stopped to rest and feed the horses at Cator's Zulu Stockade. "Well, this ain't much of a pistol compared to the newer Colts and Remingtons," the guard grumbled, "but it's a sight better than that one-shot derringer you been carryin'." The sound and recoil from the very first shot came close to ending the lesson, as Campbell almost dropped the Colt Navy and found himself wishing he had done so.

"It ain't covered in shit, you know," the guard said. "You can hold on to it like you need it, which it looks like you will." In all, Campbell fired about twenty rounds. Once, he hit a rusty milk pail ten paces distant. The guard stroked his thick beard. "On second thought, I reckon if I was you, I'd think about talkin' my way out of trouble."

When Frenchy walked out of the restaurant at the Exchange, Campbell was certain he had the revolver tucked away, but as he rose from the table, he reached inside his coat to touch the hard wooden grip and cool metal, immediately feeling more powerful and confident of his course. After all, the pistol was likely a prop; given his persuasive powers and the advantage of surprise, he doubted would need to show it at all. He wondered if the thing should be loaded. The stage guard had loaded it for him, making sure not to chamber a round in front of the hammer. In truth, Campbell was not quite sure how to *unload* the weapon, knowing only that he had to cock the hammer to move a round in the cylinder and pull the trigger to fire it.

Outside the hotel, he felt for the pistol again after he was jostled by three cowboys staggering out of Jim East's saloon, the most popular place west of Hogtown. But Campbell was sure of the moment. His surveillance had prepared him well. He knew that Frenchy, having to carry the burlap bag full of food, could not rush home. She would also have to pause to step up to the bridge spanning the creek that ran north to south, adjacent to Water Street. From there, she had a short walk to her house, not far to the northwest. There had been no rain for several days, and the ground wasn't muddy. Campbell slipped into a small alley between East's saloon and a house on the corner of Water Street and walked through a vacant lot in a crouch and unseen because the prairie grass had grown tall. Terrified of snakes, he squinted at the darkened ground before each step, but seeing that Frenchy was surprisingly near the bridge, he steeled himself to move faster.

Someone opened the back door of the saloon, throwing a broad shaft of light into the vacant lot. Frenchy paused at the bridge, glancing over her shoulder at the light and moments later seeing a strange long shadow projecting from the direction of Main Street. Her eyes tracked back from the shadow, but she saw nothing; the shadow had disappeared. Loud laughter reached her ears from the saloon, along with more whooping and hollering from Main. She had heard the express stagecoach from Dodge come in before she left the hotel restaurant, the driver shouting, "Whoa now! Whoa now, Big Bill!" She knew the passengers would be tired and sore, badly in need of the modest food and basic lodging offered by the hotel.

It was a Tuesday night, and she guessed the noise would die down around ten on her street about a mile northwest of Hogtown. She had been more careful than usual as she approached the creek, the night with a new moon not providing much light to see the ramp up to the bridge. As she reached the ramp, she heard an odd sound in the tall prairie grass behind her. Accustomed to the scurrying of rabbits and rodents through the vacant lot, she at first thought a large dog must have gone prowling there or decided to partake of its many smells.

She had never thought to be afraid when she passed by the lot. Louis Homan lived in the corner house that backed up to it, and his shutters, when he thought about them, were generally wide open. Two years earlier a drunken hand from the Frying Pan Ranch showed up at Homan's back door, having been told in jest that Rocking Chair Jane had moved there from Hogtown. He disputed Homan's blunt statement to the contrary, and the next thing he heard was the sound of Homan's .44 revolver. Homan never meant to hit him, and when the cowboy fell backward into some nettle, terrified but unwounded, the howls coming from his so-called friends were the worst pain he had to suffer. Frenchy chuckled as she thought of the incident and returned her eyes to the bridge.

"Hello, Catherine." A man had emerged from the lot and now stood less than ten feet behind Frenchy's right shoulder. She turned her head, already knowing what she would see: Campbell Harper.

She imagined him in that instant as the dark, elongated figure who had stood in the doorway of the schoolhouse back in Helena, casting his shadow down the center aisle. She felt only a slight unease as she turned fully to face him, her feet set squarely and the bag of food held tightly in front of her with both hands. "Well, you are determined."

He had stretched to his fullest height, holding his chin up, his thumbs stuck into his belt and his dark jacket in sharp contrast to the white shirt he wore. He had been certain that his surprise appearance would unnerve her; but as she stood facing him, far from unnerved, it was he who felt at a loss.

"Now that you've found me, what the hell are you gonna do?"

Was she smiling? Yes, she was. This was intolerable. He searched for a strong and commanding voice, but when he spoke it was in a raspy and almost breathless tone. "I will bring you to justice!" He fumbled inside his coat and brought out the old WANTED poster, faded and crumpled. "There!" he hissed. "Right there, in black and white, it says who you are and what you have done! You must come with me. It is your only chance."

"My only chance? Chance for what? To be hanged by the neck until dead back in Helena, Arkansas, or do I get the chance to pick a stout oak tree for my hanging on the way?"

Campbell didn't know himself exactly what he meant. Or did he? "It is your chance," he said, approximating his old preaching voice, "for redemption. Yes. A chance for freedom and redemption."

"But here I am, free as I can be and not giving a damn about redemption."

"You say. But the reason I am here is to do God's will. You believe you are free, but in your freedom, you only sin, living your life in saloons and gambling halls where our Lord is cast aside."

"I figure He can go wherever He wants to go."

He rushed toward her and grabbed her by the shoulders. "I alone can make you truly free. Together, you and I, we can—"

She tried to strike him with the bag of food, but he knocked it loose from her hands, and it fell near the creek. Her first thought was to call out for Louis Homan, but on Tuesdays he and two friends from the LS ranch played poker in Hogtown. She doubted Sheriff Cunningham would side with Campbell, poster or no poster, but she didn't want him involved. Mick was in no shape to help her, still recovering in their house less than a hundred feet away. She had glimpsed the Colt Navy revolver inside Campbell's coat. *No, I can't call for Mick, he will die.* Campbell was holding her tightly now, trying to drag her into the vacant lot. He pressed one hand over her mouth. She bit him, hard, and it was all he could do to free his fingers. He began to fumble with his pistol. When she reached for it, he struck her in the head with it, and she stumbled. The pistol in his left hand now, he used his bloody right hand to seize her hair and pull her into the tall grass. She almost broke free; he hit her again and she dropped to the ground.

She must have fainted for a while because suddenly she was aware that he was on top of her, and worse, like his filthy brother before him, he was clawing like an animal at her underclothes. She tried to bite him on his cheek or his earlobe, and on his twisted, salivating mouth, but checked herself with the thought he would knock her senseless or worse. She feigned unconsciousness, the hardest thing she had ever done, feeling his body, his aroused body, and his red, sweating face against her own. They were shielded by the tall grass but only about thirty feet from the back door to Homan's house. Turning her head toward it and trying to aim her voice away from her own house, where Mick lay, Frenchy waited until Campbell began using both hands and a knee to move her legs apart. "Help! Help!" she screamed before he cocked the pistol and held it to her head.

* * * * *

Inside the adobe house, Mick thought for a moment that he must be dreaming, imagining the sound of Frenchy's voice. But no, he was only resting, propped up in bed to ease the sharp pain in his back, where the slug had been extracted. He listened intently; no more screams. Groaning as he rose from the bed without help, he grabbed his cane and shuffled to the front door. "Hey out there! Hey!"

He thought he heard somebody struggling, over in the tall grass across the bridge. He made his way outside and hobbled onto the bridge. "Hey! Frenchy, is that you?" Groaning from the pain, he made it down the ramp and stood unsteadily on Water Street.

Lying in the prairie grass, Campbell whispered, "One sound and he's dead. I've killed once and I'll do it again. He will join your friend Mamie in Hell."

"No!" Frenchy's brain and her body were on fire with rage. The strength she brought to bear on the man holding her down was born of the trials of her dear friends, indeed their tragic deaths, and she was out of his grip and standing now, screaming, snarling, not words but primitive sounds of desperate animal ferocity. Again, the back door of the saloon banged open. The light, more yellow-hued than before, showed her there, her shoulders above the prairie grass, the man in front of her aiming a pistol at her head.

She ducked at the moment he fired, and tried to run out of the tall grass. Mick stumbled toward her, crying, "Oh God! Oh my God!" Campbell fired again. Mick fell in the middle of Water Street, his cane clattering against a rock by the road.

Campbell stared at the pistol for a moment, marveling at what he had done. Now Frenchy was almost at the back door of Homan's house, but still slowed by the grass. Campbell quickly pulled back the hammer and raised the pistol. Seeing himself in the light from the saloon, as if he were on a stage, he felt compelled to utter something to mark the drama of this, his greatest moment, when his pure righteousness and vengeance became one.

"Die, woman!"

At the sound of his scream, Frenchy jumped toward a bush and heard another gunshot. The light from the saloon cast a cone of visibility across the spot where Campbell had stood. It was joined by the jerky, shifting beam from an oil lantern, carried by one of the men spilling out from the back of the saloon. Now the shadows of the men, some carrying their own weapons, all but obscured the light. But Campbell was gone.

At the edge of the cone of light, Frenchy stood up, her face a mask of rage. "Kill him! Give me a gun! I will kill him!" But the men quickly fell back, forming a semicircle as the lantern light shone on a figure standing alone, pistol in hand.

"No need, I reckon," Mamie said. "You'll find him yonder." She pointed the pistol at another bush, not ten feet from where Frenchy stood. She looked over at Frenchy and grinned, her big front teeth easily recognizable now that the lantern was fixed on her. Covering part of her forehead was a tidy white bandage, with no hint of blood. Above it was a dark bonnet tied loosely under her chin with a velvet ribbon.

One of the men was helping Mick to his feet. "Frenchy, are ya all right, girl?" He limped toward her. "Goddammit to hell, I've been shot again!" He struggled to retrieve the cane but finally gripped it and stood on his own.

The barman from East's saloon had wrapped his apron around Mick's right thigh. "Son of a bitch almost gelded you, Mick."

Frenchy for once could not speak, though the pure hatred on her face yielded to something like awe as her brain gradually accepted the astonishing reversal she had witnessed. She turned first toward Mick and saw that he was standing and quite animated, talking and gesturing and sending a grateful, loving smile her way. Slowly, she walked over to Mamie, even as she heard Mick in the background, and encircled her dear friend with her arms. "Oh, Mamie, you are such a beautiful sight."

* * * * *

"So Dale done gave me a derringer which had dropped out of his coat pocket and into a dang horse trough at his daddy's farm." Mamie was finishing her story to Frenchy about the struggle with Campbell Harper in the Topeka hotel. They were sitting in the front room of Frenchy's adobe house. Doc Shelton had seen to Mick, and he was presumably resting in the bedroom. "Turns out Dale's daddy finally found it days later after a old bull knocked over the trough, and it run flat out of water. Dale, he confessed all this to me and made his own mark in a letter his new wife wrote to me once he heard I'd been shot. Doc McLaren read the letter to me and let out a whoop at the end, 'cause Dale said he was so happy that he'd done saved my life by givin' me a little gun that warn't worth a shit. Saved my life. Hmm. Well, that's Dale for you. That little gun, it made a noise all right, but what with the bullet hittin' my head at a angle and the powder being kinda bad, this big old brain of mine"—here she elbowed Frenchy and laughed—"you know, the one you was always goin' on about, well, I reckon it still works. The doc says that part of a brain, it ain't exactly empty but it's prob'ly not chock full of the most important stuff. That bullet ended up right under my scalp but still knocked me colder'n a frozen well bucket for a whole hour, accordin' to a nice man at the hotel who came in and found me there by the bed. And do you know, the doc says he didn't hardly spend thirty minutes poppin' it outta there. I wouldn't know 'cause for several days my old head didn't work right, and I couldn't hardly remember nothin'. Stitches is all there is up there now. I mean, on the outside!

"After a week or so, the doc made me stand up straight with my feet together and my arms stuck out straight. Told me to close my eyes, lower my head, and see if I could stand still for a whole minute. Girl, that was a long minute, but I done it, which the doc said meant I didn't have none of that concussing no more. So anyhow, I went out and got me a real pistol and learnt how to use it. I figured if I went to the law, it might not be the smartest thing, with us bein', well, wanted for a killin' and all. There ain't no telegraph lines from Topeka to this here place, and the fastest way for me to warn you was to get on that express stage from Dodge. I was on the one that come in tonight, and was checkin' in at the hotel when I seen the so-called reverend hurryin' out of the dinin' room. I was shore that somethin' was up. Then I heard you a-screamin' and, well, he got what he deserved. He did. I reckon that commandment about killin' don't apply to gettin' rid of preachers who do evil."

Mick could hear them from the bedroom. "I would'na doubt yer hard head had somethin' to do with your survivin' too!"

"You're supposed to be resting!" Frenchy had brought out the Double-A whiskey and had been savoring its effects.

"You might wanna calm down for oncet." Mamie aimed her words toward the bedroom door. "They ain't much left of you as it is." Some muttering came from the bedroom followed by a sharp "Dammit!" when a tin cup hit the floor.

An hour later, with Mick finally settled in, Frenchy heard Mamie's story of her infatuation with Campbell Harper. As incredulous as Frenchy was, she listened quietly, respectfully, her understanding of Mamie's religious sentiments helping her along. To Frenchy, the reverend was transparently evil, caring only for himself and his grandiose, narcissistic schemes. About this, Mamie now agreed, but how could she have gone so far as to love such a man and accept his lies and schemes, merely because he professed to be a man of God? Sister Brigid had it right: *See* the devil where he is, always. The more desperate Mamie's needs became, the less she had been able to see.

* * * * *

"Oh, Mamie, can't you stay a little longer?"

Mamie placed her coffee cup on the small pine table that Frenchy had returned to the front porch. Mick no longer needed it to keep his leg raised. He was up and hobbling around but still ornery because he wasn't strong enough to go back to the Jenkins and Dunn Saloon. They could hear him now inside, his wooden cane attacking the floor as he moved about in frustration.

Frenchy waited a moment for Mamie to answer and then put her own cup down on the table. The sun sat somewhere above the courthouse to the east now, and the cool morning air was fading. The view to the west was, as always, comforting to Frenchy, even when a storm was brewing. She had noticed that Mamie, cheerful for several days, had begun to sit quietly for minutes at a time, her blue eyes shadowed as she seemed lost in thought.

"You might as well stay and get some rest. You had a hard time of it up in Topeka."

"Your Doc Shelton done told me when he took off that bandage that my old head looks good as new, 'cept for a little scratch that'll go away with time. So I reckon I better go on back to Kansas."

A loud noise came from the kitchen. "He's dropped the well bucket again," Frenchy said.

"Now comes the cussin'."

"Goddamn you Mick McGinnis for the stupid oaf you are!"

"He's mad at himself now," said Frenchy. "That's a good sign, believe it or not. He can't stay mad at himself for long."

"He ain't really the reason I'm plannin' to leave out of here. For one thing, they ain't hardly no trees in this place. For another thing, they ain't much of a church neither, and most of the folks around here are . . ."

"A lot of them are Catholics. Including Mick."

"It ain't that I think they're all bad no more. That priest fella, he don't say much, and he don't preach no real sermons, but that man has got somethin' about him that strikes me as . . . I guess I'd say real. But the fact is there's this Baptist church up in Topeka that I went to before all that bad stuff happened at the hotel, and they sent some ladies over to visit me when I was in the hospital up there. And guess what? They had heard me singin' and they want me in their choir!"

Mamie's face had brightened, and she was smiling when she turned to look at Frenchy. "Oh girl, don't be a-cryin' now, you ain't never been one to cry!"

"You've saved my life twice, Mamie Jackson, and damn it, I'll cry and I'll cry some more if I need to. And I will. But I can see that this place is not for you. You must promise me, and I mean it, that we will keep in touch. I will never forget you, and I will always love you."

* * * * *

Mick and Frenchy shared that same front porch for more than thirty years after his recovery, with Mick's expansion of his livery stable bringing in enough to support them both until the years after the railroad bypassed Tascosa. They had saved enough to carry them through the lean years after the turn of the century, and both resolved to remain in their first and only real house until the end.

CHAPTER 31

For Mick, that end came in 1912, when tuberculosis finally took him away. He was buried at the Romero rancho east of town, not far from the bluffs above the Canadian River. For years after he passed away, Frenchy used to drive a buggy over to the rancho to visit his grave once a month. She would rake the leaves and debris from the plot and wipe the red mud off the stone. But now she hurt every time she got up and every time she sat down, and there were no buggies for hire anymore. Going outside for water and to the outhouse was about all she managed to do. From the first of every month, to once every three months or so, to now—the visits to Mick's grave dwindled the closer Frenchy got to joining him in the ground.

Mick still had his wits about him when he died, but he could barely talk because of the final stages of tuberculosis. They had spent months in Colorado Springs, along with most of their money. There was enough fresh air up there for the whole world, but it didn't help Mick. Doctors thought the cure was to load people up with food and more food, put them in the fresh air by themselves—on a sleeping porch or a little house or sometimes in a tent—and hope they would get well. Most didn't. Mick did take to the food because he liked to eat anyway. Frenchy figured the time and money spent up there in those houses on North Nevada Avenue, called "lungers' row," probably did her more good than it did Mick, since she got the fresh air without all the heavy food. Maybe that's why I'm still here, she thought. But the cost of going to Colorado Springs is why I'm more or less broke.

* * * * *

Frenchy looked around the adobe house, messy but still warm and sound. She wondered, How long will it take to crumble into nothing after I'm gone? For sixty years the place had stood, from shortly after she and Mick arrived in late 1879 to now. Frenchy had already made arrangements to move to Channing and take a room in the widow Blackwell's house. She had no desire to stay there for long. The world was falling apart, putting it a step or two behind her. At least in Tascosa she could pretend nothing had changed—nothing, that is, since she became the last woman in the dilapidated town. In place of the motley group who had lived there in the 1880s and 1890s, now there was mostly tumbleweed, dust, and those young boys down the way. Some reminded her of Tommy, and she wished them all the best. They would keep Tascosa alive.

Alive. A condition she would soon not know. She recalled the day when Miguel appeared at the house two days before Mick's funeral Mass back in 1912. It was Ash Wednesday, and Miguel had been out to the rancho. He and Frenchy had stayed on good terms since she and Mick were married, seeing each other on special occasions at the rancho but never at Mass. Mick had always been grateful that Frenchy had consented to a Catholic marriage ceremony and did not dare to press her further. On Sundays, without her, he had enjoyed spending time with Casimero, Ysedero, and a handful of other friends, sharing stories, smoking cigars, and enjoying the fine food and liquor that was their indulgence after Mass.

That day, Frenchy heard Miguel's buggy coming to a stop outside, announcing its arrival with the same sounds of clomping hooves and jingly traces. She waited for him to traverse the short path to her door. He looked exhausted and old for his age, about sixty in 1912. His fingers still bore the smudge of the ashes. Frenchy could not imagine the strain he had to endure: The physical effort of saying Mass in three towns each week, hearing confessions, administering last rites, conducting marriage ceremonies and baptisms—that alone would take its toll. But for Miguel, each sacrament he administered served to reinforce his grim assessment of his life, of all lives, of the world. Of the seeming futility of the heart. Frenchy wondered how often he felt or imagined that the raised chalice rising from his hands embodied the real presence. From the way he looked, with his black eyes, loose-fitting cassock, and dark, sagging skin somehow assuming a human form, she guessed not often, if at all. She bent to look into his eyes, shaded by the wide brim of his old black Roman hat. He raised his head for a moment. "Hello, Señora, I am here to see you, and to talk about the funeral."

* * * * *

Miguel was too fatigued to make the trip from Vega to the rancho where Mick was to be buried. So Louis Homan and some hands from the rancho loaded Mick's coffin onto a flatbed wagon and they all made the trip to Vega, where Miguel had lived since before Tascosa was a town. After the funeral, they would have to carry the coffin to the rancho for burial.

Miguel's skin had a grayish look. The circles under his eyes were wide and almost as dark as his eyes themselves, which were once again cast downward as he quietly nodded his greetings to the first arrivals. Most of his modest house was given over to a chapel that could seat no more than a dozen people. For Mick's service, the chapel filled quickly; another twenty people gathered near the door. Miguel proceeded without an altar boy, facing a portable altar on a simple dining table, with the closed oak coffin, ordered from Dodge City, holding Mick's body just behind Miguel, between him and the mourners.

Frenchy sat close enough to Mick's coffin that she could place her left hand on it, which she did as Miguel began the service. Casimero and Ysedero read from scriptures Mick had selected. When Miguel rose to begin the eucharistic ceremony, he was unsteady on his feet and took a deep breath before going to the altar. Frenchy was aware of the halting Latin, but she did not actually hear it, for her mind was concentrated on the coffin, on how the wood felt under the soft touch of her hand, on how it would soon disappear along with the fine, loving man it held.

Nevertheless, she was aware of a sudden lapse in the service. When she looked up, Miguel had almost collapsed, knocking to the floor a burning candle from the pull-out shelf of the portable altar.

Casimero and Ysedero looked stunned, and Casimero shot out of his chair. Frenchy was already at Miguel's side, holding him up, steadying him. His eyes never left the chalice he somehow managed to hold. Frenchy stood back from him, but not so far that she couldn't come quickly to his aid again if he needed it. She was surprised at how small he still looked even in his vestments, once he was repositioned on a step in front of the altar. Thus elevated, he was no taller than she was.

He raised the chalice, the Latin words little more than a mumble. Evidently, he had injured himself when he almost fell down, and for a moment the chalice tilted noticeably to the right. Frenchy rushed to his side, supporting his arm, and Miguel managed to raise the chalice higher. Frenchy could hear the murmurs from those in attendance. No doubt she had invaded a holy space, with no right to be there. She couldn't have cared less—except this was Mick's funeral Mass, and she felt an unaccustomed surge of embarrassment run through her. Her eyes met Miguel's. She tried to tell him in that brief look that she was sorry, that she had meant no harm. In that moment, the vanishing dimple near the left corner of his mouth became visible, and then it was gone.

CHAPTER 32

Channing-Tascosa, January 1941

By now, almost everyone Frenchy had known from the old days was dead. Only the boys and the staff at the home remained in the town. Mick was long buried at the rancho. Louis Homan had died of exposure on a clear, starry night, an empty bottle of Double-A whiskey neatly placed on a nearby rock. The letters from Gabe Celiot had tapered off after Louise's death; Frenchy never stopped believing that he lived on, somewhere along the river.

Mamie returned to Topeka, finding a job with another druggist, who not only appreciated her remarkable memory but married her for the good woman she was. She learned to read and write late in life. In Mamie's last letter, dated "Christmas '38," Mamie wrote that her husband, Harold, five years younger, could no longer join her at church on most Sundays. She said she was fine anyway but unable to sing in the choir because of some bad dizzy spells and a "little problem" with her words. The letter made Frenchy smile at the beginning. The grammar was incorrect, and the hand somewhat unsteady, but in the penciled words Frenchy could hear and see her friend as clearly as the first day they met at the boardinghouse in Helena, Arkansas, more than sixty years ago.

At the end of the letter, Mamie wrote,

I love my husband and all I really do. But me and him are like most people I guess. You and me and our poor Louise we was somethin special—hard as it was. We had somethin that hadnt never happened and couldnt happen agin. Me and Louise was so different. I reckon no preacher would of called her innocent but to me that is what she was. The more I thought about her

Catherine the more I came to love her. Us not bein able to save her was an awful thing. But we know that is our life—lots of it is loss. I never figured out why God made it that way but that's what He done so here we are.

Frenchy had written Mamie back, four times at last count, but no reply.

Putting Mamie's last letter aside on the mahogany bed tray that had become Frenchy's table, she took Mick's notebook from the bedside drawer in her small room at the widow Blackwell's house in Channing. The ruler with Louise Pennette's initials marked Frenchy's most recent entry, months ago, when she still lived in the adobe house in Tascosa. The crack near the ceiling had grown wider, but she didn't leave the place because the elements were getting in; she left because of the life that had gone out. Now, in her dreams, the house was a place where she was always searching for what had gone, never finding it, leaving her to fumble repeatedly with the hook latch on the screen door before she could depart, or open her eyes.

With a premonition that this entry might be her last, Frenchy sat quietly for several minutes, her brows narrowing behind the steel bridge of her spectacles. The words "loss and memory," "memory and loss," kept running through her mind. She had no doubt that the human beings taken from us vanish forever, no matter how much we try to reclaim them with constant longing or repentant words, but their voices, scents, smiles, and the feel of their touch are retained, welded by love and memory into an abiding presence. These things remain so close—in the heart, she felt—but the people, they are gone. Just plain gone. Most everything else, old cowtowns, the candle-lit chandeliers on a riverboat ceiling, and all that intensity poured into games of chance, they simply happened. They were not missed.

Her mind went back to the young Louise. She wrote, *For my friend Louise, what was lost, taken cruelly, was her very self. I am probably the last person who remembers who she really was. I loved her.*

August 10, 1880, was the day on which the Haitian manbo had foretold that Louise's spirit would be freed from the dark waters of tragic and untimely death. Frenchy had tried her best on that warm Tuesday, so long ago in Tascosa, to picture Louise the way she had been in Baton Rouge, young and laughing and free. Now, her head bowed, she tried again. Moments later, she picked up the old ruler and marked her final entry. She carefully placed the ruler on top of Mamie's letter. She had done all she could.

* * * * *

Hardly anyone attended Frenchy's burial at the rancho. Casimero had long since died, and most of his retinue had returned to the sheep country in New Mexico. The few who remained were all old or middle-aged, except for a few of their children and grandchildren. Three old hands from the ranches showed up, one of them Tom Harris, barely able to walk, having lost his right foot to frostbite all the way back in 1887. He had not been charged for the shootout with the syndicate gunmen at the Jenkins and Dunn Saloon, where Mick received his first wound. But what he had predicted came to pass. The cowboys could no longer round up a few head for themselves. They went on strike, but the syndicate quickly prevailed. After trying to make it on his own following the strike, he finally got on at a syndicate ranch, a big spread determined to show how barbed wire could remake the Plains. He got caught in a blizzard with a small herd far north of town. The sharp drift wire had been strung to protect the syndicate range; the new posts were strong, closer together than with regular wire and firm in the hard ground.

The cattle had smelled the blizzard coming their way. It was their instinct to head for a draw, one of which they knew in this north pasture, and find protection from the deadly cold. Tom could hear them bawling long before he saw them bunched tightly along a section of wire. The first to strike the wire were bound up with it, bleeding and doing most of the bawling, and the others pressed against them in a panic, trying to make a wedge to force their way through. Already about twenty of the poor beasts stood almost frozen, their heads down and tucked between their front legs, as they slowly descended to the snow-covered prairie. They were giving up. They were dying. The whole herd would die, their instincts thwarted by the sharp steel wire.

Tom had strict orders not to cut the wire. The very fact that it could hold the frantic cattle in such a storm was testament to the brand of wire the ranch owners had developed not only for themselves but also for sale across the country. The loss of a small herd meant nothing to them. But Tom cut the wire. The cattle ran snorting and bellowing toward the draw. Some ran over Tom. He lay unconscious in the snow long enough for frostbite to set in. Lucky to find his horse after he revived, he did make it back to the ranch. The owner fired him but gave him a blanket to wrap around his leg. Doc Shelton had no choice but to cut his foot off. Soon thereafter, the wire took over the Plains, finally cutting off Tascosa, leaving it isolated and deserted except for one last woman.

Tom Harris was now in his eighties, able to make his way to the gravesite only with help from another old hand. Joining him there was Father Miguel, almost ninety and so small now and so stooped that his dark eyes were mostly hidden. Standing at the head of the grave, with the plain pine coffin below him, was PFC Tommy Hollis, who'd made the long drive to the rancho in a borrowed car from Camp Bowie, near Brownwood. One of his soldier friends came with him and now helped to keep Miguel steady on his feet. In Tommy's right hand was a plain cardboard box.

Frenchy had left no instructions, other than to be buried next to Mick and to have no funeral Mass. The weather was, thankfully, above freezing, but a breeze added some chill and kicked up the prairie dust. Finally, Tommy said, "Well, I know one thing about Miss Frenchy. She liked her tea cakes. I reckon she wouldn't mind us having these here." Opening the box, he held it out to each person there, and even Miguel took one of the now-hard cookies from the box. Tom Harris waited to see if any were left. "Yeah, I will have one."

"Most folks nowadays call them plain old sugar cookies." Tommy was speaking into Tom Harris's mostly deaf ear. "Don't hardly see folks dipping them anymore. I know Miss Frenchy liked them as they was."

The teacher from the boys' ranch walked up to join Tommy, along with four boys, ruddy-faced, shivering, and fully scrubbed, there for the purpose of paying their own tribute to Frenchy. Among them were two of the boys who had pretended to shoot at her after she scorned their picture show. The teacher, Jim, took a pitch pipe from his vest pocket, blew on it once, and stood straight and solemn as the nervous boys sang out the first verse and chorus of "Home on the Range."

A few of the older household workers from the rancho slowly came forward, standing alongside the grave and making the sign of the cross. Tommy carried the box over to them. A young girl quickly grabbed one of the cookies and put it to her mouth but hesitated, her eyes on a small, solemn, gray-haired woman, her grandmother Luciana, almost six decades removed from her childhood on the rancho. Lifting her black veil, Luciana appeared doubtful, but seeing her granddaughter's disappointment, she whispered her approval. Then she walked around the grave to stand beside the priest. Gently touching him on the shoulder, she said, "It is good to see you, Father."

Afterword, by the Author

The idea for *The Last Woman* had its origins in a chance discovery of the life and legend of a colorful woman of the Texas Panhandle, Frenchy McCormick (ca. 1852–1941). I do not remember the exact circumstances of my first encounter with her story, but early on I read a summary of her life in the *Handbook of Texas*, became intrigued, and sought out more information about her long journey from Baton Rouge to Tascosa. From the beginning, I knew what it was about her story that interested me the most: Having moved to Tascosa in the early 1880s with a man named Mickey McCormick, she remained in the town for almost thirty years after his death and the eventual death of the town they both loved, much of that time as the town's sole resident. Why?

Life inevitably entails loss. It is natural to cling to what we can, remember what sustains us, and struggle to accept what has been lost. Yet the real Frenchy's devotion to what had vanished was exceptional, requiring her to bear solitude and privation for decades in a harsh and desolate place. Surely she survived by making the past especially vivid and present. How did she do that? Who else had been in her life? How did she manage, at such a young age, to travel from Baton Rouge to Tascosa?

The slim historical record suggests that she journeyed from Baton Rouge to St. Louis and from St. Louis to Dodge City. More is known about her move from Dodge City down to Texas, in the company of young Mickey McCormick. And we know that in Tascosa she remained, for many years the town's sole inhabitant. The novel tells the rest of the story, as it might have been, while describing her as a few years younger. Thus it is correct to say that *The Last Woman* was "inspired" by the life of a real person, Frenchy McCormick, but the novel does not claim to tell her true story. That story was hers alone and, like old Tascosa, is now one with the dust of the prairie.

About the Author

John Willingham's fiction and non-fiction have appeared in *Southwest Review* (SMU Press), including the lead essay on the themes of Texas writers John Graves (*Goodbye to a River)* and Larry McMurtry (*Lonesome Dove)* in the 100th anniversary edition of *SWR*. More recently, his essay, "Paulette Jiles and the 'Aura' of the News" appeared in the *San Antonio Review*. In April 2023, the *Southwestern Historical Quarterly* published his long essay "Should We Forget the Alamo? Myths, Slavery, and the Texas Revolution," which challenged some recent interpretations of the famous battle. His 2011 novel, *The Edge of Freedom: A Fact-based Novel of the Texas Revolution,* explored the relationship of the Alamo to the tragic events in Goliad a few weeks later. A native of Waco, Texas, he now lives in Georgetown, near Austin. He received a BA with honors and an MA in American social and religious history from the University of Texas at Austin.